THE CHU[illegible]
MEMORA[illegible]

CW01596932

BY SEAN GABB

The Moving Finger writes; and, having writ,
Moves on: nor all thy Piety nor Wit
Shall lure it back to cancel half a Line,
Nor all thy Tears wash out a Word of it.
(*The Rubaiyat of Omar Khayyam*)

The Hampden Press
London
2011

The Churchill Memorandum, by Sean Gabb

This first edition published in January 2011

© Sean Gabb, 2011

The right of Sean Gabb to be identified as the author of this work has been asserted hereby in accordance with the Copyright, Designs and Patents Act 1988.

All rights reserved. No reproduction, copy or transmission of this publication may be made without written permission.

Any person who does any unauthorised act in relation to this publication may be liable to criminal prosecution and civil claims for damages.

With the exception of Alan Greenspan, all characters who appear in this novel are dead or fictitious. Any resemblance to other real persons is purely coincidental. Any resemblance to the famous dead is fully intended.

Published by
The Hampden Press
Suite 35
2 Lansdowne Row
London W1J 6HL
England

Telephone: 07956 472 199
E-mail: *directors@hampdenpress.co.uk*
Web: *www.hampdenpress.co.uk*

ISBN: 978-1-4467-2257-2

British Library Cataloguing in Publication Data: A catalogue record for this book is available from the British Library

I Dedicate This Book
to Professor Hans-Hermann Hoppe
who suggested its subject
for my speech to the 2010 conference
of the Property and Freedom Society

And to my dear Wife Andrea
without whose patience
it might never have been written

And to my Daughter Philippa
despite whose best efforts
it was completed

ACKNOWLEDGEMENTS

The quotation on smoking in Chapter Twenty is from Ayn Rand, *Atlas Shrugged*, 1957. The two other quotations in that Chapter are also by her.

The front cover image was produced by Mario Huet.

NOTE ON CURRENCY

Following a return to the gold standard, the price level in this alternative 1959 has fallen somewhat below that of 1914. Whether we take the current price of gold, or the various cost of living indices, this gives a rough conversion of £1 to £200 of our own as of 2011. This makes 1s. worth about £10, and 1d. about 80p. A halfpenny, therefore, is worth about 40p, and a farthing and half farthing 20p and 10p respectively. There is no smaller coinage.

CHAPTER ONE

"Of course," he said, dropping his voice so it could be heard only half way down the queue, "the Americans have never changed over. They still call today March 6th 1959. Their custom is to put the month before the day. It makes good sense, as the month is more significant than the day." As if looking for support, the old bore pointed up at the calendar that hung just beside the concrete statue of the President. It was a wasted gesture. The departures hall of Anslinger International may have its excellences. If so, these didn't extend to its calendar. Through dust-covered glass, it was still showing a date from January.

"Next!" the check-in clerk snapped. The New York accent is never friendly. New York bureaucrats, I'd long since found, go out of their way *not* to sound friendly. Somebody muttered, from a few places behind me, about the interminable wait. We shuffled forward another eighteen inches. One of my coloured porters strained with his box. Since the others didn't think it worth the effort of moving theirs, he scraped it an inch or so across the uneven floor, then went back to sitting on it. I took a new standing position as I came to my own halt. It didn't do to scratch in public. Even so, my left buttock was itching again like mad. Had I been bitten by something? I wondered. I'd been told you might pick up some nasty things in America.

"Mind you," the bore struck up again beside me, "the computer chappies go one step further. They put the year in front of it all. They write today as '59-03-06'. That lets them put dates into a numbered list where they follow each other in fully logical sequence—most significant number first. Just before I retired in '56, we had a new computer fitted in Calcutta. The Marconi people had shipped it out in pieces for fitting together *in situ*. Big thing, it was—needed its own building, you know." He took out his pocket handkerchief and, holding it in his left hand, blew his nose hard enough to start an echo round the cavernous dump where we'd all been shivering half the afternoon. I was one place from the check-in desk, and I saw the clerk look up disapprovingly from her inspection of yet another exit visa. Unimpressed—or perhaps unaware—the bore sniffed loudly and rearranged the very large and very white moustaches that covered his very large and very red face.

"I did ask the boy in charge," he went on, "what would happen when the century number changed—what would he do when '00 came *after* '99? Gave me a fishy look, the little blighter, and muttered something that boiled down to 'sufficient unto the day'." He chuckled. Would he drift into recollections of his Indian days?

I could have kicked myself. Buttonholed—and even before check in—by the voyage bore is bad enough. Buttonholed by a bore who'd served in India was surely as bad as things could get. Unless I was to spend the next three days locked in my cabin, all my thoughts of a pleasant flight home were looking decidedly iffy. I looked again at his tie to see if it gave any indication of what he'd been doing before he retired. But the nearest fluorescent lighting was on the blink, and I couldn't see the details of its pattern.

There was a loud crash behind us. Fifty bored, impatient faces turned to see who'd got the double doors unlocked that led back out into one of the less ghastly areas of New York. It was whole squad of Republican Guards. In their regulation fedoras and trench coats, they paused at the entrance and looked round. Most carried hand guns. A couple had sawn-off shot guns. One of them pointed in my direction and held up a folded sheet of paper. Coming at a brisk march, they set out across the fifty yards that separated us.

I fought to keep a blank face. Even so, I could feel my guts turn to vinegar. Forget voyage bores. Things had just gone horribly to the worse. And this wouldn't be the end of it. For what it might be worth, I put a hand up to reach for my passport.

"Hands out of pockets, dear boy," the bore breathed into my neck. His voice had a soft urgency wholly different from his calendar monologue. He was right. I'd been here long enough to know the drill. Trying to control their trembling, I stretched out my fingers and pressed my hands against the fabric of my trousers. Looking neither to right nor left, on the men came through the now silent hall. I thought of the permit I'd bribed out of the Repository Office in Chicago. Would it mean anything against these people? I prepared to clear my throat, and tried for an easy smile.

But it wasn't me they were after. They stopped beside me. But it was the man right at the front of the queue they were surrounding.

"Alan Greenspan?" their officer snarled. He unfolded his sheet of paper. It was covered in typewriting, and there was a photograph in its top right hand corner. "You are Alan Greenspan—enemy of the people!" The little Jew in front of me cowered backwards and got out a few words in the sort of English accent you hear in Hollywood films from the old days. The officer laughed unpleasantly and took up the British passport the clerk had been in the process of stamping. Holding it in his left hand, he rubbed one of the pages between the thumb and forefinger of his right. He sniffed at his fingers and held them out to show how blue they'd turned. "Take him down," he said to one of his men. The man's face took on a gloating look as he put a hand on the Jew's collar.

"I'm a British subject," Greenspan squealed in an accent that now said he clearly wasn't. He looked at me as if for confirmation. I forced myself not to step backwards, and looked steadily down at the floor. "You can't touch me," he cried again, desperation in his voice. "I'm a British subject." A hard poke in the stomach sent him to his knees. The officer turned to face the flight representative who was hurrying over to protest.

"He's none of your concern," he said in the cold voice of authority. "He's not a British national." He put a hand on the obvious shape that bulged through his trench coat. The young representative opened his mouth to speak, but thought better of saying anything at all. It was now that Greenspan found his own proper voice.

"Free Ayn Rand!" he shrilled quickly. "She's been in solitary for a year now. They're killing her with neglect." He was taking in breath for another slogan. But a knee in his face sent him straight down on the floor. The officer snapped an order to his men. They pulled Greenspan to his feet and three of them began dragging him back towards the doors. "Restore the Constitution!" he managed to shout.

"Anslinger's a tyrant!" But that was it. With a last despairing wail of "A is A!" from Greenspan, the doors closed behind him and his keepers, leaving the rest of us in total silence.

"I can smell a Jew at five yards," the officer said, now looking directly at me. He smiled and flexed backwards, showing still more prominently the bulge of the metal in his pocket. "And I can smell subversion. You were beside him. You were with him?"

I wanted to tell the man very smartly I'd never seen Greenspan before in my life. It was the truth. He'd pushed in front of me not half an hour before, and had been giving me funny, sideways looks ever since. I thought of claiming friends in high places. Instead of all this, though, I opened my mouth and found that I couldn't even breathe out. The officer was looking triumphant. Already, I could fear, he was turning to give orders to more of his men. Before I could open my mouth and try for gibbering, the bore had an arm on my shoulder.

"My dear fellow," he said to the officer, "you'll find this young man really is a British subject. He had nothing to do with your felon." The officer's face turned a kind of puce. I thought for a moment he'd pull out his gun and try some pistol whipping. But he controlled himself. He took the bore's offered passport and looked long and closely at it, comparing face with photograph.

"Stanhope," he said at length to the bore, separating the syllables into *Stan Hope*, a slight emphasis on the second syllable. He twisted his thin face into an apology for a smile. "Reginald Stanhope. Do your friends in England call you Reggie?"

"They call me *Major* Stanhope," came the reply in a tone that avoided all hint of rebuke. The officer turned the pages of the passport.

"Well, *Major* Stanhope," he said, now mockingly, it says here you're subject to Imperial immigration control. You sure don't look like no nigger."

"British bred," came the now breezy reply, "though born in Cyprus. The law is very strict, you know—doesn't just apply to Her Majesty's coloured subjects. One law for all and all that." The officer continued looking at the much-stamped pages.

"What was the purpose of your visit?" he asked with a lapse into the official. He pointed at the dense mass of previous visa stamps. "Is it family business?"

"Not in so many words, dear boy," Stanhope said with a wave. "But there's a brotherhood among those of us who served in the War that's very like blood." I tried not to look at the black glove that covered the stillness of his right hand. He saw my attempt and laughed softly and held the hand up. "I got this on the fourth day at Paschendaele," he said. "Jerry machine gun bullet—went in through the knuckles, lodged in the elbow. Whole lower arm had to come off in the end." He waved the artificial limb and looked the officer in the face. "You might say I was lucky. Whatever the case, life goes on. You learn to get by with the other hand. I can't complain.

"I sit on the Veterans' Relief Board in London," he said, pulling himself back to the main subject. "Not many Americans in the War, of course—came in too late for that. But they took quite a few casualties. All old men now, those still with us—some older than me. But American war pensions don't buy much with all this inflation. We do what we can. You'd be surprised the difference a few shillings a week can make between want and dignity."

"They fought in England's war," the officer said with quiet contempt. "It's only right that England should look after them now." He gave Stanhope back his passport and now took mine. "Anthony Markham," he said with the same division of syllables. "Born in Rei-*gate*, January 17th 1930?" I nodded and managed a feeble smile. I wondered if Stanhope was laughing inwardly at the unconscious reversal of the dates. I could feel the sweat running down my back. "And the purpose of your visit?"

"I'm an historian," I said, trying and failing to match Stanhope's easy assurance. "I'm researching a biography of Winston Churchill. You—you may have heard of him. He was half-American—his mother's side. He left all his later papers to Harvard. I was out here to consult them. I—I…" The officer had lost interest, and I trailed off. Avoiding his face, I looked up at the statue of Anslinger. It had been cast in the early days when he was modelling himself on Mussolini, and there was still black paint on areas of the uniform. Somehow, the artists had got a smile on the man's face. He was looking down at the little girl he held in his arms. She looked back adoringly. I tried to think of something flattering to say about my trip.

Just then, though, the sound of a gunshot came though the doors. Stanhope raised his eyebrows. "Well, really!" someone said from far along the queue behind me. All about, there was a buzz of quiet outrage. I looked past the President's statue, though the single sheet of plate glass that gave a view over the landing field and the huge body of the airship that quivered two hundred feet up in the breeze. The cabin was painted in the Imperial Airways colours, and had a Union Flag at each end.

I felt a hard bump in my chest. It was the officer handing back my passport. Before I could gather any words for thanks, he and his men were already heading back for the doors.

"Next," the clerk grated. It was my turn. Still trembling, I put my passport on her desk and pulled out the paper copy of my exit visa. She ignored the documents and pointed at the five wooden boxes my coloureds were still attending. "There's a forty pound weight limit for non-stowed luggage," she said. I pointed at the handwritten amendment on my ticket. She waved it aside. "There's a forty pound weight limit for non-stowed luggage," she repeated in exactly the same tone. I stared up at the ceiling and tried to pull myself together.

"I am a personal friend of the British Foreign Secretary, Harold Macmillan," I said with an attempt at firmness. "These boxes contain papers for a project in which he has taken an interest." She gave me the dead look that only officials in a down at heel police state can give.

"There's a forty pound weight limit for non-stowed luggage," she replied, for all the world as if there were a gramophone record in place of her mind, and the needle had stuck in a groove. I smiled weakly. Normally, I'd have called the representative over and got him to explain things. Now, I was even willing to leave the boxes behind. For all they meant to me, the safety of that cabin hovering in the sky outside meant more.

"If I might be so bold, Dr Markham," Stanhope whispered conspiratorially from behind, "I would suggest the offer of a supplemental fare. £2 should do the trick." I swallowed and reached into my pocket. There was obviously no point offering any of the thousand dollar bills that still bulked out the paper section. Instead, I took out one and two half sovereigns, and pushed them quietly across the desk. The clerk stared at them. She took up one of the smaller coins and bit into the gold. She covered all three coins with a sheet of paper. Without another word, she stamped my documents. Well she might. That must have been a month's salary for her.

"Next," she cried. I glanced at my coloureds and pointed at the boxes. There were hours still to go till boarding. But I could at least get out of this bloody queue.

CHAPTER TWO

As we passed out of American air space, and the black escort helicopters turned back, the bar opened in the first class saloon. I tore at the cellophane on a packet of Woodbines and jammed a cigarette between my lips. Ever since taking the railway train from Chicago, I'd been counting the days till I could light up without risk of a coshing from some thug in uniform with an Irish name. Now, after a month of forced abstinence, the first lungful of smoke came straight back out in a stuttering cough. But I suppressed the burning sensation and squeezed my eyes shut. I took in another drag and held it this time until the tension of the dreadfulness of Anslinger International began to drain away. I let out a stream of bluish-grey smoke and reached for the treble brandy I'd ordered. According to the waitress, it would be seventy five hours before I could see the greens and browns of an England in late winter. But it was enough for now that I was out of America and out of American air space. Here, even the Republican Guard couldn't intercept an Imperial Airways ship. If I looked left out of the window, I'd still be able to see the Anslinger Monument on Ellis Island. The sun would be going down behind it.

But I had my eyes shut again, and was savouring a lungful of fresh smoke. I thought of the Atlantic, cold and silver a thousand feet below. On one side of that vast expanse, the Americans might grow ever more beastly to each other. On the other, the comic foreigners could jabber and gesticulate themselves black in the face. But England, safe behind the wave-swept grey of the Home Fleet, was the same England as always. The Queen was on her throne. The pound was worth a pound. All was right with the world—or with that quarter of it lucky enough to repose under an English heaven. I breathed slowly out and wondered what might be on the dinner menu.

"Funny things, dates," I heard Stanhope say. I opened my eyes and sat up. Large gin and tonic in his good hand, he was seating himself on the other side of the little table. "Without Lord Chesterfield's Act, we'd still be on the old calendar. That would make today the 17th February—the 17th February *1958*, you know. But it would still be Friday. That cycle never changes. It's followed in unbroken sequence at least since the time of King Solomon. It really makes you think, don't you agree?" I nodded and took another sip of my brandy. No doubt, I was to be held fast by the voyage bore. But I now owed the man. If he wanted to give the whole crossing to lectures on the French Revolutionary Calendar, or whatever else took his fancy, it was nothing less than his right. I perched the remainder of my cigarette on the ashtray and pushed up another one from its package.

"Thanks for the offer, dear boy. But I've already availed myself of the young waitress's hospitality." He took a pipe out of his blazer pocket. Clamping it between the jaws of his artificial hand, he broke the seal on a small tin box and pinched out a plug of something black and greasy. I reached over with my lighter and helped get it going. Stanhope sucked hard. Pipe smokers aren't supposed to breathe in. He did. A moment later, he blew out a cloud of acrid smoke that had a hint of cannabis about it.

Now that the American music laws no longer applied, the piano quartet struck up with an arrangement of *Non Piu Andrai*. As with tobacco and alcohol, real music was another sign that we were passing back within the realms of civilisation. Anslinger's present taste ran to mournful folk songs and a few hymns, and, like all his other tastes, he'd imposed these on his subjects with grim enthusiasm. The Republican Guard was always breaking up private gatherings where "anti-American" music might be played. Almost every day in Chicago, I'd seen trucks going back and forth in the street over heaps of confiscated gramophone records, and seen those caught with them paraded up and down with placards about their necks. The only public dissidence I'd heard was from a decrepit Jew, who would get up in Lindbergh Square and sing pieces from Irving Berlin. For some reason, the authorities never touched him. It didn't do, however, to stand about and listen to him.

"I'd like to thank you for your help back in the airport," I said, once the band had moved on to selections from Gilbert and Sullivan. "I would have had the boxes stowed. But I didn't want their contents to risk a soaking in the hold." Stanhope smiled and puffed out another cloud of black smoke. At the table next to us, a man dressed in American business clothes looked round and scowled. He waved ineffectually at the smoke with what looked like a list of stock prices.

"Oh, think nothing of it—nothing at all," Stanhope said with a smile that now showed two lines of cracked, brownish teeth. "For my own part, I feel honoured to have been of assistance to one of our most distinguished younger historians. I read the first volume of your Winston biography when I was still in Calcutta. He's not popular out there, you may be aware. The natives don't like him for the trouble he made over the India Bill. Our own people don't like him—it's all to do with that Birmingham speech he made back in '43. But I read your first volume, and I think you did as much for him as could be done. No doubt of it—after all, he was a fine writer."

Stanhope might have said more, but the cannabis in his pipe tobacco was now kicking in. He stretched his legs forward and leaned back in his chair. As his head rolled sideways and his mouth fell open, I thought he'd suddenly nodded off. Another thirty seconds, though, and he'd pulled himself up and reached again for his pipe. It had gone out. I leaned forward again to help get things going properly. He acknowledged the help with an expulsion of air that set his moustaches an inch from his face. He sucked hard and blew out a cloud of now astonishingly dense smoke. The American he'd earlier annoyed started an impatient cough and, this time, put a handkerchief over his mouth. We ignored him.

"I suppose it's Churchill stuff in your boxes," he said. I nodded. Trust the old fool to have left virtually all his later papers to the Americans. Then again in that sad, final decade of his life, his affection for the land of his mother had grown regardless of its troubles. So, his executors had begged and scraped to endow the Churchill Collection, and had deposited the last papers there just before the student uprising began that had reduced Harvard and most other university towns to an imitation of Ypres *circa* 1915.

"The family asked me for a second volume," I explained. "It won't have the drama of his main career. But there was much of interest in his last quarter century." Or so I hoped. I thought of the mound of paper I was bringing back—unsorted originals, mostly, but also photographic copies of copies held under lock and key in Chicago. To justify the bribes and all the attendant risks, I'd have to work these into a bloody interesting narrative. Indeed, if, since about half way through the first volume, I'd changed my mind about the man and his times, I really couldn't afford to let that show in the second.

"You didn't have any problems in America?" Stanhope asked with an effort at delicacy. I could see he was looking at my hands. Instinctively, I put them together, covering the fingernails. "They can have some rather hurtful rules in their hotels and restaurants," he added. I was thinking to change the subject. But there was nothing accusing in Stanhope's voice. Besides, he already seemed to know enough about me. And he'd served in India. No point trying to evade the point.

"My father was a headmaster in Karachi," I said quietly. "He retired to England with my mother in '26. It was a late marriage—she was one of the teaching assistants. You heard from the American that I was born in Reigate."

"I thought as much," Stanhope said, dropping his own voice. "I'd have said your mother was from the north—that, or you took most of your father's colouring. Well, we're all subjects of the Queen-Empress, even if some of us"—he tapped the immigration control card he'd been issued—"take a little longer than others to get into the Imperial Motherland." He laughed and raised his glass. "Yes, England isn't America—and praise be for that!" He looked down for an inspection of the dinner menu one of the waitresses had just laid out. In the resulting silence, I transferred the Woodbines to my cigarette case. The American at the next table was still making his quiet fuss. Now I took the trouble to give him a proper—and what I hoped an insolent—inspection, I could see his face and clothes had the most decided look of a man who'd done well out of the Great Pacification. Certainly, he was drinking only mineral water. If he wanted to bring his country's laws with him, that was his affair. They didn't apply to me. I lit another cigarette and breathed easily in. For all I'd have no one waiting for me at Croydon, I was looking forward to England. For the moment, my bottom had stopped itching.

I got up and stretched.

"If you'll pardon me," I said to Stanhope, "I feel the need of some fresh air." He stared up at me, another smile on his lips.

"I could do with a walk on deck myself," he said. "It'll set me up nicely for dinner. Besides, it can be most inspiring to lean on the rail and look out at the setting sun."

I tried to look pleased at the offer of company. *No peace for the wicked*, I told myself.

CHAPTER THREE

It was three days later. A favourable wind had got us in early, and I stepped off the bullet tram at Victoria shortly after 1pm. From here, I walked through a light drizzle to *The Drivers' Arms*, just off Regent Street. The pavement heating was still on at full pelt, and the resulting clouds of steam had given London the appearance of an old-fashioned fog. If the kerb lighting hadn't switched itself on, I'd surely have fallen under one of the newer and more silent electric cars. As it was, one of the pedestrians bumped into me, and there was a whole minute of apologies and hunting about as he helped me recover my hat.

At last, I settled myself in my usual place in the pub and called for a dish of pork chops and a quart of ale. As I tucked in, I felt myself sinking back into the dull certainty—no, the *safe* certainty—of life among my own in *my* England.

And this is a good place for being in England. You get a mixed crowd in *The Drivers' Arms.* There's the usual mob of lawyers and other professional men, come to skive off their management of and dipping into the great river of gold that runs through London. There's taxi drivers, come in for a quick drink. You get the occasional off duty police officer. Mostly, though, it's actors and their hangers-on. Even the ones who aren't queer act queer, and their raucous screams keep the saloon bar lively all afternoon till theatre business begins to call them back.

Sadly, though, the landlord had given in while I was away, and installed a television set. I was burping my way through a second quart when someone insisted on having it switched on. It was one of the new models, with bright, exaggerated colours and stereophonic speakers. Even through the smoke and chatter of the theatrical set, I had trouble keeping my eyes from being drawn to the beastly thing.

It was the last item in the home news. This was about the heart and lung transplant man. He'd been out of hospital now for a hundred days, and was setting off for a golf tournament in France. The overseas news was less cheerful. Then again, it might have been worse. The big crisis that had filled every newspaper front page and news bulletin before my going away had fizzled out. I'd already learned on the flight home that the Dalai Lama had caved in and handed over the Tokyo metro bombers. The Japanese had then withdrawn their army of three—or was it seven?—millions from the Tibetan border, and we'd returned our bombers to their base at Peshawar. All was lovey-dovey again with the Japs, and the more lunatic writers for Lord Beaverbrook had given up insisting that this was an opportunity to see if atom bombs really would set fire to the atmosphere.

The only sadness in all this was that gold had collapsed even lower than before the crisis blew up. Bad news for me, I thought gloomily.

But even if war was right off the cards, the East remained unsettled. While they'd been breathing fire at Lhasa, the Japanese had taken their eye off the puppet Tsar they'd set up in Ulan Bator. He'd slipped his leash and called for a Crusade against Moscow. Or perhaps he hadn't. I couldn't quite make out the nutter from the Moslem League. But he seemed to be claiming the Tsar had converted to Islam and was preaching *jihad* against the British in India. Except he was making his usual call for moderation, the man from the Indian National Party looked equally insane, with his dry lips and swelling eyes. Certainly, Bombay was back under martial law. With equal certainty, Beria's foreign propaganda fronts were all talking up a double or quits war with Japan. Adding to all this, word was drifting in that old Goering was about to make a speech in Warsaw, threatening his own long-delayed crusade against Bolshevism.

There was another story I couldn't follow above the loud chatter that had footage of the Indian Ocean Fleet airships floating over what looked like somewhere in Africa. This was followed by footage of Lord Halifax inspecting the Suez Canal. Again, I'd already gathered on the flight that he was going about his Prime Ministerial duties by chairing some conference in Nairobi that involved the French and

Belgians. I could hear nothing of what he was saying to the cameras. But there was no mistaking how doddery he was beginning to look. I'd seen him only the previous September, walking up Piccadilly. Though seventy seven, he might have passed for sixty. Now, six months on, he was looking well past eighty.

The noise diminished somewhat when the football came back on. It was Jamaica *v* Sudan for the Vickers Cup. Through some technical marvel that involved rockets, film of the previous day's match had been rushed in from Wellington, and was now being broadcast as if live. I'd have had little trouble watching that—assuming I enjoyed the sight of coloureds running about in the sun. Some of the theatrical set did, which is why the pub had fallen into comparative silence. "Once you've tried black," someone shrilled, "you'll never go back!" There was a little shriek of laughter. This was immediately drowned by a cheer as a goal was scored, and then by a groan as a burst of interference turned the screen to white noise.

It was as it ought to be. In America, I'd soon learned that listening to the news was compulsory. Breakfast every morning in my hotel had been suspended for a full quarter hour, as everyone had to stand and shake his fist when the names of the newest traitors were read out over the wireless. One evening, when I'd retired early, the management even sent a wireless into my room, with someone to stand over me as I listened to President Anslinger's sermon of moral uplift. It was just one more sign of being back in a free country that football was more important than the news. No one in *The Drivers' Arms* had paid much attention to the painted newsreader. Now she was gone, about half the pub was glued to the screen.

"You finished with that glass, love?" Old Elsie whispered. I smiled and pushed the glass across the table. If no one else had, she'd been glad to see me again. It was a pity I had nothing to say about America that corresponded to the crisp, black and white celluloid version that, after all these years, still played in her head. She sang a few bars from an old musical and asked about the dark magnificence of Chicago. I, of course, had been better informed about conditions there when I set out. Even so, I hadn't been prepared for the smell of burst sewers, and for the burnt-out cars and no-go squatter camps that filled the wider streets. No point telling her about the endless turf wars between Italian and coloured and Jewish gangs that had kept me awake night after night until I was used to the sound of gunfire. Nor any point telling her about the black helicopters that hovered by day above the streets, and that only ever came down to snatch pedestrians, seemingly at random, off to probable torture and death in one of the Fellowship Camps. Elsie had the vision of America common to people of her generation, and it would have been cruelty to tell her exactly how it had all been broken in pieces. I smiled as she sang again and cleared the little table. As she came back with a damp cloth, it looked as if she'd forgotten again about the bill. I put a shilling on the table, and told her to keep the change. I pushed my chair back and got to my feet.

It was as I came out of the gents that I saw Stanhope. He was sitting across the public bar in what, even at twenty feet I could smell was a cloud of pure *hashish* smoke. With a deft use of his claw, he was reading the English edition of the *Völkischer Beobachter*. In honour of the coming Sad Anniversary, this had a huge picture of Hitler on the front and back pages. Whatever he was reading on the inside pages, his huge body was shaking with laughter.

What was he doing here? I thought I'd seen the last of him when I breezed through passport control at Croydon. A continental flight was in, and the alien entry queue was fifty yards long. He'd absolutely insisted I shouldn't wait for him. And his final lecture had been forbidding and interminable—all about the new Russian calendar, with its ten months called variations on the name Stalin, and about the placing of its fifteen days of Socialist Rest. No one could have blamed me for taking my chance and bolting. I'd already given instructions for delivery of my boxes. So it had been straight onto the tram just before it pulled out. Now, here sat Stanhope—for all the world as if he'd come up on the following tram.

I might have wondered how he'd got so fast through alien entry. I could have marvelled how, of all the establishments in London, he too had chosen this one. What really mattered, though, was that he didn't appear to have seen me. Nor would he see me. Voyage friendships are seldom worth prolonging. This was no exception. I dropped a sixpence into the China Mission collection box and dodged into the street.

Now it had stopped raining, I could see that London was reassuringly unchanged. It was the same noisy bustle on the streets, the same shiny cars of the higher classes trying to push their way through the swarms of smaller vehicles, the same smell of electricity from all but the grandest traffic. I thought of stopping a taxi. But I wanted the normality of London. Here, there'd be no machine gunning of pedestrians from unmarked black vans, no terror bombs in the restaurants, no endless stops and searches by men in and out of uniform—no swooping by those wicked black helicopters. It would surely come on to rain again in the next quarter hour. But I'd walk to the Richardson offices. Besides, where even English beer is concerned, two quarts still make half a gallon. I'd need a clear head for this meeting.

***

I was half way up Charing Cross Road when it did begin to rain. This time, it fell in sheets that overwhelmed the pavement heating. The danger now wasn't so much stumbling into the road as being soaked by water thrown up by the trolley busses and other large traffic. Having no umbrella, I dodged into the main entrance of Foyles. I stood there, fumbling with a packet of fifty and looking in at the display of new books. My own first Churchill volume was now over a year old, and had been promoted to the general chaos of the shelves. There might be a few copies on the second floor, or they might be in the basement—always hard to say, of course, with Foyles where anything might be shelved from one day to the next. I scratched a wet fingernail over wet cellophane until I could make a breach in the seal. I gave an annoyed grunt as I pushed the packet open. While I was away, the larger packs of Capstan Super Strength had gone filter tipped. I broke off the cork tip and flicked it onto the pavement. I was trying to get my lighter going in the gusty, rain-soaked wind, when someone who'd taken shelter beside me reached forward with his own gas lighter. I lit my cigarette on its intense blue flame and nodded my thanks.

"Iss it true, my friend, zat ze Archpishop of Canterbury is not a priest?" he asked with slow deliberation in a very thick German accent. He waved at the central book on the display. It was the defence of the Thirty Nine Articles that had come out to such acclaim just before I left England. I watched as the stream of smoke I let out was dispersed in the wind and gathered my thoughts.

"It was a controversial appointment," I replied in German. "But C.S. Lewis was, of course, ordained before the position was formally offered. And I don't think anyone can doubt that he has been a success by any reasonable measure. It isn't every day that a Cardinal Archbishop of Westminster and a dozen other Romish priests are converted in the course of a public debate." I'd lost him there, and I didn't feel inclined to explain myself. The man smiled and went back to looking at the display. About my own age, he was dressed in English clothes. If he hadn't opened his mouth, I'd not have guessed he was a foreigner. I could have kept the conversation alive by asking how long he'd been in England. But that isn't something you ask of Germans. It was still raining, but the sky was beginning to lighten. I took another draw on my cigarette and got ready for a complex sentence all about the weather.

"You have just returned from Germany?" he asked with a downward look at the one suitcase I'd brought with me from Croydon.

"Sadly not," I replied. "I've been in America. I'm having my main luggage delivered to where I live." It sounds a redundant amplification. But you weren't there to see how the man looked at me and at my luggage and back again.

"It iss as it should be," he said, back now back in his slow and hesitant English. "But you should come to Germany soon. Dresden is an extremely beautiful city in ze spring—*ja*, ze most extremely beautiful city!"

I had no doubt it was. But it had now left off raining. I stamped my cigarette out and made my parting excuses. Normally, I'd have made some effort at politeness—you can strike up some interesting friendships in this way. On the other hand, conversations, in English or German, about the whereabouts of my luggage or the joys of yet another chocolate box German city were not on my agenda for that afternoon.

CHAPTER FOUR

"So, our good Dr Markham is back from the wars!" Gwen snapped. She looked up from her typing and took off her spectacles. "Back, and still in one piece, I see," she added with a look of bitter contempt. I tried for an easy smile, but found myself wilting in the blast from that chilly stare. "Since you're back this early, I suppose you've been wasting money on one of those nasty little aeroplanes." She ripped the sheet from her typewriter and muttered an obscenity as she reached for her bottle of correcting fluid. "Well, the Boss is out to lunch," she said without looking back up. "I don't expect him back this afternoon. I suggest you call in tomorrow. I'll see then if there's an appointment free." She stabbed viciously at the sheet, sending a splash of whiteness over bad text and good text alike.

"Oh, dearest Anthony!" I heard a voice behind me. "Oh, dearest, *dearest* Anthony! We really weren't expecting you until tomorrow at the earliest—tomorrow, or perhaps even Wednesday." It was Vicky. Poured into a dress that couldn't have left much change out of fifty guineas, she stood in the doorway. Holding it out carefully to avoid getting dust on that shimmering green silk, she carried a stack of marked up typescript.

She put the stack on the one patch on Gwen's desk that was clear and came over to embrace me. I brushed my lips against her very soft cheek, noting the slight and doubtless expensive smell of lemon.

"If only you'd telegraphed ahead to say when you were coming, Daddy would surely have been here to welcome you home," she said. She put her hands on my shoulders and looked me affectionately in the eye. "Oh, darling, dearest Anthony," she breathed. "You really are the most beautiful writer in all of Daddy's stable. And we missed you so—didn't we, Gwen?" The old secretary coughed venomously and lit one of her cigars. Vicky smiled and led the way through towering piles of other typescript into her father's office. Old Man

Richardson's office was, if possible, still more cluttered. Vicky moved a pile of new books from the chair in front of the desk and poured me a very small sherry. As I sipped at the disgusting fluid—the contents of Gwen's correction bottle might have been more palatable—she fitted a cigarette into her long holder and looked about for the desk lighter.

"How was America?" she asked. "The only news in the papers while you were away was all about the new round of show trials in Washington. The Prosecutor-Judge sounded perfectly frightful." She smiled and fiddled with the lighter. Except for a difference of forty years and about twelve stone, she managed to look exactly like her father. I ignored the question—in any event, it was probably more an evasion than anything else: and I had nothing to say about Richard Nixon, or any others of the Anslinger attack dogs—and cleared my throat.

"Your father told me he wanted something sexy for the second volume," I said. "Well, I've evidence that Churchill was taking money from Czech Jewish interests to get him out of trouble. There was a payment of £15,000 in late 1939, and another of £5,000 in 1940. The payments ceased after his first stroke and when it was clear there wouldn't be a war." Vicky smiled again and lit her cigarette.

"Such ghastly people, these Jews, don't you agree?" she said. "But does this really add to our picture of Winston? More to the point, I'm not sure it gives the impression Randolph wants the world to have of his heroic father." I gave her a stony look. Yes, the family had specified a thick cover of whitewash over the old beast's reputation. On the other hand, Richardson & Co. were putting up the money. Bearing in mind how Churchill's last failed cause had been his turn against the Jews once they'd kissed and made up with the Germans, this *was* as near to sexy as anyone could have wanted. But Vicky was reaching down for one of the books she'd taken off my chair. She held up the thick hardback. *Hitler: Colossus of his Age*, its title screamed from the glossy cover. A picture of the man had been found that didn't make him look barking mad, and this had been stuck over a *montage* of his more extravagant building projects.

"We sent this one to the printers while you were away," she said. Daddy's throwing a big party on the twentieth anniversary of the death, and another next month on what would have been the seventieth birthday. Hitler always sells. Even at 9s.6d, we think we'll shift a million of these." She stopped and gave me another of those exaggeratedly loving stares. If my American trip had spared me the build-up, I'd known this was coming. Most galling it was, too.

"But, surely," I said, trying for a tone of gentle mockery, "the author's a foreigner. Besides, the last I heard of her, wasn't she banged up in some American jail?" For perhaps half a second, Vicky dropped her loving act, and her face turned as expressionless as the display on a calculating machine. Then she was all smiles again, and fussing with her cigarette holder.

"It's sad, of course," came the reply, "she was caught while crossing back into America. But she'd already put the last touches to the manuscript. As for being foreign, she has a big following here—aren't we the nearest, after all, to what she wants for mankind? And she has a growing presence in Germany. Indeed, it was their foreign minister who put pressure on Washington to have her charged only with tobacco smuggling. We'll shift a million here for sure. And we've already sold the German rights. Daddy's even wangling an introduction to that edition by Goering himself." Vicky put the book down and gave me what passed for her full attention.

"The problem with Churchill," she went on, "is that he did nothing big after Gallipoli. If you think a bit of corruption can make up for all that arid financial stuff from the twenties, and then his long, piss-stained descent into something close by the gutter, you really will have to think again. I'm sure Daddy will agree.

"Did you find any sex scandals?" she asked with a sudden change of tone. I shook my head. "Any truth about his deathbed conversion to Rome?" I shook my head again. "Did you find anything except this Jewish scandal that might be dressed up as an explosive revelation?" She varied the question, now putting an emphasis on the *anything*. I smiled frostily back at her. "Well, you see, my darling Anthony," she went on, now motioning at what looked like the telegram I'd sent once we were out of American air space, "Daddy can't see how we can add to the advance we agreed. £500 is a lot of money. You can buy a house with that." I shifted uncomfortably in the chair. £500 might buy many things. It might even keep Vicky Richardson for a whole month in shoes. But I was in a tight spot, and I needed more.

"The American trip was more expensive than I planned," I said firmly. "The Safe Zone in Chicago is at least three times London prices." Where was her father? He must have known I'd be round today. He'd probably have been just as flinty about the cash. But it's always easier to talk money with a man.

"I really do feel for you, Anthony," she crooned. "Did you lose *all* your money in that gold mine?" My face tightened. How did they know about that? "But I did hear Daddy urge you to do the work from Montreal. That would have been ever so much cheaper." She stood suddenly up. "Now, we do need the manuscript by October. Publication date, you'll recall, is set for next March. We absolutely must catch the tenth anniversary of Winston's death. This aside, Randolph will explode if we don't have the last volume out before he also drinks himself to death." I thought of a more insistent plea for money. Of course, she saw it coming and cut me straight off.

"The first volume is still doing rather well, and you'll get your royalty statement in the next fortnight," she said with a little pat on my back. "I *might* persuade Daddy to consider a further advance on the second volume—but you'll need to persuade me that it can rise above the dull worthiness of a second volume.

"Can we get you a taxi?" she asked with a brief glance at her watch. She fitted another cigarette into her holder.

As I left, Vicky was almost cuddling the Hitler biography. I'd never before realised how much I hated Ayn Rand.

***

The pavement heating was being repaired in Chamberlain Street, and the taxi took an age to get me through the resulting traffic. At last, though, I was able to walk through the glass doors of Victory Mansions. Looking dejected, there were two Indians sheltering from the drizzle in a doorway across the road.

"Glad to see you, Dr Markham," the porter said, getting up from his desk and giving a brisk salute. "I heard you'd be back tomorrow. I'm afraid I had your boxes taken up to Dr Pakeshi. There were too many to keep down here. I do apologise. I…."

"Think nothing of it, Hattersley," I said with an open smile. "I suppose you've enough other post to give me." He had. There was a whole box load of the stuff. "Don't worry about carrying it up," I said, taking delivery. There must have been a hundred letters and packages in there. I'd sort through them all in due course. For the moment, all I wanted was to sit down and relax after a week of travelling.

I bumped into Pakeshi as I came out of the lift on the second floor. Had he put on weight since I'd last seen him? Certainly, his face had swollen slightly and taken years off the fifty whatever that I'd always taken him to be. Sleek in the fine, outgoing clothes of a medical man about his visits, he'd been plucking hairs off his face in the reflection of the brass plate on his door. He smiled and said something in Hindi.

"If you can't speak English," I snapped at him, "you should consider sodding off back to wherever you bought your medical degree." If I thought I'd got him there, I'd forgotten my neighbour's thick skin. He smiled again and held up a bristle for inspection in the glow from the recessed light overhead.

"Did they make you sit with the other coloureds in America?" he asked with a giggle. I swallowed and tried to look contemptuous. "But please, O most learned of neighbours," he went on, his flabby, brown face creasing into a smile, "accept my felicitations on the safety of your return from the great toilet bowl in the west." He stopped for another giggle before changing tone. "There are five wooden crates shedding splinters into my hall carpet," he said coldly. "And it looks as if someone's smashed the lock on your main suitcase. Shall I ask the most excellent Hattersley to help you move them into your own flat?" Smiling again, he pushed his door open and pointed at the boxes. I held my breath to avoid the blast of heated, curry-laden air that I knew was coming my way.

"Oh, there are two darkies outside in the street," I said, stepping back from the open door. "Shall I call out of my sitting room window at them that dinner is ready?" That wiped the smile from his face. He darted a nervous look over at the lift door and fiddled with something in his overcoat pocket. There was something deeply unpleasant now about his face—far less pleasant than his usual oily grin. In the long silence that followed, I stepped forward and looked once more at my boxes. They were heavy, I knew, and I was shattered.

"Can't we just leave them there for this evening?" I asked, suddenly emollient. I didn't even comment for once on the smell. "I'll drop round in the morning." Pakeshi put his smile back on and nodded. He went inside his flat. Almost at once, he was back with a little cardboard box. He seemed to have changed his mind about going out. At any rate, he'd taken his overcoat off.

"Welcome home, O dearest neighbour," he intoned, holding the box under my nose. "We were *so* worried about you in America. Mrs Dale was convinced you'd be locked away for smoking. And that was the least of our worries." With his free hand, he stroked a bristle just under his nose. As if marking it for future attention, he tapped it twice, then let his hand drop down again. I smiled wearily and looked at the box. I reached up and took it from him. Like everything else about him, it stank of Indian spices. If I didn't get my own stuff out soon, it would all need a month of fumigating. "A gift, and only 4s.6d," he said quickly. I stared at the open hand. Four and bloody sixpence? Christ—you could hand over a shilling for that in Boots, assuming the pharmacist there was in the right mood, and get a farthing change. But Boots was far away, and I was shattered. I reached for my wallet. "No, no, no, my esteemed Anthony," he cried with his oiliest smile. "Tomorrow will do—tomorrow, when you come for your boxes."

I was beginning to feel sick from the smell of curry. I nodded, and moved towards my own door and reached up to unlock.

CHAPTER FIVE

Except it was musty from the long absence, my flat was just as I'd left it. The funny thing about homecomings is the momentary sense of being simultaneously in two different time streams. There's the knowledge of everything said and done while away. There's the feeling of never having been away. There, on the kitchen table, was the bottle of generator reagent I'd bought the morning of my departure. There, at the end of its long cable, was the television remote control on my bed. There, indeed, was the bump on otherwise neatly-folded bed coverings where I'd sat and flicked through the news channels for the Atlantic weather forecasts. It's a sensation that passes quickly enough. No doubt, it would vanish altogether once I began sorting through the bills and begging letters in that box Hattersley had given me. But that, like the boxes cluttering up Pakeshi's flat, could all wait.

I went into the spare bedroom that I'd fitted up as my office. I sat behind the desk and looked at the self-correcting typewriter. I swore as I realised I'd left the thing switched on. No wonder all the lights were flickering. Another few minutes, unless I opened that bottle of reagent, and I'd sit in the gloom of a late afternoon in March. I got up and went into the kitchen. The Hotpoint Home Generator was tucked under the sink. I went on my knees and unscrewed the metal cap. Five guineas down, the salesman had told me, and wave goodbye to gas and electric bills. That had been the truth—though there had been nothing about the 2s.6d for top-ups every month or so, or the danger of some very nasty burns if you didn't pour with a steady hand. Still, I got through this top-up without mishap. Another half hour, and I'd be able to put the kettle on. I might even manage one bar of the electric fire in my sitting room.

I went back into my bedroom. I took off my overcoat and then my jacket and sat down beside the bed. I tore the packaging from

Pakeshi's ready-filled syringe. He was a shifty creature, that was for sure. How he managed to practise with that stamp in his passport was anyone's guess. But he'd saved me the trouble of going out and negotiating with some pharmacist. I rolled up my shirtsleeve and looked at the veins of my left arm. The pale flesh around them would surely have passed as Italian or perhaps Spanish at worst. I put the syringe down and stood up. I went over to the mirror and stared at my reflection. Vicky's praise, perhaps, had strayed into flattery—though plain buttering up was more likely. But, if you like fine bones and a Mediterranean tint, you'll not deny a certain handsomeness—a certain *boyish* handsomeness, if you want to be specific. If only, though, I'd taken on a little more of my father's colouring. Why couldn't I have looked more English?

Oh, here, in England, I nearly always passed. It would have been rude to take me as other than Dr Anthony Markham, son of the Rev. Richard Markham, and author of *Churchill: Lion of Empire*, and of those monographs on the national recovery since 1931. The Americans had been far more brutal. In the end, I'd just let them think I was Jewish. It had got me barred from the indoor swimming pool. But at least I'd been able to check into the hotel. Perhaps Vicky was right. Perhaps I should have done everything through agents from Montreal.

I sat down again and looked at the coloured portrait of the Queen above the fireplace, and at the crossed Union Flags that were above it. Bible in one hand, her husband and son stood modestly behind, she was dressed in her coronation robes as Empress of India. It had been my mother's last Christmas gift to me. I bowed solemnly without getting up, then looked away.

I tapped at one of my veins and reached once more for the syringe. I laughed, breaking the cold quiet of the flat. No point whining about America, I thought. I really had to think how I'd get that bloody manuscript in by October, and how I'd live in the meantime. I had £34.8s.2d in my account. Once the next quarter's rent was paid, that would give me £23.18s.2d. Based on the last cheque I'd had, the royalties Vicky had mentioned would bring in another £25. Put 15s in the income tax account, and it would leave me the grand total of £48.3s.2d. That should keep me going in moderate comfort well into the summer. But I didn't know what would be in my broker's letter. It had been on top of the box of post Hattersley had handed over. I'd open it tomorrow and see the full ghastly truth.

No—I'd open it now. Some things you can't put off. I ripped at the envelope and scanned its contents.

"Bastard money people!" I snarled. I threw the letter down and went back to looking at my veins. It was no consolation the broker had himself lost money in the venture. What mattered to me was that he had, in advising me to buy those shares, helped turn £20,000 into slightly under £2,000. Unless gold recovered pretty sharpish, I was stuffed—no more swanning about as the gentleman-scholar.

But you don't inject in this frame of mind. I got up again and went back to the mirror. Was the faint slittiness about my eyes more or less pronounced? Hard to say in this light, though it couldn't be much changed from the day before. I put up a hand and stretched an eye wider open. The larger patch of whiteness only showed up the dark brown of the iris.

I felt I was about to cry. Instead, I stiffened my upper lip and smiled. That certainly increased the slittiness. But, whatever the change in the past day, it had been far more pronounced when I was a boy. I'd been in my second year at Lord Sittingbourne when the Japanese bombed Pearl Harbour. For a week, I'd been the most popular boy in my form. I'd even put on an all-purpose Oriental accent picked up from Saturday morning pictures.

"You are what you are, old boy," I said to myself. I smiled again. If I wasn't of the pure Imperial Race, Stanhope had been right about my mother. She'd been a fine-looking woman from the north. In her veins—and now in mine—had run the blood of another imperial race that had swept out of the deserts and imposed its own sway on the inert, trashy peoples of the hotter south. Whatever his endless mockery, I had no fellowship with Pakeshi or any of the other trouble-making *babus* who fancied themselves as the rightful lords of India. "Courage, and shuffle the cards!" had been my mother's last words to me. Now, if I'd shuffled badly, I could at least try to look brave.

Yes, I'd lost out on the venture. But I'd been the one to say yes—no one had put a gun to my head and made me sign the transfers. And it had all looked set fair for success. Ever since we'd gone back onto the gold standard, the price of gold had rocketed. We'd gone back on in 1950, then the Germans, then the French and Italians, then any number of riff-raff countries. Within five years, the Ministers were all wittering about changes in the silver ratio. Should there be a new fix of twenty four shillings to the pound? Or should we keep the old numerical ratio, but mint heavier shillings? Who could have expected the Russians to pay off some of their debts by dumping a straight thousand tons of gold on the market? That had killed all talk of the reminting. And it had buggered the South African mines good and proper. One day, the union leaders out there and the mine owners had all been at each other's throats. A single announcement to the cameras in Moscow, and they'd all fallen sobbing into each other's arms.

Once again, I smiled. I stretched out on the bed and undid my collar buttons. A week after the bottom had dropped out of gold, I'd sat with Harold Macmillan. He and Churchill had been close in the '30s, and, now Eden was back on the lithium salts, there was no better source for opposition to the first Munich Settlement—the failed one, that is, where Hitler had tried to make us look stupid. We'd sat for an hour, going through the diplomatic and financial meltdown that had looked inevitable in March 1939. Scary stuff it had looked too, even if Big Mac was still—though quietly—more bullish about its longer outcome than I now felt. More interesting had been his relief about the gold collapse. If wages hadn't fallen much, the headlong drop in all other prices had caused havoc in the rental markets. The Government's official line was that the fall in general prices below their 1914 level should be welcomed. In private, Macmillan was still talking up his old friend Keynes and his schemes for printing everybody rich. He'd been out of office when gold was restored. Now, he was rubbing his hands at the thought of the boost the fall in gold would give to computers and drugs and chemicals and electricals and all the other goodies in the "family silver". Perhaps he was right. Perhaps, whatever embarrassments I might be facing, it would be good for the country.

I looked over at the Queen and gave her a brief salute. She was on her throne, and the pound was worth a pound. And, failing an actual bankruptcy in my gold company, I remained a player in the game. For the moment, I was stuffed. I needed those royalties. And I'd need to make a few economies. But the game was by no means over.

I jabbed in the needle and winced at the now unfamiliar pain. Just a few days earlier, possessing even an empty syringe would have let the Republican Guards do to me what they'd done to poor Greenspan. Now, I was at home with all the comforts of home. In a moment, I'd feel much better. Much later on, I'd think how to avoid the indignity, some time before Christmas, of a begging letter to my cousins in Sheffield.

CHAPTER SIX

I sat on my bed and pressed the remote control to switch channel. I might as well have switched the set off. It was another documentary.

It was Thursday the 16th March 1939, went the solemn commentary over the usual black and white footage. The Fuhrer had spent twenty two hours in Prague to inspect his latest conquest. During this time, the people of that city had barely been aware of his presence in the Castle. But as the Mercedes accelerated to carry him back to the railway station, one of the armoured cars forming his guard got stuck in the tramlines that lay just beyond the Wenzelsplatz. The Fuhrer's car swerved to avoid this. On the frozen cobblestones….

And so it went on with leaden predictability. How anyone watching this hadn't seen it all a hundred times before was a mystery. But it had been made for morning television. There might be a backward schoolboy somewhere in England watching it for the first time. I pulled the blankets back over my knees and took another sip of the hot coffee. We were now being shown the gigantic funeral in Berlin—all Wagner and fluttering banners. Then it was a surprisingly youthful—not to mention still rather slim—Goering giving the eulogy. You'd never think from the tears running down his face that he'd already signed the arrest warrants for everyone else who might get in his way. But now we were back into colour, and there was some Jewboy with a Swastika on his arm smoothly explaining how the Nuremberg Decrees were only ever meant to be a short term defence against the Bolshevik Menace. There was what should have been an entertaining divergence between the spoken German and the subtitles. But I was in no mood for entertainment, and the subtitles were now being distorted by some most provoking interference.

"How much more of this fucking drivel?" I snarled softly as I flicked through the other ten channels. It was all Hitler, Hitler, and more bloody Hitler. And there were still six days to go till the actual anniversary. But I do exaggerate. One of the channels was showing an Enid Blyton cartoon. Another was nearing the end of a Hollywood film from the old days. But there was no Churchill. Had everyone completely forgotten him? "Nothing big after Gallipoli!" that bitch had claimed. "Arid financial stuff!" Did the first restoration of the gold standard count for nothing?

I pressed the wireless button on the remote control and got the Third Programme. It was Carl Orff's *Requiem for the Fuhrer.* I ground my teeth at the percussive mournfulness and the hissy interference, and stabbed viciously at the off button. I threw the blankets aside. At least, the heating was fully up. Good old Hotpoint. Even if I couldn't eat, I'd not freeze. I went into the bathroom for a pee. Then I washed a dead spider down the plughole and ran a very hot bath. I was still stewing there over my second cigarette, when the telephone rang. I reached out with my free hand for the extension receiver.

"Bayswater 27 3532," I said. There was a muffled voice on the other end of the line. "Can you speak up?" I called. "I can't hear you."

"Professor Markham?" someone said in a foreign accent. There was a loud crackle and an electrical hiss.

"You could call me that," I said. I waited for more. Suddenly, with a click, the line went dead. I swore and reached for the dial to see who'd been calling. It was out of reach. Well, I wasn't getting out of the bath. I would eventually get out—but that would be to inspect my bottom in the shaving mirror. I could feel a boil the size of a child's marble coming up. If the call was important, the telephone could ring again. I pulled a face and shifted position in the bath. I took up my *Daily Telegraph* again and peered at the now smudged ink of the Situations Vacant column. It was a bit below me. But there was an advert for a History master at a school in Balham. There was the hint of a need for Latin as well. It was, indeed, a bit below me. But I could do it. That would bring in about £75 a term. The duties might not be onerous, and would leave time for turning out a few thousand words every evening on the second Churchill volume. I lay back again and thought of the Underground connections. It would be Bayswater to Earl's Court, then to Charing Cross, then the Northern Line straight down. Or I could change at Notting Hill and Tottenham Court Road. Then again, Tottenham Court Road was always a bugger for changing….

There was a loud knock at the door. I groaned. It was too peremptory to be Pakeshi wanting his flat emptied of boxes. It sounded more like Hattersley with a special delivery. I wondered what that might be. Welcome back flowers, perhaps, from Vicky or her father? I laughed bleakly.

"Hold on," I shouted. "I'm just getting out of the bath." I heaved myself out and rubbed at myself with the towel. I hurried into the sitting room and over to the front door. I lifted the flap covering the inspection hole. I suddenly realised I was naked—and there was a puddle forming on the carpet where I stood. I left the flap open and stood back to dab at myself again with the towel. I could at least wind the thing round me before opening the door.

There was a loud crack that made the whole door shake, and a smashing of glass behind me. I turned and saw that the picture of the Queen in my bedroom was on the floor. There was a hole in the wall where it had hung. Puzzled, I looked back at the door. Where the inspection hole had been was now a much larger hole. It was smoking, and there was a smell of cordite. I rubbed at my face with the towel and looked again. I was about to call out, when I saw what looked like a metal spatula poke through where the door joined the frame. It moved quickly in and out around the lock. I looked at the catch on the door lock. It was down, and both bolts were drawn back. Through the still smoking hole in the door, I heard someone swear in what sounded like German. It was a high-pitched squeal, and, not expecting to hear any foreigner at my door, I couldn't catch the words. Nor could I understand any of the much lower, defensive reply. The door rattled as it opened against the chain, then shook as a man's weight crashed softly against it. With a loud *snap*, the chain gave and the door flew open.

I finished wrapping the towel about my waist and stepped back. In Chicago, I'd been warned repeatedly by the hotel people about this sort of raid. I'd never imagined it could happen here, in London—not in my own home. I held up both hands and stepped further back. I looked at the two men who stood looking back and me from just beyond the open door.

"So, *Herr Professor* Markham, you are still alive—*Ja?*" someone sneered in a thick accent. He stepped jauntily across the threshold and glanced round. A smallish man, in perhaps his late twenties, he had the entire look about him of a comic Nazi from the stage—the thin, scarred face, the wire-framed spectacles, the black leather overcoat, the slightly oversized hat. He looked back at me and smiled nastily. "You are alive, which is exactly according to my instructions. And, since you have, most fortunately for yourself, survived our entry, you may save us the trouble of a search." He dug an elbow into the much larger man beside him—he was the one carrying the pistol—and rapped out an order in German to check that I was alone in the flat.

"What do you want?" I gasped, still holding my hands up. "There's money in the teapot behind me." I'd been told you should always try to establish eye contact with robbers. That's easier said than done. The smaller man had got over what may have been his initial concern that I'd been killed, and was now looking rather pleased with himself. I still didn't feel up to staring him in the eye.

"*Schwein*! *schwein*!" the larger man shouted, coming out of my kitchen and jabbing the gun at me. He was much larger than the other man. He was larger and an altogether more desperate-looking sort. Farting softly, I stepped back again. I found myself almost at once against the far wall.

"*Nein, nein, Dumkopf!*" the small man said impatiently. He stood forward and took the gun. He balanced it in his hand and smiled again. He repeated the order to check the flat. Standing a few feet away from me, he levelled the gun straight at my stomach, and then downward at my crotch. "You will obey if you wish to stay alive," he said with a Teutonic cheerfulness. His smiled broadened till it stretched from one side of his face to the other. He looked briefly at his gun, as if to check that the safety catch was off, and waved it about the flat. "You will tell me where it is—now!"

"Please," I croaked through chattering teeth, "I don't know what you mean. Tell me what you want, and I'll give it to you." The response was a look of annoyance, and also of confusion. He covered this with another wave of his gun and a snarled insistence that I should produce whatever he'd come to take. I was getting enough

German together to explain that I'd give him whatever he wanted, if only he could tell me what it was, when the larger man came out of the bedroom, carrying the portrait of the Queen. The smaller man barked at him in German to put it down. Suddenly, he laughed. He walked over to the picture, and, gun still levelled in my direction, stamped on the broken glass.

"I spit on your filthy Elizabeth," he said bitterly. "I spit on your contemptible Empire and what you are pleased to call your place in the sun. You will not live to see it, but you shall be the means by which *we* become the masters that it is our destiny to be.

"*Heil Hitler!*" he shouted, transferring the gun to his other hand so he could click his heels together and give the required salute. He might have continued the lecture. But the larger man called out with what sounded like alarm. The smaller man looked away for a moment. I felt my legs buckle, and, back still pressed against the wall, I slid gently down onto the carpet. I drew my knees up under my chin and hugged my knees with both hands.

"Please, tell me what you want, and I'll give it to you," I moaned in German. "Just don't shoot me—please…."

But no one was paying attention to me now. There was another shout from the larger man. Then there was a crash that almost deafened me. I squeezed my eyes shut and pressed my face harder into my kneecaps. I heard the small man squeal what may have been a plea for mercy. Then there was another crash. Next thing I knew, something large and hard had landed on me and then bounced off.

There was a long silence. I waited for what seemed an age for something else to happen. But there was nothing. I opened my eyes. Twisted, but mostly on his back, the small man lay just beyond my feet. The gun had dropped from his hand, and, pointing straight at me, lay on the carpet. I picked it up and looked at it. I put it carefully down again. Over by the bedroom door, the larger man was lying on his back. Where his face had been was now a mass of red, and there were splashes of red and grey all over the settee. Otherwise, I was alone.

I tried to get up. But my legs wouldn't work. Naked, I huddled myself back into a ball on the sitting room carpet and began to cry.

Not very dignified, you may think. But it saved me the trouble of trying to work out what had just happened.

The next thing I distinctly recall is the glass of spirits Pakeshi held against my lips.

"In my professional opinion," he was saying—"a professional opinion attested by more than one degree—it is highly probable that these men are dead." I looked at the body of the smaller man. There was a large hole in his forehead where the bullet had entered. His face still carried a look of surprise. The whole back of his head was missing, and there was a spreading puddle on the carpet where he lay. "All that my diagnosis could possibly want," Pakeshi went on, "is some indication of who these men were, and of who might have killed them."

Ignoring him, I reached again for my towel. It had fallen off on my retreat to the wall. Now it was splashed with blood. Even so, I wrapped it about myself as I stood up. Still shaking, I took a step towards the bathroom, where I'd left my cigarettes. Where I'd been sitting, there was just the overpowering smell of cordite. Now I sniffed the air.

"Have you been smoking cannabis?" I asked with an irrelevant giggle. There was still cordite in the air—and now the usual smell of curry that indicated Pakeshi was within a ten foot radius. But no one can mistake the dry and aromatic smell of cannabis.

"Now, just you tell me, Anthony," he smirked back at me, "what a man in my position should be doing with a sedative that can be bought in any tobacconist." His face would have lit up with the smile that spread over it—except his eyes were cold and were looking very carefully in my direction. How a greasy, fat wog in late middle age could keep such presence of mind was something I'd consider in due course. He should have been the one ready to void his bowels—not me. As it was, he stood with easy assurance just a few feet from me. He uncocked his revolver and pushed it carefully into his trouser pocket. I made another effort to pull myself together, and sniffed the air again.

And it was cannabis. You really don't mistake that for anything else. I thought again of my cigarettes. I felt the need of *something* for my nerves, and I needed to give some indication in front of Pakeshi that I was in control of myself. I didn't make it to the bathroom. I had another look at the body of the smaller man. His spectacles had come off. What I'd taken for the scar on his face, I could now see, was simply stuck on. Ignore the hole in his forehead, forget about the fake scar—and I was looking straight at the man who'd lit my cigarette outside Foyles the previous afternoon.

I looked again at Pakeshi's stony face and tried to say something. Instead, I collapsed onto the settee and vomited into my towel. I was dimly aware of a shrill screaming from somewhere beyond the still open front door.

CHAPTER SEVEN

I lit another cigarette and stared defiantly ahead. Inspector O'Brien sighed and relit his pipe.

"Now, Dr Markham," he said gently, "if you really want a solicitor, we can sit here until one can be found. However, I must remind you that you aren't under arrest. All I'd like is some answers."

"I didn't kill anyone," I said quickly. "If my prints are on the gun, it's because I picked it up." O'Brien sat back, his battered face now faintly impatient. He shook his head at the policewoman who sat beside him. She put her pencil down and looked at the wall.

"Dr Markham," he said again, "this is not a television play, and we are not completely stupid. The only gun we recovered from your flat was a .22. The shots that killed your intruders were fired from something much larger. Now, since we are not accusing you of anything at all, can you please try answering some of my questions?" I could have replied that I'd answered every question that I was able to answer—first to the uniformed officers who'd turned up at the flat, then to his younger colleague at the station, and now to him. But he had a senior look about him—everyone else, to be sure, had been *very* deferential—and I didn't feel up to another argument.

I looked down at the cigarette. My hands were shaking again. Despite the blast from the radiator in that interview room, they were cold as ice. I gathered my thoughts and explained again about the smell of cannabis. O'Brien's face took on a pitying look, and he tapped the message that had been brought in ten minutes before.

"I told you," he said, "we've checked with Imperial Airways. There was no Major Stanhope booked on your flight. We've also checked with the India Office. The only Reginald Stanhope on record is a foreman in the rope factory at Calcutta Dockyard."

"But what about witnesses?" I cried. My voice came out as a tight squawk. I stopped and took another deep breath, and then a drag on my cigarette. "Everyone saw him. He was an old, fat man, with an artificial right arm." O'Brien waited for me to stop. He leaned forward across the table.

"That, of course, is something we shall look into," he said firmly. "For the moment, the facts are as they are. Whatever you say about a smell of cannabis in your flat—and this is hardly decisive evidence—we have no reason to believe that your intruders were shot by a one-armed old man with whom you may have travelled from New York. Two grouped kills with that precision aren't things one associates with an aged left hand.

"Now, can we put aside these particular suppositions, and go back to the matter of what these men may have wanted?" I shook my head. I didn't need confirmation that they'd been foreigners. Besides, Pakeshi had been through the smaller one's pockets, and pulled out a German identity card. Beyond that, I was as much in the dark as the police.

O'Brien got up and went over to a chair against the far wall. Draped over it was a German flag. The black swastika in the centre still showed clearly enough. The red and white, though, were splashed with brown gore. He held it up for my inspection, then rearranged it on the chair.

"It's fair to assume that this was intended to be left beside you, or even covering your body," he said. "Or is it possible that they didn't intend to kill you, but were planning instead to take you somewhere and leave the flag behind?" I swallowed hard and waited for O'Brien to come and resume his seat opposite me. "Or is it possible, sir, these men were angry with you?" he asked with a change of tone. I looked back in confusion. O'Brien smiled politely. "I didn't read your book about Churchill. But I am aware of the articles you wrote for *The Daily Express* last September. Your speculations on how things might have turned out had Churchill been Prime Minister when the Germans wanted to break up Czechoslovakia were most interesting. I believe they were the subject of sharp complaints in the German press.

"Do you *really* believe the world would be a better place had we gone to war with Germany?" he asked suddenly. It was an odd question for a police officer to ask. But it put me firmly on my own territory, and I felt calmer than at any moment since I'd got out of my bath. If I didn't believe it any more, I could certainly put the case.

"It is arguable," I said carefully, "that, with Germany crushed, we could have taken a firmer line in the Near East. We could have stopped the emergence of the Jewish Free State as a German satellite, and kept Turkey from renewing its alliance with Germany. We'd certainly not have signed the Petroleum Accord that stopped the development of oil as a replacement for coal. The alternatives we had to develop were less convenient than cheap, unlimited oil would have been."

"And you suppose, Sir, that we *could* have crushed Germany?" O'Brien asked. "Did you have any family members in the Great War?" I shook my head. My father and his brother had been too old to serve. One of my mother's people had volunteered as an Arabic and Persian translator under Allenby—but I'd not be mentioning any of *those* people. "Well," he went on, I lost my father and all my uncles on the first day of the Somme. I wouldn't have wished a repeat of that on my own generation. Besides, it would be interesting to see how, without Germany, we'd have kept the Russians from pressing south towards India." He shrugged and gave me a questioning look. I might have continued the defence. But, if I'd been willing to breathe fire for Beaverbrook's readers, I'd long since realised what luck it had been that Churchill wasn't in charge back in '38. I'd not try any more silly arguments on O'Brien.

"Are you suggesting," I asked, returning to his original point, "that German agents were sent to punish me for slighting Hitler's memory?" O'Brien raised his eyebrows.

"No," he said with calm assurance. "I don't think that at all. We may have had the occasional difficulty when Mr Bormann was Chancellor. Since Count Stauffenberg took over, what you suggest has become unthinkable. Besides"—he paused and now he was speaking carefully—"Do you suppose the German Government would send out someone dressed as your man was, to murder you and then drape his country's flag over your body?" he paused again and waited for what he'd said to sink in. "Is it not more likely, Sir, that some of the fifty thousand German refugees who remained here after the amnesty have hatched a plot to make trouble between the British and German Governments? You would make an obvious target.

"On the other hand, Sir," he continued, "you assure me your attackers were searching for something—though you don't seem able to say what they wanted. Indeed, there may be some doubt that they knew what they wanted. This doesn't fit in at all well with our hypothesis. It might suggest that your attackers were simple robbers, sheltering behind an elaborate mask for their actions. On the other hand, armed robbery of a private dwelling is so rare in London that I really don't wish to entertain that as a theory either."

O'Brien might be enjoying himself in a quiet way. But I simply felt sick. I needed a walk in the fresh air. I stood uncertainly up.

"If I'm not under arrest," I said, "can I go home?" O'Brien smiled, now reassuring.

"You're free to go whenever and wherever you please," he said. "I'd only ask you to tell us of any travel plans. If you see a plainclothes officer outside your block, please be assured he is there only for your protection."

"You think they'll come back?" I gasped. O'Brien smiled again. If he was about to try for reassurance, he was cut off by a knock on the door. A uniformed officer came in with a grim look on his face. He handed a note to O'Brien, whose own face now turned very dark.

"If you will sit down again, Dr Markham," he said coldly, "I have some possibly interesting news. Behind some dustbins, about a hundred yards from your flat, two more bodies have been discovered. Each had been shot through the back of the head. They were dressed as police officers. Since four in one day doubles the number of shootings we've had all year in London, I find it difficult to believe they are not somehow connected.

"Can I ask you to look at the bodies with me?"

CHAPTER EIGHT

I pushed my current bun aside and lit another Capstan Super Strength. I was in the fifth floor tea shop of the Bayswater Army & Navy. It was an improvement on staring at the saggy but stiffening faces of the dead, and an improvement on O'Brien's renewed questioning. It was certainly an improvement on shuffling up and down Westbourne Grove in the rain, wondering if everyone walking in my direction might be about to pull out a gun. But didn't make thinking any easier. I needed desperately to think through all that had happened. What had those Germans wanted? What connection had their raid with the other killings? Why had one of them first approached me outside Foyles? Instead, I found myself nervously eyeing everyone in the tea shop who was or might be a foreigner.

It was no help that the man at the next table had now turned out to be an American. When I arrived, he'd already been slumped there, morosely nursing a giant cup of coffee. I'd given him an understandably nervous inspection. But I'd been pulled at once into other thoughts by the uniformed waitress and her menu. Now, he was being joined by another man, dressed in American clothes, and I could hear from their accents that both were from one of the western States.

Not bothering to take his hat off, the other man grabbed at the offered packet of cigarettes and lit one.

"God, it takes you back," he said with an appreciative expulsion of smoke—"just to sit here in public and light up without having to look about."

"So why don't you stay on?" the first man said. "So long as you're white, the Irish don't look too closely at the documents you present. With a green passport, you can go where you like in the Empire."

"Because I'm an American!" the second man said firmly. "Besides, as long as you can pay off the right people, you can still make a lot of money in New York. Kowalski was a fool when he built that house in Brooklyn. Showing off is a red flag to the Guard." As if the management had also noticed there were Americans on the premises, the recorded music that played softly through the shop was now Cole Porter's *Begin the Beguine.* The two men fell silent and listened without moving. As it finished and something English took its place, the first man lit a cigarette.

"It was all a dream," he said in a voice of bottomless sadness. "It was already unravelling when we got into the Great War. We thought we were through that. But then there was the Depression, and then Roosevelt. By the time he was shot, the dream was over. Do what all the other smart people are doing, and stay on here. I know a man who can get…."

"So what is the news over here?" the second man broke in. "The New York papers say Lord Halifax is dying of syphilis. Any truth in that?" The first man laughed.

"Nah," he said. "He's on the way out, but not because of that. He was expected to call an election for May. There's still time under British law. But no one thinks he'll go and see the Queen. But there's gotta be an election by December at the latest. The smart money says that he'll resign after the Budget, and give his successor time to settle in before the people get to vote."

"Well, that's an old-fashioned way of doing things!" the second man said with a bitter laugh. "The Limeys have had Halifax forever. Now, he'll just step down and go off to sit in his garden. No bombs or bullets in sight!" He laughed again. "So, who's the next Prime Minister?"

I picked up a knife and cut my bun into quarters. I then cut each into tiny slices and thought of spreading on some butter. Whatever these Americans were doing in the Army & Navy, it was plain that neither had a machine pistol under the table cloth. Even so, trying to make sense of things with them next to me was about as unthinkable as playing chess on the Underground. I'd got as far as ruling out Pakeshi as the man who'd killed my intruders, and was back to speculations on Stanhope. There I was stuck.

"Halifax has been in since Chamberlain died in '44," the first American now said. "The papers say he wants some guy called Butler to follow him. He's the Chancellor of the Exchequer—which is something like a Finance Minister. This is a big surprise, as number two in the Government is Harold Macmillan—he's their Foreign Secretary. He's the one with an American mother." The first man nodded vaguely. I had found Macmillan's American connection occasionally useful out there when dropping his name. Most Americans, of course, knew nothing of our politics beyond Lord Halifax. This one was of the ignorant variety.

"But it will be Butler," the first man was saying with the condescension of the foreigner who knows something about the country where he is living. "Richard Butler's his full name. He's got the full trust of the Tory Party, and the country sees him as a safe pair of hands. You just can't say the same for Macmillan. He's got a superficial popularity with the working classes—they call him 'Big Mac'. But for every ten who like him, I'll bet there are only three who trust him.

"It's Butler, then. And, once Halifax is gone, it will be the knife for Big Mac. He'll be out. So will Heath, who's Home Secretary. He's too close to Macmillan. There's a couple of other young men about him. They'll all be out as well. If Butler wants youth in his Cabinet, his own man is Powell at the India Office—Enoch Powell, that is. He used to teach Greek or something in Australia. He'll soon be in line to take over as Prime Minister when Butler finally steps down.

"Never a truer word you've said, Kennedy. They sure do things the old-fashioned way, these Limeys!"

The men were now moving to the real purpose of their meeting, which was an elaborate fraud connected with grain shipments from New Orleans. In better days, I'd have sat there very still, taking in its details so I could run straight off to my broker with instructions to play the futures markets. But these were by no means the best of times. I'd had enough. I got up. I dropped a sixpence on the table and walked out of the tea shop. I got onto the moving stairs, and made my way past the crowds and the brightly-lit merchandise towards the exit back into Westbourne Grove.

***

"Could you possibly spare a minute of your time, Sir?" someone called as I walked past one of the moveable stands. Normally, I'd have shaken my head and continued walking. Today, there was something just sufficiently authoritative in the salesman's voice to remind me of the Police. It was a feeling that passed almost before I'd stopped. By then, it was too late. Like the Wedding Guest, I was held immovably fast. I looked at the mass of dark curls and the cheap suit and sighed inwardly. To call this worse than anything else that had happened since getting out of my bath would be absurd. In its own way, though, it was no less unwelcome.

"Did you know, Sir," he opened in a confidential and doubtless well-rehearsed patter, "that the average electric bill—for those who still have them—is £2 a year? That's almost a factory worker's weekly earnings." I saw my chance and told him about my Hotpoint Home Generator. No good. He smiled and changed his angle of attack. He led me over to his counter and showed me a light bulb that was glowing away under a glass cover. He put both his hands over a black surface about one foot square and looked at me as I watched the bulb dim and go out.

"It's photovoltaic cells," he explained—"to you and me, electricity from light. It can be sunlight. It can be daylight. It can be your neighbour's own electric lights. The Germans have got them up to thirty eight per cent efficiency and a payback time of two years. By 1965, Sir, every house in Germany will be powered by these." He took his hands off the panel and the light came back on. "No messy reagents here. No annual maintenance. Just one payment down, and, after your first two years, all the free electricity you can ever use. Looked at another way, it's six kilowatt hours to the half farthing. Your Hotpoint won't beat that, Sir."

"Sounds attractive," I said—and, to be fair, it did. "But you've got to me a year too late. I've gone with Hotpoint, and I'm in no current position to think of changing." No good again. The salesman was now unrolling a large coloured poster of a grinning driver parked in the countryside, a large glass of spirits in his hand.

"Just think of it, Sir," he urged—"all the flexibility of petrol, but at a cost of farthings in the pound. Eighty seven per cent of drivers nowadays have electric cars. These are good enough so long as you stay within the web of charging points in the towns, or along the trunk roads. If you want to get out, though, and see the *real* England, it's so far been a question of petrol at 10s the gallon. With our Photovoltaic Conversion Kit, one hour of charge will give you forty miles of driving. From the last charging points in Bromley, you can get to places like Ashford with that."

If I'd been a driver, I'd have signed up on the spot. As it was, I let him chatter away, loading me with more and more of his brochures and the facts and statistics he delivered with expert ease. All around, the crowds of late afternoon shoppers streamed or dawdled. Self-moving irons, washing up machines, filmless cameras, massage devices explained by young women so prim that none dared snigger openly at the device shapes—yes, I'd been button holed in the New Age departments of the shop. Twenty feet above, the lights glared down at us. The noise and bustle about us was suffocating. I reached up to loosen my collar. It was no longer a matter of finding somewhere to think. It wasn't even a matter of feeling safe. I needed just to get out and breathe.

CHAPTER NINE

Normally, I'd have have been pushing things, but still on time. This was Tuesday afternoon, though, and the Boots in Westbourne Grove had closed early for staff training. My overcoat pulled up and my hat down, I looked into the brightly-lit window. One of the young men—the one who always served me with a smile—looked back at me as I stood in the pool of light. He was rearranging things on the shelves. Headphones clamped over both ears, he was jiggling about to some rhythm from the cassette player that was hooked to his belt. He pointed at his wristwatch and then at the closed sign in the door. I nodded and continued looking at the advertisement for diet pills. Combined with drink, these were useful for getting things written late at night. I hadn't gone there, of course, for stimulants. The plan had been to wheedle as much morphine as the pharmacist on duty felt inclined to dispense. Failing that, I'd have bought a few grains of codeine. But I was too late. I looked a while longer at the young man. Though slim, how he'd got himself into those tight trousers was a mystery that almost took my mind off the horrors of the morning.

"Of course, you're younger than I am, dear boy," I heard a voice drone behind me. "But do even you really understand the mind of the generation now rising in England?" I turned and looked Stanhope in the face. Wearing an old sports blazer, he stood a few feet away. He'd got out of a taxi that was still ticking away by the kerb.

"Who are you?" I whispered. I looked round. Apart from a few smartly-dressed women staring into the hat shop next to Boots, we were alone on the pavement. I pulled myself together. "Who were those men you killed in my flat?" He shrugged and sucked hard on his pipe.

"Two generations of peace and prosperity," he continued as if he'd not heard me, "and the young just don't worry about anything nowadays but their funny clothes and music. See that boy in there?"

he asked with a sudden shift of tone. He pointed through the Boots window. "Apart, naturally, from sexual intercourse, do you suppose there's much more on his mind than gyrating his hips in some smoke-filled basement where, all night long, darkies play their trumpets and guitars?

"What do you suppose he'd think if he had to cut his hair and put on a uniform? Would he climb out of his trench into No-Man's Land as willingly as I did? Would you think less of him if he refused?"

"Who are you?" I repeated, now louder. "What do you want?" If, despite O'Brien's assurance, I'd been vaguely worried about bumping into more German assassins, Stanhope was the last person I'd been expecting to see in the street. He laughed and stepped towards the kerb. He raised his good hand to clutch at the open door of the taxi. He settled himself back in and looked out at me from the darkened interior.

"You, I am given to believe, take a different view of Queen and Country," he said with a chuckle. "How would *you* respond if called on to serve?" he pulled the door shut and rolled the window down. "Would you be as selfish as Ayn Rand preaches? Or would you be as self-sacrificing as her follower was back in New York?"

"I'm going straight back to the police," I said, pointing back in the direction of the station. "If you won't speak sense to me, you will to them." What was all this to do with some ludicrous American woman, or her followers? I raised my voice. "You'll tell me here and now what is going on. Or I'll have the police on you."

"I don't think that would be a wise move," he said with another laugh. "You just keep an eye on tomorrow's news, and then think about *your* duty to Queen and Country. Yes—tomorrow. That will, of course, be the 11th *Epiphi* in the Ancient Egyptian calendar. That makes it the Festival of the Risen Osiris—a most auspicious date, you'll readily agree." I dropped my arms and looked hopelessly at the grinning old maniac. He rapped on the window separating him from the driver. The taxi began to move off. Stanhope looked out at me again. "Yes, dear boy—you pay attention to the news tomorrow. I'm sure you'll find it interesting. Believe me, Dr Markham, *I did*!"

There was something gloating in these final words—gloating in their deliberate lack of meaning. Stanhope looked back and me and might have said more. I followed his taxi for the first few yards. But it accelerated and the window began to close.

"What is going on?" I yelled. "What do you want with me?" But the taxi was now heading in the direction of Queensway, and I found myself with no one to shout at but the two women, who'd left off their inspection of the hat shop and were giving me funny looks.

In Boots, the young man had his back to me. With bright flashes from the overhead cables, a trolley bus glided past, on its side a big advertisement from the South African High Commission. A land of endless sun and endless promise, it said. In the background of the picture of the ideal emigrant family, a coloured servant pushed happily on a broom. No mention of failed gold mines. Here, in Westbourne Grove, it was coming on to rain again, and I had no umbrella.

***

"But what could a man of my standing have to fear from the Metropolitan Constabulary?" Pakeshi asked with one of his greasy smiles. "Are not my papers in order? Do I not contribute valuably to the life of our Imperial Motherland?" He moved forefinger and thumb with practised efficiency over his chin and plucked out a white bristle. "I answered the good Inspector's questions and returned to my professional duties."

"Professional duties," indeed! I thought. If you count the ability to direct a knitting needle and write out morphine prescriptions a "valuable contribution", there was no doubt Pakeshi was on firm ground. But I was in no mood for sneering, and I was grateful for his whisky, and its bitter undertaste that was reviving me by the moment. With much rubbing of his sore head, Hattersley had got the front door patched up, and I was back in my flat. Of course, the bodies had been taken away, and Mrs Dale's cleaning lady had done her best with the stains. The Queen was propped up on the settee and was covering up one of the larger blood stains. Otherwise, things were back to a semblance of normality. I had a sudden thought.

"Are my things still in your flat?" I asked. Pakeshi nodded. "Could those men have been after something in my luggage?"

"Goodness gracious me, Anthony!" He burbled in an exaggerated Indian accent. "Did you think of that all by yourself?" He got up and looked at one of the larger stains on my sitting room carpet. "Surely, you are versed in all the ways of the white *Sahib*." I ignored the mockery in his voice and took another sip on his drugged whisky. He was back in the dark suit he always put on for visits to his patients of quality. The only metal in evidence now about his person was the gold watch chain that no medical man could be without—unless, that is, his ambitions went no further than 2s.6d consultations. O'Brien, I was told, had asked a few questions about the bodies in my flat. I'd said nothing about his gun. I was sure he'd said nothing. Pakeshi didn't appear to be under suspicion of murder. The exact nature of what questions Pakeshi had been asked remained unclear. But they didn't seem to have troubled him. He stood over me, holding out a hand to help me up. I ignored the offer and got unsteadily up by myself. With a final look at the hole where the Queen's nose had been, I followed him towards the door.

How the smell of curry didn't pass through the wall between our flats and gas me in my own bed was another mystery beyond solving. I'd never actually gone through Pakeshi's front door. All I can say is that his patients must have been pretty desperate to brave that ghastly miasma. The cooking smells were joined by the smoke from a dozen joss sticks that filled the place with the sort of fog you only get elsewhere from a chip pan that's caught fire. Except I had an equally overpowering reason for being there, I'd have run straight out for a vomit.

"Oh, Dr Markham," said Mrs Dale, "how delightful to see you looking so well." She looked tipsily up from the settee where she was sprawled, and pulled her dress down so her knickers were no longer on display. "Don't mind me at all, Dr Markham," she tittered. "I'm just a silly old woman who's had a little too much of Dear Srindomar's nerve tonic." She burped and stretched out to get at the remote control box that governed Pakeshi's gramophone. She knocked it instead onto the carpet. As she tried to reach it, her wig slipped, showing cropped, grey hair. With an obsequious remark, Pakeshi walked over and lifted the tracking arm from the record. I suddenly realised she'd been listening to the slow movement of a symphony by Bruckner. The smell had taken my mind off all else in the flat. It had the disturbing incongruity you get with educated Indians. There was the smell, of course, and the brightly-coloured pictures on every wall of gods with many arms and elephant heads. There was also, however, a mass of the heavy, dark furniture that had last been popular in the days of Queen Victoria. All that took away the sense that I was in the home of some retired officer of the *Raj* was the picture, right above the sitting room fireplace, and level with the native gods, of Mahatma Ghandi. From the sad look on his ravaged features, it may have been taken just before his last and fatal hunger strike.

"Do please be seated, Dr Markham," he said. He went over to a sideboard and poured three glasses of something bright green. He then put on another record—of Schubert *lieder*, sung, I think, by Elisabeth Schwarzkopf—and sat down. We listened in silence. I sipped carefully from my glass. Its base was alcoholic, though its other contents were beyond my understanding. All I can say is that it settled without dulling my wits. As the last piano accompaniment died away, I got up and went over to my things. They were just as Pakeshi had described them the previous evening. One of the suitcase locks had indeed been prised off, and someone had gone through everything inside. My dictating machine was missing. So were my walking boots. Apart from that, all was just a mess. The other bags were untouched.

"And what might be the contents of these forbiddingly large crates?" Pakeshi asked. "Since, without the intervention of your good friend Major Stanhope, they might have attracted visitors to my own front door, I suggest a certain right to an answer."

"Oh, that's only my Churchill stuff," I said. "If there's anything among them to interest anyone, I'll almost be glad." I managed a feeble laugh and kicked one of them. Someone had tried to pry this one open. So far as I could tell, though, the nails hadn't been lifted. Inside all of them, the papers were probably as neatly sorted and packed as I'd left them. "The only person who might have any interest in taking that off me would be Churchill's ghost," I said with another laugh. "What the begging letters show would give Randolph a stroke. Other than that, it's the increasingly disjointed ramblings of a dying drunk."

"I hope Flora made some order in your flat," Mrs Dale said in a dreamy voice. "She and her husband were with me in Bengal a few years ago—when we had to send out the whole army. She is used to clearing away the evidence of sudden death." She smacked her lips and laughed softly. "I find it so hard to find anyone at all nowadays—let alone anyone decent. If only we didn't have that criminal three shilling supertax, I'd ask her to move in with me." She broke off and spoke to Pakeshi in one of the Indian languages. He smiled and took her glass.

"Well, my dearest of neighbours," he said from the sideboard, his back to me, "I am no friend of your Mr Churchill. More importantly, though, since you have raised the possibility of some connection with your unfortunate experience of this morning, I think I'd rather like everything moved without delay into your own flat."

Mrs Dale drained her glass with a long cry of ecstasy, and managed to reach for the remote control. She stabbed at one of the buttons. I heard the click of the cassette tape engaging and then the opening strains of something Indian with flutes and a drum accompaniment.

CHAPTER TEN

We were straining over the last box of papers when the lift doors opened and Inspector O'Brien stepped into the hallway. In his hat and mackintosh, he looked for a moment like some British version of a Republican Guard.

"Ah, Dr Markham," he said, sounding almost pleased to see me. "The porter did assure me you'd still be awake, so I'll not bother apologising for the lateness of my call." He stopped and looked at Pakeshi, who'd beaten a sharp retreat through the doorway of his own flat. "You gave your name earlier as Dr Srindomar Pakeshi," he said in a suddenly official voice.

"Indeed, O most honourable Inspector of Police," came the greasy reply. "Are there further questions you wish to put to me?" O'Brien looked back at him for a moment.

"I have no further questions, Dr Pakeshi," he said. "However, there were two Indian gentlemen downstairs as I came into the building. Your porter refused them entry. But from the nature of what they were saying, it is possible you will receive a visit from several of my colleagues tomorrow." Pakeshi's face lost its cheerful look—no, it turned suddenly grey. The door slammed firmly shut, and we were alone in the hallway.

I led O'Brien into my flat and shut the door. He refused my offer of tea, but sat down at the kitchen table and took out his pipe.

"Have you found Major Stanhope?" I asked. There must have been a good reason for this unannounced visit. He shook his head. I thought of mentioning that I'd seen him again, but remembered what Stanhope had said. Besides, I wondered if I'd be believed. "Have you had any more out of the Imperial Airways people?" I asked again. There was something final about that shake of the head. O'Brien opened his bag and took out a small notebook.

"The men dressed as police officers and the larger man who called at your flat remain a mystery," he began. However, we've managed to identify the small man in the leather coat. He was German, sure enough, though his identity card was forged. He was a refugee called Krystoff Buchbinder. He'd been living in England six years. Before then, he was an official in the German foreign Ministry. According to his asylum application, he'd been accused of spying for Soviet Russia, and was afraid he'd not receive a fair trial in Berlin." I said nothing, but looked at the notebook O'Brien was holding.

"His landlady identified the body," he went on, "when she came to report that men had forced their way into her house earlier and tried to break through his door. Fortunately, she was able to scare them away with a shotgun. We made our own search. I can't say much of what we found there. But we did find this." He held out the notebook. I opened it and stared at the spidery writing.

"It looks like a note on my movements in the weeks before I went to America," I said nervously. "I'm not too good with German handwriting," I added. "But I could read more if you left it with me."

"That won't be necessary, Sir," he said, taking the notebook back. He put it on the table. "I have already had a full translation made." I tried to look steadily back into his face. The effort was too great, and I lit a cigarette. I'd run out of Capstan Super Strength. Woodbines would have to do.

"There are references here to an address the dead man wrote as *Orwellstrasse* 37," he said carefully. "I take this to mean a 37 Orwell Street. Are you familiar with this place?" I swallowed and flushed red. "My question," O'Brien prompted, "is purely connected with the matter in hand. I believe that the 37 Orwell Street off Euston Road—there is one other Orwell Street in London—is a place of resort for men of a certain inclination." I swallowed again and looked at the notebook. I'd have liked to pick it up and turn the pages.

"Did you know the dead man?" O'Brien asked gently. "Did he come here this morning asking for money?" I shook my head firmly. This much I could deny. I repeated the story of our meeting outside Foyles. That at least confirmed that he had been following me about. "I will assure you, Sir," O'Brien finally continued, "that my question is purely connected with the attempt on your life. The more I can know about Mr Buchbinder and his interest in you, the better it will be for my investigation."

"Until yesterday afternoon," I said, recovering my voice, "I'd never seen Herr Buchbinder before in my life. It really isn't as you think it might be." We sat for a while in silence. O'Brien lit his pipe and stared at the open notebook. He lifted it and turned to the last completed page. He pushed it across the table.

"Then we must look at other possibilities beside blackmail," he said. "There are several references here, I am told, to a 'Churchill Memorandum'. You know that I have some familiarity with your professional work. Are you in possession of any document that might correspond to this?"

I thought of the boxes that now covered the larger bloodstains on my living room carpet. Unless my memory was at fault, I must have had several hundred documents that could be described as memoranda. But I'd read them all. It made no sense that someone could have wanted to kill me to get possession of any one of them. I thought again of Stanhope. I would now have mentioned the meeting in Westbourne Grove. But O'Brien had got up and was looking through the door into my living room.

"Is this all the Churchill stuff you have?" he asked. I nodded. "You surely won't object if we borrow them for a while?" I nodded again. "Tell me," he said with a change of tone, "did your Major Stanhope show any interest in these boxes? I'm told you had them with you in your cabin. Did Major Stanhope visit you there? Did you leave him alone with these at any time?"

I lit another cigarette and thought. How did O'Brien know where I'd kept the boxes? If he knew that, how was it he still seemed to know nothing of Major Stanhope? I was glad I'd said nothing of the Westbourne Grove meeting. O'Brien was looking closely at me. I shook my head. My conversations with Stanhope, I told him, had all been in the first class saloon. A few insignificant comments aside, he'd shown more interest in calendars than Winston Churchill. And I was more worried now about O'Brien's mention of the establishment in Orwell Street. I needed time to sit down and think. If I was to tell him anything more, it could wait until I'd had time to compose myself.

O'Brien turned off the kitchen light and went over to the window. He moved the curtains gently aside and looked down into the street. He dropped the curtains and went back to the light switch.

"I don't wish to alarm you, Dr Markham," he said in a tone that was anything but reassuring. "But can I ask you not to leave this flat tonight? Can I also ask you not to answer the door unless I telephone you first? Would you also object if we collected these boxes from you tomorrow morning? It may be that there is nothing there of interest to us. But we should be grateful for the chance to look for ourselves."

I stubbed my cigarette into the ashtray and lit another. Whatever Pakeshi had given me earlier was wearing off with a vengeance, and I could feel a heavy trip to the lavatory coming on. But I tried to smile and look less perturbed than I felt.

O'Brien fished out another card and handed it over. If anything odd happened overnight, he said—he lingered on the word *anything*—I should call him. In the meantime, I should keep the door locked. I might also keep the curtains drawn.

***

A few minutes after O'Brien had eventually left, there was a gentle knock on the door. I froze and sat down on the floor. There was a louder knock. Then I heard Pakeshi calling through the bullet hole.

"Anthony, Anthony," he said with soft urgency, "open the door."

"Go away," I quavered. "I'm not allowed to come to the door. It's too dangerous." There was a hiss of annoyance.

"Anthony," he said, now louder, "if you won't open the door, I'll stand out here until you do!" Keeping my body against the wall, I unlocked the door and opened it a few inches.

"If I had the slightest inclination," he sneered, "I'd already have blown your arm off." He pushed hard and walked in past me.

"What do you want?" I whispered as I closed and relocked the door. Ignoring me, he walked into the kitchen and poured himself a cup of tea. He came back and seated himself on a patch of the settee that wasn't too stained. He'd now taken off his professional clothes, and was wearing the silk pyjama clothes of a wealthy native. There was a red dot on his forehead. His pupils had the contracted look of someone who's been eating or smoking opium. In other circumstances, I'd have made a sarcastic reference to his consultations with Mrs Dale. But I looked at the half bottle of brandy he'd produced from within his robe. He topped up his teacup and passed the bottle to me.

"It may not be my business to know what the most excellent Inspector O'Brien could have wanted with you so late in the evening. But I do regard it as my business to know what is in those boxes. Perhaps it is not in my interest to know. But it is my undoubted wish." He smiled coldly as I came back from the kitchen with an empty teacup and filled it from his bottle. There was no reason why he should know about any personal matters. But he might as well know the rest. I drained the cup and gave him an edited account of the conversation.

"Have you any tools in this flat?" he asked. I shook my head. With an expression of disgust, Pakeshi got up and went over to the front door. I thought to lock it again after him, but decided to go into the kitchen for a cup of tea. A few minutes later, Pakeshi was back, now carrying a canvas bag. He dumped it on the floor and fished inside for a hammer and chisel.

"What are you doing?" I asked wearily. I drank half my tea and topped it up with more of the brandy. "The police will be round in the morning to take everything away. I'm not sure if it's a good idea to go opening them now."

"I am, Dr Markham," he said in a voice that didn't welcome objection—and that didn't now sound particularly Indian—"proposing to open those fucking crates. If you don't wish to see what might be in them, *I do*!" With surprising force, he jabbed his chisel under the lid of one of the boxes and strained to prise it off. It was no more of a success than the effort someone else had made on the box. With a muttering of something in Hindi, he threw the chisel down and set to work with his claw hammer. With a squeal of nails within wood that might have woken Mrs Dale in whatever drug-induced slumber she'd been left next door, that got the lid off.

"Those are copies of his accounts for 1934 onwards," I said, looking at the neat bundles of yellowish paper. "There's a loan agreement secured on his country property that I'll never be able to mention. But that's everything of any interest." Pakeshi stared at me a moment, then set about another of the boxes. I had to pick up the chisel and help lift the lid off this one. This time, he made me go through the bundles of typed and mostly undelivered speeches. These were Churchill's later Philippics against Germany, and his calls for a witch hunt against pro-German Jews throughout the Empire.

"And what is this?" Pakeshi asked, pointing at the cardboard file right at the bottom of the box?" He had me there. This wasn't anything I'd packed in Chicago. One of the unopened boxes was crammed with miscellanea I had found the time to organise properly. But this shouldn't have been in with the speeches. I'd been very precise about sorting the contents of this box. Confused, I took it out and lifted the flap. Charred about the edges—doubtless from the fire that had ravaged the main collection—these were original manuscript pages in the old man's later hand. I lifted the top sheet and held it up.

"Be careful, you idiot!" I snapped, pulling another of the sheets back from Pakeshi. "Can't you see how scorched it is?" I put both sheets back into the file and took the lot into the kitchen. I put the file onto the table and lifted out all the dozen or so sheets. If they had been numbered, the lower edges were gone from every sheet, and I made sure to look at each in order. Pakeshi leaned over my shoulder. I could smell the garlic on his breath as he read them. I would have started an argument—only I was far too busy trying to control my now racing heart.

CHAPTER ELEVEN

"When was President Anslinger ever in London?" Pakeshi asked. Now standing behind me, he still looked down at the heap of scorched paper. "When did Anslinger leave his bunker beneath the White House, let alone visit a hostile foreign country?" As if it had been cold tea, I took another mouthful of his brandy and cleared my throat.

"It says here he came over in the spring of 1948," I answered. "He wasn't President yet, you can see. He was still Lindbergh's strong man. They'd settled the Houston Mutiny, and there was another six months to go before Lindbergh was killed. It seems that Anslinger was on a secret mission to get a big foreign policy success to bolster Lindbergh in the Congressional elections he'd promised for that year. He got us to repay the whole Great War debt and open our colonial markets to American manufactures. We also promised to bully the Japanese into vacating Hawaii and the Philippines, and we promised to guarantee the Pacific coast of America against further attack. You may remember how the announcement of the deal nearly did for Halifax as Prime Minister."

With hands that, no longer shaking, were still sweaty, I turned the pages over again. The bargaining, it seemed, had taken place over a dinner hosted by Churchill. Halifax had been there—though not, so far as I could tell, continuously. The main bargaining on our side had been left to Butler, who, as Leader of the House, represented Halifax in the Commons, and by Anderson, who was still at the time Foreign Secretary.

I might have supposed the minute Churchill had taken of it all was as unreliable in its account of his own contribution as anything else he wrote near the end. There was a page of self-justifying rhubarb that didn't fit in at all with the ruthless plundering we'd arranged of what he persistently called "the Great Republic". But there was no reason to doubt that its burden must be correct. Apart from some skipped pronouns and a few repeated sentences, the general tone was of Churchill in his better days. Either for the dinner or for the time spent on the memorandum—perhaps both—he must have been off the brandy.

Besides, it all made sense. No one had ever explained why Halifax had given away so much from a position of overwhelming strength. The defences he and Butler had made in Parliament—all about the brotherhood of the Anglo-Saxon race—had been grotesquely out of character. Even in the Lords, Halifax had been repeatedly shouted down. In the Commons, only heroic whipping had fought off the no confidence motion. The strain of the debates had even shortened Anderson's life.

"So you gave all that to the Americans," Pakeshi said. "All they had to do in return was hand over all research into the uranium bomb, plus the scientists who were directing it. A most estimable man was Sir John Anderson. If only he hadn't withdrawn the promise of India's dominion status, I might even praise him."

"Anderson was a scientist in his younger days," I said, ignoring the comment about India—and what would anyone have done once Members of the Indian Parliament began shooting each other instead of debating? "His thesis at Leipzig was on the chemistry of uranium. He made sure we got the Bomb even before the Germans did. Bearing in mind the Dual Possession Treaty he and Halifax made with Goering, it's no surprise he'd have given anything to stop the Americans from following." I straightened the heap of crumbling papers and lit a cigarette.

"Do you not fear cancer?" Pakeshi asked irrelevantly. I blew out a long stream of smoke and looked up at the light fitting.

"If you believe that nonsense, I'm glad not to be one of your patients," I said. "Everyone knows it was petrol fumes that caused all the cancer." I'd finally controlled the beating of my heart, and was now thinking hard. As with O'Brien the day before, I was back on my own territory. Churchill's account made sense. We'd all watched with hypocritical regret as the Americans tore themselves apart, and then lost a war they should have won with both hands tied behind their back. But there's a time when the disintegration of a great power becomes inconvenient. What Halifax and Anderson had been about was to help stabilise America. Plainly, it hadn't worked at once—there was still the terrible collapse that followed Lindbergh's assassination. But, for all his anti-British rhetoric, Anslinger had followed his own restoration of order with a complete withdrawal from foreign affairs, and no perceived inclination to acquire nuclear weapons.

"What are the Pressburg Accords?" Pakeshi asked, breaking the long silence that had followed our discussion of cancer. I looked at the last page of manuscript. I had wondered that myself. It put a snag in the simplicity of the narrative I was imposing on what Churchill had written. But I cleared my throat again and looked knowledgeable. If I put my defence into words, I'd see how well my narrative stood up.

"It could be a slip for the Treaty of Pressburg," I said. "Remember, we are dealing with a long work by a man who'd already had two strokes." Pakeshi was looking blank at the reference. I smiled and waited for him to go back to his seat opposite me.

"The Treaty of Pressburg, 1943," I said at last. "Once Goering was properly in the saddle, "Chamberlain hurried off for a second agreement at Munich. Then Goering had his second purge, and it was decided we all needed something more formal. So Chamberlain's last real outing on the foreign stage was to get together with Goering in some potty little town about fifty miles east of Vienna. They sorted everything out face to face. Germany got a free hand in Central and Eastern Europe and the Balkans excluding Greece. In return, Germany accepted all its Versailles losses in the West and the loss of its colonies, and agreed to scrap its entire fleet. Both sides needed large air forces. So we agreed to turn the skies over Western Europe into a neutral zone and to install a special telephone link between London and Berlin."

Yes, it had been Chamberlain's last and greatest triumph. It had put an end to exactly ten years of strain between us and the Germans. What might easily have bubbled over in some repeat of the July Crisis that had got us into the Great War was stopped with a settlement that fully reconciled the two great powers of the world. And it was all so logical. We gave the Germans what we couldn't stop them from taking. They left us with what they couldn't take. Chamberlain resigned the next year at the top of his career. Halifax easily won the election that followed. By the time the Japanese attacked Pearl Harbour, Chamberlain was dead. But, if this began a new round of complications, it didn't shake what had been settled at Pressburg. Indeed, we and the Germans had come even closer together for managing the pace of the Japanese expansion.

"But, my most learned and subtle Anthony," Pakeshi broke in with an oily smile—it was almost as if he'd been reading my innermost thoughts—"the Great Winston has referred to the Treaty of Pressburg on the third or fourth pages of his memorandum. He quotes Anslinger as referring to the Pressburg *Accords* right on the last page. It could be that he is quoting a misstatement. On the other hand, you will see that Anslinger is turning down the offer that Sir John Anderson has made. He is then referring to these Accords as if he were not expected to know about them. Does not the memorandum break off here? Could it be that Anslinger is about to explain the burden of these Accords, and that some further British concession will be sought before a deal can be made?"

He was right. I'd already noticed how the memorandum broke off in mid-sentence at the sixteenth page. Yes, Anslinger had rejected the deal as put to him. And if we'd got the Japanese to vacate Hawaii, we'd gone along with their annexation of the Philippines. Whatever final deal had been reached must have come after discussions much deeper into the night than these pages covered.

I got up and went back into the sitting room. I looked at the boxes. I turned to Pakeshi, who'd followed directly behind me. He shrugged and raised his eyebrows.

"It would make sense to begin with the boxes that are already open," he said.

I could have told him without a second search that there was nothing there. But we went carefully through every sheet. The missing pages weren't here. We opened the other boxes. One of these showed undeniable evidence of having been searched. But nothing appeared to have been taken or added.

Back at the kitchen table, Pakeshi shared out the last of his brandy.

He glanced again at the sixteen sheets of scorched foolscap and pursed his lips.

"There are various questions worth asking about this lot," I said, "The first is why let a garrulous old fool like Churchill in on the deal? I can see why a half-caste American might be seen as a good intermediary. But why Churchill? The second is how even the first part of his memorandum was allowed out of the country. What were our people doing?"

"And the third," Pakeshi broke in, "is why it was planted on you. And the fourth is why someone is trying to kill you to lay hands on it."

Trust Pakeshi to lead me straight off the path of high politics to the brownish stains all over my sitting room. I looked into his grinning brown face. Time for another cigarette, I thought.

"Did you see the story in yesterday's papers?" He asked. "The one about the big American loan being floated in London?" I hadn't. But it was reasonably plain that his own mind was moving along the same course as mine.

"This agreement," I said, "effectively made America into a satellite of Britain. Enough of it came into effect to show that Anslinger is our man. If this 'Churchill Memorandum' gets out, however, he'll be torn apart by his own people."

"And then the Americans will pull themselves together and look outwards again," Pakeshi said with a snarled giggle. "And that will be the end of British world supremacy," I took a long pull on the cigarette that turned half of it to ash. I smiled calmly back at him.

"I must correct you, my dear Srindomar," I said—though more by reflex than from conviction. "A nuclear and fanatically anti-Communist America would put immediate pressure on Russia. That would divert all Russian interest from the Orient—no more funded subversion among your lot!"

"Whatever you say," he said with a shrug. "But you know it will be the beginning of the end. England's power has always rested on the weakness of everyone else—that, or playing off one stronger power against another. You see how long the Empire will last once America's back in the world. All else aside, do you think they will forgive you for castrating them? It's no secret how the Royal Navy watched the Japanese as they crept across to bomb Pearl Harbour. Didn't Lindbergh himself threaten war over the rebel bases you allowed to operate in Canada?"

I would have gone through the motions of arguing with him. But it was clear he knew as much about diplomatic chess as I did. I could have speculated about some German interest. But what O'Brien had said couldn't be denied—that the Germans would never have sent out an assassin got up like Herr Buchbinder. I also didn't suppose they would have been interested to lay hands on the memorandum. Like us, they had everything they wanted. Why bank on the Americans to do other than start another civil war?

If it wasn't the Germans who'd tried to kill me, it would obviously have to be some other person or persons. Who were these, and how had they known when and where to come looking? How, indeed, had it got into my luggage in the first place? I thought of Stanhope and swallowed. How he'd done this I couldn't say. But he'd plainly set me up. I'd kept the boxes with me on the railway journey from Chicago. But there had been a good half day when those coloured porters in New York had had them all to themselves. Once more, I was back off the path of high politics.

Oddly enough, thoughts of Stanhope had steadied my nerve. He'd spoken about my duty to Queen and Country. Well, that was something in which I'd never fail—whatever it might be. I sat back and lit another cigarette. Other thoughts were now pouring into my mind. O'Brien would be back in the morning. He'd take the memorandum away. I could probably insist on his letting this be known to anyone who might otherwise still have some interest in killing me. I might even insist on some kind of explanation.

More important than any explanation, though, I now had the second volume of Churchill drifting into my head. I might not be able to tell the complete story. Indeed, I'd never be able to breathe a word of the truth. But there was enough left over to give an entirely different and more exciting tone to my second volume. At least once more, before the end, he'd taken his part in great events. And I might even squeeze another few hundred after all out of Richardson and his daughter.

I got up and poured myself a cup of water at the sink.

"We'll leave that file on the table for Inspector O'Brien," I said. "Everything else can go back in the boxes. I'd like to hang on to those. I won't bother explaining their suddenly heightened value as source material."

CHAPTER TWELVE

The morning news was all about a speech Goering had made unannounced the night before—not in Warsaw but in Prague. It was a rambling, semi-senile performance. For some reason that no one bothered to explain, half of it had been in halting Czech. Nor did anyone in the studio notice the differences between the German subtitles and the English voiceover. The key passage—and this had been in German and was correctly interpreted—was a question he'd asked near the end. Bearing in mind British-backed Arab aggression, he'd bellowed round the half-empty stadium, was there any reason why Germany shouldn't provide nuclear weapons to the Jewish Free State? This had already set off a run on all the markets, and there were calls for Halifax himself to fly home by rocket jet to make a statement that afternoon in the Lords. There was footage of the Prime Minister looking relaxed in Nairobi at the unveiling of a statue of the Queen. There was then a long interview with some doctor, who was talking about the way Goering's face had kept drooping throughout the speech. Was this evidence of another stroke? Someone else with a faintly German accent came on to speculate on how much of the speech had been cleared in advance with Stauffenberg and Hayek.

I switched channel, and caught the end of an interview with the leader of the British Communist Party. In his whining staccato, Michael Foot was calling for Jewish working people everywhere to redouble their opposition to the "cancer of bourgeois-Teutonic Zionism". No one could doubt this was the line that Moscow would confirm once Beria could be made fit with injections and vodka to face the cameras.

It was a change from Hitler celebrations, and even kicked the renewed communal rioting in Calcutta and Bombay out of the headlines. Normally, I'd have been straight on the telephone to *The*

Daily Express, trying to flog another article about Churchill's plan for a knock-out blow against Germany once Hitler was dead. As it was, I sat in front of the telly, enjoying my first smoke of the day, and making up the first paragraph of an article that would bring in much more than the usual tenner. Why, the larger crisis might even puff up the price of gold! O'Brien hadn't said what time his people would come calling.

Even as that thought drifted into mind and prepared to sink straight below the level of consciousness, there was a knock on the door. I hadn't time for jitters about the lack of a telephone call. It was only Pakeshi again. He now sounded panicky through the bullet hole.

"I've got to go away," he whispered. "I'll not blame you, my most esteemed and learned neighbour. But you are the vehicle by which troubles came to my door. I must beg the loan of two of your smaller suitcases." Unshaven, still in my pyjamas, I unlocked the door again and let him in. He'd washed the red dot off his forehead, and was now dressed as if for going out to a home consultation. There was a rawness on his chin, where he'd been plucking again at the bristles. He looked at his watch before stuffing it back into his pocket. No point arguing. Fair's fair—I had got him into trouble, and even three guineas worth of cowhide was the least he could ask of me. I took him into my bedroom. Before going to bed, I'd unpacked everything, and the suitcases lay empty on the floor. I'd been thinking to put them away on top of the wardrobe. But tiredness had finally got the better of me.

I was about to ask if Pakeshi had any religious scruples about the leather, when I heard a cough just beyond the still open front door.

"Dr Anthony Markham?" the police officer asked in the loud, flat voice that almost abolished any need for his uniform." He and his colleague stepped through the doorway. They looked at me, overlooking Pakeshi, who'd come out of the bedroom with me, and now had vanished straight into the kitchen.

"I thought more of you would be coming," I said vaguely. "Still, you won't be needing the boxes." I nodded towards the kitchen, then paused. "But I think I'd rather wait for Inspector O'Brien to come round," I added. "I'd like to explain things to him in person." Indeed,

I would. For the first time, I'd be the one to do all the talking. One of the officers turned to close the door.

"Inspector O'Brien has been taken off the case," he said reassuringly. He turned to his colleague and opened his mouth to speak. Suddenly, they'd frozen, and were looking past me.

"Goodness gracious me, my dear officers!" Pakeshi said in his most bubbling Indian accent. "You cannot possibly take my patient before his tests are complete." He'd come out from the kitchen, and stood framed in the doorway. He looked at me and then with professional disapproval at his watch.

"And you might be, Sir?" the officer who'd spoken to me asked. Was there a slight tension in his voice—or just annoyance? Pakeshi's voice was bubbling away with the insistent lilt of a sub-continental carpet salesman.

"I am Dr Markham's neighbour and physician," he said with another glance at his watch. "He told me you would be coming for him. But I cannot possibly allow him to leave without completing my examination. Considering the shock of the past twenty four hours, I cannot speak with any surety about the state of his heart." He took my arm. "Come, my dearest patient," he said. "The nurse and my colleagues await you in my consulting room next door." I gave him a confused look and tried to break free. But he had me as if in a steel vice. He led me briskly over to the front door.

"I assure you, officer," he said, looking back, "my examination will be the work of a moment. Once mine are complete, your own duties may once again be paramount."

"What, in the name of God, are you about?" I muttered once we were out in the hallway. "I told you—these men are here for the documents, not me." Pakeshi's answer was to pull me though his own front door. He closed it softly and put on the main lock.

"My dear Anthony," he said with a chilly smile. "Since when have the most excellent police of this country gone about in brown suede shoes? Since when have their pockets shown the most suspicious bulges that I saw in your flat?"

"What are you talking about?" I gasped. "Have you gone mad?" There was a sudden rap on the door. Pakeshi propped a chair against the door just under the handle and pulled me into his bedroom.

"Those men are here to kill you," he hissed with cold passion. "The reason I've saved your worthless life is that they would have killed me as well the moment they entered your kitchen. Now, if you want to stay alive, you'll come with me." Even before I could see the red flashes, my stomach had turned to ice. He took an overcoat from one of the wardrobes and threw it at me. "Put that on." He ordered. "Forget about the slippers."

There was a heavy thump on the door, and then another. This was followed after a few seconds by the crash of a bullet through the door lock, and then a renewed thumping on the door. Pakeshi got the window open and pushed me out onto the fire escape. His own flat was at the end of the corridor, and the bedroom looked over a side street. I stood there alone for a moment, looking down through the painted steel grating at the empty street. As my body warmed its thick cloth, I began to smell the curry on my borrowed overcoat. Then Pakeshi was beside me, a leather briefcase in his hand. He paused for a desperate look back into his flat, as if he'd left something. He might have been about to dash back in, when there was another sound of shooting through his front door. With a mutter of something unpleasant in Hindi, he took my arm and hurried me down the steps. He swore wildly as he strained to get the rusted ladder down to the ground. We'd just got down into the street, when I heard a shout from two floors up. There was another gunshot, and I heard the bullet ricochet from the cobblestones.

"Keep against the wall, you fool!" Pakeshi shouted as he pushed me along towards the opening into Chamberlain Street. There was another gunshot and another ricochet. Then I heard the frantic crash of shoes on the fire escape.

We ran down Chamberlain Street. No surprise that I ran like the wind. But, for all his age and probable weight, Pakeshi more than kept pace with me. As we turned into Westbourne Grove, we hit a group of about a dozen market traders who were rolling out from one of the all night pubs.

"Watch out! Watch out!" one of them shouted as we pushed our way through. "Oh, you bleeding yids and niggers—no manners!"

Pakeshi shoved him hard in the chest and his hat fell off. One of his friends bent forward to pick it up, and we hurried through the gap. We raced about twenty yards along the mostly deserted street. A trolley bus was just pulling away as we reached the request stop. Pakeshi jumped onto the open deck and lifted me clean on behind him. If the conductor had bothered looking back, or the driver had looked in his mirrors, two apparent police officers would have been obvious on the road behind us. That would have brought us all to a sudden halt. But neither did look. The men ran heavily after us, shouting and waving. We came to another request stop, but no one flagged us down. The trolley bus hurried along Westbourne Grove towards the eighty floor monstrosity of the Pemberton Tower. I looked back. Far behind us, out pursuers had managed to stop a taxi and were arguing with the driver. The lights we were passing changed suddenly to red, and there was a build up of traffic as if from nowhere.

I reached within the overcoat to the breast pocket of my pyjamas and took out a now crumpled cigarette pocket. I begged a light from the conductor, who gave a funny look at my pyjama trousers. I breathed in the smoke, and waited for the tightness in my lungs to relax and my heart to come back to something approaching normal. Good for me that Pakeshi's talk of a bad heart was a lie. I slumped into the long seat we'd taken at the back of the trolley bus.

"Who were they?" I asked. Still on his feet, Pakeshi was looking intently back. Without taking his eyes off the still busy road behind us, he pulled out a few coppers and gave them to the conductor.

"Who they *are* doesn't presently matter," he whispered. "What does matter is the guns they seem willing to use even on the streets of London." He reached over and pulled on the bell cord. "We need to put far more distance than we so far have between them and ourselves."

We got off by the entrance to George Street Underground Station and hurried down the steps. Pakeshi announced in a purely English accent that he was a doctor on emergency and pushed his way to the front of the queue at the ticket office. With two threepenny tickets, we jumped onto a departing Coronation Line train. I begged another light and smoked in silence all the way to Euston, where we got off.

Euston Road was reassuringly crowded. Dressed in smart hats and coats, the office workers scurried about to coffee bars or to late 9am starts. It wasn't a cold morning, but the pavement heating was on at full blast, and I could feel its warmth through the soles of my slippers. Keeping close by Pakeshi, I hurried along in the crowds. Far over on the right, obscured by second hand bookstalls, was the entrance to Orwell Street. So far as I did look about, it was to my left. The redevelopment was finally over, and the scaffolding had come down from the gleaming neoclassical *facades*. On both sides of the road, from Portland Street, all the way to King's Cross, the new buildings ran in a blaze of magnificence that even a Roman Emperor might have envied. The boundary between the twenty foot pavements and the road was lined with plinths, most already filled with toga-clad statues of the famous dead. One of the new buildings would soon house the offices of Richardson & Co. The Old Man, no doubt, would have been happy to sit forever like the bloated spider he was in the dingy courtyard behind Southampton Row. But Vicky had nagged him into moving, and my second Churchill volume would be their first launch from the new premises.

However, I was in no mood for basking in the magnificence, or my own small future share of it. The road itself was crowded with traffic. The massed hum of all the electric engines was like the feedback from a pair of headphones with the volume turned full up. The air was thick with the smell of electricity. I looked at Pakeshi. Though somewhat darker, his face was as drained of expression as the new *facades*.

***

"So, what do we do next?" I asked. Pakeshi put down his knife and fork and stared thoughtfully at me. Half an hour in Marks & Spencer, and 23s.6d of his money, had got me out of my pyjamas. I hadn't quite the cultured look of Dr Markham's usual self. But no one would now be giving me sideways looks as I hurried past. We were still in the Baker Street branch of Marks & Spencer, and the late English breakfast was a welcome break from a random hurrying along streets that, sometimes wide, sometimes narrow, were always crowded.

"I might suggest a visit to the telephone boxes in the basement of this most luxurious emporium for a call to your Inspector O'Brien," came the reply. Pakeshi took up his folded overcoat and fished into one of its breast pockets. Folded, so it had cracked down the length of its scorched foolscap, was the Churchill Memorandum. I straightened my face out of the scowl I was beginning at the sight of the damage. Pakeshi smiled. He leaned down and opened his briefcase under the table. He put in the document, still folded, and closed the catch.

"It is this that your supposed police officers wanted—isn't it?" he asked. I nodded. It was for the best he'd taken it, I told myself. I couldn't see what else the men had come for. They'd have killed me and walked off with the Memorandum. If we'd left without it, they'd still surely be after me. With it, we might be in a better position. Certainly, I could show it to O'Brien.

"And what about you?" I asked. "You'll come with me to the station, won't you? If it's a matter of immigration status, I don't think that will be a problem after this." Pakeshi smiled and gave me a satiric toast with his teacup.

"This is, my dearest Anthony," he said, "a matter to which I had given no consideration whatever before you raised it. I saved your life purely out of the deep love I bear you as my neighbour. Now you mention it, however, it was rather fortunate that I brought Mr Churchill's memorandum with me." He looked sideways at me through slitted eyes, and, with unerring aim, plucked a bristle straight from the left side of his upper lip.

"I need to visit the gents," I said, putting my napkin on the table.

After washing my hands, I stood awhile smoking and looking at myself in the mirror. A comb and a razor would have been useful. But I put the cigarette down and rubbed at my face to try and smooth off the hunted look. I'd never see twenty five again. But, on a good day, I might pass for somewhat less. And there was no reason why, today, I should look considerably past thirty.

There was a flush in one of the cubicles behind me. The door opened and a man in late middle age stepped out. We'd seen each other perhaps a dozen times. For just a moment, our eyes met in the mirror. Then we both looked away. He stood beside me and washed his hands in silence. I patted a lock of hair into something like its normal outgoing position and walked back out.

Pakeshi was waiting just outside the door. He pulled me over against one of the screens separating the restaurant from the rest of the shop and shoved one of the mid-morning newspapers under my nose. Half way down the front page was a picture of Goering and an account of some "clarification" von Mises, his Finance Minister, had made to try settling the markets. Pakeshi waited until one of the waitresses had gone past with a tray of coffee. Then, with an impatient grunt, he stabbed at the main headline. I stared in total confusion at my own photograph. It was the one Richardson had commissioned for the first Churchill volume. Odd it hadn't been the first thing I saw on the page. I looked back at Pakeshi.

"But this can't be," I said in soft despair. "We must go at once to Inspector O'Brien. He knows I didn't kill those men. Besides, how can I be wanted for murdering you, when you're alive and standing beside me?"

CHAPTER THIRTEEN

The police were out in force by all the platforms at King's Cross. For the hundredth time that afternoon, I resisted the urge to put up a gloved hand and touch the brown face paint. Instead, I showed my ticket to the inspector. He nodded and I stepped with Pakeshi through the barrier.

"THE 6:27 WILL SHORTLY LEAVE FROM PLATFORM EIGHT," the announcement boomed crisply overhead, "CALLING AT…." Where it was calling didn't matter. I was in Pakeshi's hands. Where we went was his decision.

The motor was already revving up as we boarded, and I nearly tripped when the magnets came on and raised everything an inch off the single rail. We found our way to the first class compartment marked on the ticket. Pakeshi closed the door and pulled down the blind. I sat gloomily and looked again at the newspapers we'd picked up on our way through the concourse. I was on every one of the front pages. My face burned red beneath the paint as I looked at some of the horrid things that had been written about me. Leave aside the details of what I was supposed to have done to Pakeshi and the two Germans—the incidentals were perfectly beastly.

"The books a man keeps on his shelves at home are none of the world's business," I wailed softly. "Can't they understand that I'm a scholar, and that I need to have all sorts of research materials ready to hand?" Pakeshi smiled and looked up from an account of the rioting that had now spread to Madras. Reading the upside down headlines, I was able to see there had been thousands of deaths, and that the Moslem League was now preaching *jihad* against us and the Hindus. No doubt, the Hindus in turn were rioting against us again and the Moslems. So far as I could tell, this had all blown up from a sermon given in Seringapatam by a French Catholic priest. I'd normally have followed this with moderate interest. But there were other photographs of me all over the inside pages. I couldn't imagine how the newspapers had laid hands on *those*.

"I don't think, Anthony dear," Pakeshi replied with a glance out of the window—the platform was floating gently past as we left the station—"any of your neighbours will be surprised by the details of your private life. The eminently perceptive Mrs Dale spotted your little weakness a day after you moved in. I hope you will appreciate my reticence if I do not ask what 'objects' were taken from your flat that 'are not suitable for a family newspaper to name'" Pakeshi gave me his first greasy smile of the day, and went back to the Indian news.

I sat a while in silence. I tried not to think about the newspaper reports. I tried not to wonder what had gone so dreadfully wrong with everything in the past two days. I tried not to think about many things. I ended with all of them jumbled hopelessly together in my mind. King's Cross was already several minutes behind us, and there was a rising hum from the motor as it took us towards our cruising speed. I put a cigarette into my mouth and reached for my matches. Without looking up, Pakeshi pointed at the No Smoking sign on the window.

"It was the only first class compartment they had left," he explained. "Would you have had me procure tickets for the second class carriages?" I ground my teeth and stood up.

"I'm going outside," I said. Reading what looked like the dog track results, Pakeshi sniffed.

"There is a lavatory if you go left along the corridor," he said. "The lights will soon be fully on, and I'm not sure if your facepaint would bear close inspection in the corridor."

I sat on the toilet and struck a match. As I took the cigarette away from my mouth, I noticed how I'd got brown paint over the base of my forefinger. I held both hands in front of me and willed the shaking to subside. I might as easily have willed the loud and omnipresent hum of the motors to die away. I drew hard again on the cigarette and held in the smoke. That might eventually have worked. Worse luck, though, I could hear two women had already formed a queue on the other side of the door.

"It's plain, if you ask me," one of them was saying, "the papers can't tell the half of what they must all have been doing together in that flat. Those nasty black hands, all over that poor German boy, and then shooting him afterwards—it fair makes the flesh creep." There was an expression of agreement from the other woman. The picture of Buchbinder that had been supplied to the newspapers bore no resemblance to the grinning sadist who'd tried to murder me in my own sitting room. But there was no point shouting that through the door. I sucked hard on the cigarette and tried to blot out the conversation. I failed. "It's that hot, foreign blood, of course," she went on. "Perversions aside, it sends them fighting mad if you give them so much as a funny look."

"Did you see that programme on the telly the other evening?" the other woman now broke in. "It was about a whole street of them in Nottingham. No? Well, every one of the houses is filled with them. All you can see in the street is the brown faces of their children. Once they've lived there a week, you know, you can't get an English family to move back in—not without taking all the plaster off back to the brick. It's their cooking, you see. The smell seeps into the plaster."

"Oh, but he's not pure Indian," the first woman replied. "His father was English. And you must agree"—there was the rustle of newspaper—"that he's not half bad looking. You can see he's a bit less than white. But he's got that pretty look about him you often find in half-castes. Shame about his tastes…."

"Well, I'm not one to judge," the second woman jumped back in. "Down my street, there's a woman who's moved a Jamaican in with her. No one speaks to her, of course. Still"—she paused and drew breath—it's not my business if she's too ugly to get a white man. Live and let live is what I've always said. If they're happy together, I'm not one to go judging." She paused again. "Mind you," she added at last, "it's the children I feel sorry for. They just don't know which side they're on."

I jammed my still glowing butt into the ashtray and shot the bolt. Not looking at either of the now silent women, I walked straight past and made for the end compartment. Even Pakeshi's company was an improvement on this. As if hurrying to the toilet, there was a man coming towards me. I pushed myself against the window and waited for him to squeeze past. Instead of going past, though, he stopped in front and looked carefully at my face.

"In you come, Tony!" he said in the flat voice of the working classes. He put one arm about my shoulders and, with the other, jammed a gun against my chest. I opened my mouth to cry out, but thought better of it. The man glanced into the compartment just beside us, then pushed me back down towards where one of the women still waited with her back to us. The man got the door opened and shoved me so hard into an empty compartment that I went sprawling on the floor. It was as if I'd been grabbed by one of those trapdoor spiders you see on the nature documentaries. I lay a moment on the compartment floor, too confused even to feel scared.

"Right, Tony my lad," the man said with a grin, "I don't think we need no introductions. You don't need to know who I am, or how I caught up with you. You just hand over that document you've got about your person, and I'll leave you here in one piece. That's a promise, sure as anything—none of us needs no friction."

I looked up into the battered face. He was right that gunshots would suit neither of us. Though the motors were now so loud that he had to speak up to be heard over them, any gunshot would surely be heard in the next compartment.

"So, what do you want with it?" I asked with a better than fair appearance of self-possession. I swallowed and looked the man in the eye. "And I might ask who's paying your bill. You don't sound German, and you haven't tried a Hitler salute yet. But I don't suppose you're working for anyone with an English accent." Keeping my hands in front of me, I got up carefully and seated myself on one of the plush benches.

"Well, who isn't the cool fucking cucumber?" the man answered. He pushed his hat back and laughed. "But German, Germans? You're barking up the wrong tree there, mate." He laughed again and waved his gun at me. "You see this?" With his free hand, he took a railway compartment key from his pocket and held it up. "You be a good shit-faced little queer and get that document out of your pocket. You give it here, and I'll just lock you safely away till the next stop."

I smiled and held up both hands. Behind him, on the other side of the glazed door, Pakeshi was looking in. I saw him reach up to put a hand on the sliding door and push it—ever so gently open. I've said the electrical hum was omnipresent. Door open or door closed, there'd be no change in its tone. It was a matter of keeping the man occupied.

"Then, if you aren't working for the Germans," I said loudly, "would I be wrong to guess that the Russians were paying your wages?" The man laughed again. "Might you even be a member of the Communist Party?" I hazarded. "Not everyone left there, I'm told, is an intellectual." Another laugh. Pakeshi now had the door open wide enough for him to step noiselessly through the gap. I thought of another question—anything to keep the man from turning round. But Pakeshi now had both hands up behind the man. As if moving in some Indian dance, he brought the bony parts of each wrist hard together, until each smashed simultaneously against the man's temples. The hat tipping forward, the man went straight down like some stricken beast in the slaughterhouse.

"I did tell you, Anthony dear, to be careful" Pakeshi said calmly, a hint of disapproval in his voice. He stepped fully into the compartment, and slid the door shut. He pulled down the blind and turned back round to kick the fallen man in the crotch. No movement. Pakeshi bent down and went quickly through the pockets. He took out a wallet and flipped it open. "Do have these," he said, handing over a £5 note and some silver. "The £8.12s.9½d you owe me for clothes, syringe, lunch, makeup and railway incidentals, we can discuss another time. But you can at least pay when we visit the dining carriage." He went back to his inspection of the other wallet contents. There was nothing to take his interest. He looked down at the fallen man.

"Is he dead?" I asked nervously. Pakeshi reached carefully down for a pulse and shook his head.

"Not dead—not dead yet, at least," he said with a look back at the closed door. "But, if you'll get that window open, that can be our next business." I shrank back into the seat and fought to control the horror.

"I'll be no party to murder!" I gasped. Pakeshi put his face close to mine. I held my breath to avoid the smell of whatever he'd eaten for breakfast.

"This creature will wake within a half hour at the latest," he said softly. "I don't think this is the time or the place for questioning him. As for murder, there's already a rope about your neck. Now—get that window open!"

With shaking hands, I pulled on the leather strap, and fell back at the sudden wall of air that hit me at two hundred miles per hour. Its high roar blotted out all sound of the electric motors. Straining with the unexpected weight of unconscious flesh, I helped Pakeshi get the man off the floor and pull him over to the window. We had to turn him sideways to get the shoulders through. For a moment, he balanced on the open window, arms pressed left against the carriage by the blast of air. With a casual motion, Pakeshi lifted the legs and waited for the air to suck the man fully out. Next, he threw out the wallet and then the gun. He pulled up the strap and rubbed both hands together.

"Come along, Anthony," he said brightly. "The ticket inspector will not be pleased if he finds us in the wrong compartment. And I will note"—he pointed at the sign on the now closed window—"that this too is a non-smoker."

CHAPTER FOURTEEN

"Make mine a double," I muttered to the waiter. He nodded and finished taking the order. "How can you know," I said to Pakeshi once we were alone again, "that there aren't more of them?"

"I don't," came the reply. I looked once more round the brightly-lit dining carriage. The two women who'd been waiting outside the toilet were sitting a few tables down. Deep in some chattering conversation, they paid no attention to us. The other diners all seemed reassuringly respectable. They'd given us a look of collective but faint hostility as we entered—my brown paint had now been repaired with a second coating. They'd looked put out by the colour of our faces. Perhaps they were more put out by my failure to remove either hat or gloves. Perhaps it was Pakeshi's smell, and the smell that still clung to the overcoat he'd lent me. If I was aware of this, others ought to be. But these considerations had, in themselves, been reassuring. Now the waiter was back already with a large glass. I put my cigarette down and drained its contents.

"Another, if you please," I said, forgetting to bother with my accent. The waiter raised his eyebrows and went away with the glass.

"From your description of what was said," Pakeshi went on, "I should say he was alone on this railway train. I could, I must accept, be wrong. But my brief tour of the second and even third class carriages revealed no obviously unwelcome truths. I fear, even so, that we shall need to change our travelling arrangements. This is an express, but there will be a stop at York, where we can get off and change. What does most concern me, however, is what could have enabled your friend to catch so unerringly up with you. I can assure you, Dr Markham, that, when I wish not to be followed in a place like London, I am *not* followed!"

"What are these 'travelling arrangements?'" I asked, ignoring this last point. "Where are we going?" As I spoke, the lights flickered in the carriage, and there was a rattle of glass and china as the railway train began to slow. I felt my face turn pale under the paint.

"There is nothing to fear," Pakeshi said in the sort of voice I could imagine he kept for his dying patients. "There is a long stretch of unmagnetised line somewhere between Ely and Lincoln. My understanding is that we shall not stop, but must continue forward with some less modern form of locomotion." The waiter was now back with my drink. Another was carrying our dinner. Pakeshi beamed at his cheese omelette and unfolded his napkin. "Such excellent service, would you not agree, the London and North Eastern Railway provides to its first class passengers?" He reached into his bag and took out a glass jar filled with some yellow powder. He scattered it liberally over the plate.

I picked miserably and in silence at my reheated lamb cutlets, and tried to ignore the vomit-inducing smell of Pakeshi's curry powder. Sure enough, the electric hum died gradually away, and the smooth forward motion gave way to the more traditional rumble of metal wheels on metal rails.

***

Back in our compartment, Pakeshi used the round key he'd taken to lock the door. It wouldn't prevent a determined attack, he said, but might slow things down. Still, with two shillings worth of spirits sloshing about inside me, I was feeling moderately safer. I looked at one of the late edition newspapers Pakeshi had called for after dinner. My face had now vanished to the inside pages. In its place was news that the entire German Government had got together and "clarified" old Goering's threat into a rhetorical flourish. Von Mises had spent all day soothing the markets. Hayek was, even now, risking himself on an aeroplane flight to London to discuss things directly with Macmillan. Another crisis that wasn't leading anywhere.

I thought of what Stanhope had said the previous day about the coming news. This morning, I'd supposed he had some wind of the Goering speech—it made sense, considering his preferred reading material. Obviously, I'd dropped this supposition the moment my own face had turned up in the newspapers. I was now back to wondering if my first supposition had been so wrong.

The other overseas news remained grim. Communal rioting had spread to every main Indian city. The Viceroy had declared martial law in three Provinces, and all the Sikh Regiments were being called to New Delhi. There were unconfirmed reports of clashes between units of the Russian and Japanese armies somewhere on the Mongolian border. The Jews were threatening to drop poison gas on the Arabs unless they evacuated Beirut. The Turks were trying out some of their new German weapons as they put down the rising against them in Teheran. On a lighter note, the wife of the French President had been dancing naked again in some Parisian theatre.

The home news was unusually placid. The Liverpool dock workers had settled their strike. Penguin had brought out an unexpurgated *Lady Chatterley's Lover*, and was daring the authorities to prosecute. Three monsters had apparently been photographed at Loch Ness. A bus driver in Rotherham was claiming that aliens had abducted him from his night shift and sexually molested him. The Federation of British Industry was calling on the Chancellor to cut income tax to 1s.3d in his budget, and make up the lost 3d with an excise on generator reagent. That would be ignored, no doubt—though, if I made it far enough into the new tax year, I calculated it might make me £5 better off on balance.

Because there was so little else to report, I dominated the rest of the home news. Pakeshi's body had supposedly been fished out of the Surrey Canal in Deptford. I'd been sighted in Exeter and in Deal. That turd Barlow was cashing in on what he still claimed I'd done with him in 1952 in the basement of the LSE Library. If I hadn't already been numb with the horror of all that had happened, I'd have got up and shouted at the unfairness of the newspapers.

But it was late. No one else had come knocking on the door to murder me. Looking at the few lights that went past outside, we were crawling along this stretch of line—crawling and gently swaying. It was the soporific swaying you used to get on long railways journeys before magnetisation of the main lines. I could feel the drink tightening its hold on me. If I nodded off for an hour, I might contrive to feel more cheerful. If I nodded off and more killers broke in, I'd at least be rested when they finally shot me….

I pulled myself together and looked quietly round. I had been dozing. I might even have been sleeping. Since I had no watch, it was impossible to say how long I'd been slouched back with my eyes shut. I could ask Pakeshi for the time. I might also start badgering him for some facts about where we were headed. I might also suggest at least a call to O'Brien. I didn't fancy putting myself into his hands. But a short conversation might reveal something about what had been done to me.

But Pakeshi was asleep. Mouth open, eyes shut, he sat opposite me, pressed into the corner formed by the window and the wall of our compartment. I looked at him awhile. Every so often, he'd mutter something under his breath. More often, he'd let out a gentle snore. I looked at the leather briefcase he'd snatched up in our escape from his flat. The Churchill Memorandum was in there. I felt the sudden need to see it again. There might be something else in it that I'd overlooked in my only and hasty reading of it the night before—something that would better explain why I was being hunted by our own people, and by some other person or persons unknown. It might also be worth seeing what else Pakeshi had brought along with us. He'd risked a good twenty seconds on getting that case—twenty seconds while I was waiting on the fire escape and two armed men were trying to smash in his front door.

It was just between his feet. With the swaying of the railway train, one of his legs knocked against it every so often. Otherwise, it was untouched. I watched and waited and got the rhythm of the swaying. I reached forward and pulled the case towards me. It was surprisingly heavy, and I had to grab it with both hands to stop it from scraping on the carpet. I took it onto my lap. Holding my left thumb over the latch, I pushed gently down on the opening button. I'd already seen it wasn't locked, and the latch came away with a soft click. With a stab of excitement, I pulled the case open and looked in.

I looked up at the ceiling and squeezed my eyes shut and then open again. I looked back down into the case. It must have been after midnight, and the compartment lights had been dimmed. But you can't mistake banknotes when you see them. The Memorandum was right at the top of the case, just where Pakeshi had dropped it in the Marks & Spencer restaurant. From what I could see, the rest of the case was stuffed with money—bundles and bundles of white Bank of England notes—fives, tens, fifties, hundreds—all thick bundles, neatly held in paper bands of the Midland Bank. How much was in there I just couldn't say. It might have been £50,000, or £100,000. The thing about money above the usual amounts is that, unless you work as a bank clerk, you can't estimate sums from their physical mass.

I heard a sound opposite. I looked up into the barrel of Pakeshi's gun.

CHAPTER FIFTEEN

I dumped the still open case on the seat beside me and sighed wearily. This was only my Third look into the barrel of a gun. But it was my third in only two days, and I was learning fast.

"Come now, Srindomar," I said, "you surely wouldn't kill me after such devotion to keeping me alive." I reached into the case and pulled out a bundle of fifties. "I'd never have thought the medical profession could be so profitable." I laughed softly and dropped the bundle back into the case.

"What a man cares to do with his money in this country is his business alone," Pakeshi said. He put his uncocked revolver back into his overcoat pocket and reached across for the case. "If no one in the bank presumed to ask questions of me yesterday afternoon, can you give me any reason why you should ask any now?"

"Oh, I can think of many reasons, my dearest Srindomar," I said with what I hoped was a bitter smile. "In the first place, the clerks who counted it for you weren't on the run with you for murders they hadn't committed, or that hadn't taken place. They also weren't being chased by God knows who. Now, would you care to enlighten me on your own part in this pantomime? Any chance that you're one of Stanhope's old Indian friends?" Now it was Pakeshi's turn to laugh—not the high giggle of the East, but a parody of the English guffaw.

"Oh, Anthony, Anthony," he mocked. "Always the historian! Always ready to make patterns and impose them on the most disparate events. Such a blessing all the Gods in Heaven heaped on suffering humanity when they never inclined you to study medicine!" Now, he sniggered in his usual way, and plucked twice at a bristle on his upper lip. Silent, I stared back at him. He snapped his case shut and put it back under his feet.

"Very well," he went on, "if you must know all, I will tell you something. The money is my business, not any of yours. When I saw the accursed Mr Churchill's document last night, my third and final decision was to remove myself from London. At the best of times, your Inspector O'Brien's colleagues would have been hard on me. I had no wish to involve myself in further complications. When those men arrived at your flat, I was there wholly to beg the loan of your fine suitcases. I saved you because there was no other way to get myself out of your flat alive. When they followed us, I naturally ran with you. As we finished our belated breakfast in Marks & Spencer, I decided it would be in my interest to represent myself to Inspector O'Brien as your saviour, and therefore the saviour of England. When I opened the newspaper, and had recovered from my own shock at what it contained, I dropped that plan and decided on the plan we are now executing." He paused and stretched his arms. He fell back into his dozing position and smiled at me.

"And your current plan—what might that be?" I asked, breaking the silence that had followed. Pakeshi smiled again.

"There is no benefit in handing you to your own authorities," he said. "But, while I accept it may not have been they who tried to kill you for it, the Germans might be persuaded to pay good money for Mr Churchill's memorandum." He grinned into my tight, suddenly angry face. "The plan, since Marks & Spencer, has been to get you to Hull. From there, we can take a ferry to Rotterdam. Holland, you may be aware, has no passport control for visitors from the United Kingdom, which solves the difficulty of our having left Bayswater unequipped for overseas travel. From there, I expect an easy time in the German Embassy. It will be easy, that is, for me. For Her Majesty's Government, it will entail the greatest embarrassments. Published to the Americans, it will be some measure of German revenge for the Zimmermann Telegram that got America into the Great War on the British side." He giggled and let his right foot kick against the briefcase. "An aroused America will be staunchly anti-British. It will also, as you pointed out last night, be reliably anti-Russian. On either count, the Germans will not be displeased."

"I won't allow this!" I said fiercely. I got up and stood over Pakeshi. He shrank deeper back into his corner and went through the motions of looking frightened. "What you're proposing is treason—treason against the Queen-Empress, treason against this country, treason against the Empire. I'll not let you get away with it." I bent down to get at the briefcase. If it was the last thing I did, that Churchill Memorandum was going, one torn up page at a time, out of the window.

Without seeming to move any other part of his body, though, Pakeshi's right leg shot up and smashed with overpowering force into my chest. I found myself back in my seat, my head ringing from where it had knocked against the wall above the back of the seat.

"Please, my esteemed and most learned neighbour—please, my dearest Anthony—do not test my patience. If I saved your life this morning, it was, as I have said, in my own interest. If I broke my medical oath before dinner this evening, it was because I like you. I do not think you will be of much use to me in my negotiations with the Germans. The document you have most kindly allowed me to retain is all that I really need. Be grateful for my charity—and do not test my patience." He got up and now he stood over me. It was now my turn to huddle back in my seat. The railway train rumbled again on its tracks, and Pakeshi had to steady himself by holding onto the luggage rack. But he continued standing over me, and looked pityingly down.

"Your talk of treason is wholly beside the point," he continued. "Continued British rule of India has been a disaster for the Indian people. You were not in Bengal when the rice crop failed. You did not see the multitudes who wandered in the country districts, having abandoned their towns and villages—the sunken eyes, wan faces, lips flecked with foam, lower jaws projecting, bones protruding through skin, stomachs hanging like empty sacks. You did not see them howling with the pain of hunger, begging alms. Can you imagine the very children sold by parents, and the collective suicides? Can you imagine how the starving even split open the stomachs of the dead or dying to eat their entrails? Millions died to the point where the country was covered with the corpses of the unburnt or unburied. And then there was the pestilence that carried further millions away. All this was the work of English rule of India. Do not accuse me of treason when revenge is a better word."

"Then you're a bloody fool," I snarled. Yes, Pakeshi had a gun, and he knew how to use his hands in ways I hadn't conceived. But I knew nonsense when I heard it. "The rice crop failed because the virus used by the Japanese in China spread to India. The plague was also Japanese work. We did everything possible to relieve the distress. How would you and your Congress Party friends have fed fifty million starving beggars? As I recall, it was the Congress Party that machine-gunned the corn meal distributors, and lied that the meal was contaminated with beef lard. Don't tell me about Indian patriotism when all you want is to add German gold to English paper."

Pakeshi smiled and sat down. He'd spoken about the famine with what seemed genuine passion. The virus had "escaped" from a Japanese laboratory in 1942, and he was old enough to have been practising then. But he was now his usual ironic self, and it was hard to tell if he'd believed a word about his pity for the Indian poor. He took out his watch and looked at the time. In defiance of the No Smoking sign, I took out my cigarettes and lit up. Pakeshi glowered and reached for the leather strap to pull the window down an inch. He controlled himself and went back to his cold smile.

"Mr Kingsley Wood might have done more than he did from New Delhi," he said, quietly giving in. "And do you recall how the potato famine killed Irish nationalism for a generation? If British rule has lasted this long over India, is it not because a fifth of India lay dead by 1943?" He waved at the newspaper reports of the Indian rioting. "How do you suppose this would be controlled if India were not still prostrate? Leave aside air power—there are currently not ten thousand white soldiers in the whole of India." I gave no answer, and the argument died. Pakeshi looked again at his watch and sighed.

"But do tell me, dear Anthony." He asked, "what better plan you have than my own. The men who tried to kill you this morning were not police officers. But I saw no inclination at Kings' Cross to give yourself in to the real police."

"I was wrong," I said. "I want to get off this railway train in York and turn myself in to the first uniformed constable I meet. I want that document back, so I can hand that over as well. If you want to continue to the Hull ferries, that's your concern. I'll not tell anyone." Pakeshi raised his eyebrows.

"And you will trust the authorities not to hang you?" he sneered.

"The authorities would never knowingly hang an innocent man," I said with firm assurance. "I don't understand what's in the papers. But I trust the honesty and good intentions of the men who rule this country." That shut Pakeshi up. He sat opposite me, his mouth open. Once or twice, he looked as if he'd burst out laughing. But he obviously found no reply. We sat in silence for perhaps ten minutes.

The carriage swayed again, and there was a grinding of metal on metal. Pakeshi put a hand to his pocket, then sat up and looked out of the window. We were coming to a stop at a platform where all the station lights were burning bright. I heard shouts further along the platform, where a conversation had started with the drivers.

"There is no scheduled stop at Sleaford," Pakeshi said flatly. "Your wish to have a rope put about your neck may have been granted sooner than you expected." He might have said more, but we'd now stopped, and there was a man on the platform just outside our window. He had his back to us, and all I could see was his hat. "Get down!" Pakeshi whispered urgently. He pulled me to the floor. We huddled together. I saw the man's shadow as he seemed to be putting up a hand to see into the compartment. There was a laugh and a muttered comment I couldn't hear through the glass. Pakeshi looked briefly over at the locked door. He pulled out his gun and held it uncertainly.

"If you try using that," I said, "we'll both hang for sure." I could almost hear my heart banging away inside my chest. I wanted to persuade him to put the gun away and stand up. But my throat was suddenly tight, and I was going into a fit of the shakes. Had they already found the dead man all those miles back along the line?

There was a loud hiss of steam and a long shudder of steel as the locomotive engine started up again. I saw the glow from the platform lights move as we began to pull out of the station. As everything outside the window darkened again, Pakeshi stood up. I didn't know which was worse—Pakeshi gloating and self-assured, or Pakeshi nervous to the point of dithering. Each was awful in its own way. I'd spent all day with the former. Now, I was having a glimpse of the latter. He took hold of his gun in both hands, as if each might cancel out the tremor in the other.

I remained on the floor. We must still have been some way till the magnetised line started again, and the railway train was still only rumbling along. Even so, we were moving, and it was only a matter of time before the carriage to carriage search reached our own compartment.

"My plan of getting off at York has just changed," Pakeshi said. He reached for the strap to get the window open. Suddenly, he froze. There were men in the corridor outside our compartment. The blind was still down, but I thought I could see a shadow on the thin cloth.

"He's in there," one of them was saying. The door handle rattled, and the compartment door slid open about an eighth of an inch. The man swore and seemed to let go of the handle. "Get it unlocked," he snarled.

"I don't know about that," the ticket inspector said. "You can't get me opening first class compartments without proper cause. The Railway by-laws say very clearly—here, you can't go pointing that thing at me!" There was a muffled thud outside, as if of something hard on flesh and bone. There was then another muttered conversation. Pakeshi put a knee on my back and pushed me harder against the floor. He pushed himself as far as he could against the wall of the compartment. The door rattled again.

"Dr Markham," another man said, now in a strong London accent, "we know you're in there. Just unlock the door and come out. I promise we won't hurt you."

"They aren't the police—are they?" I whispered through chattering teeth. Pakeshi pulled the window down and reached down to get me to my feet.

"Help, help!" the ticket inspector suddenly cried outside. "Help!" he now yelled. There was a muffled gunshot, and then silence. I wanted to try squeezing myself under the seat. But Pakeshi held me fast with one hand, his gun in the other. Now the door was rattling again, and I heard the sound of the inspector's key in the lock.

"Tell them you'll throw the Memorandum out of the window if they try coming through the door," he whispered. Teeth chattering uncontrollably, I looked blankly at him. "Tell them that," he whispered fiercely. "Play for time if you want to stay alive." I found the voice to do as he said. The door lock ceased rattling, and there was another conversation outside.

"Come on, Anthony," Pakeshi urged, now very calm." Climb out of the window and jump when I tell you."

"No—please! Have you gone mad?" I managed to say. But, still holding me with his free hand, he pushed me closer to the window. There was a gunshot that shattered the window of the compartment door. I felt the bullet go straight past my head into the darkness outside.

"I have the window open," I somehow found the voice to shout. "I only have to let go, and you can forget about your document." There was another bullet. This one seemed to brush the collar of my overcoat. There was an incredibly loud crash as Pakeshi fired back. I looked at the window blind. Holed now in three places, flapping slightly in the breeze from our open window, it was all that separated us from the men outside. But there were no more shots. The men must have stepped back along the corridor.

"Come on, Anthony," Pakeshi urged in his best bedside manner. "It's now or never. We must go before they think to get the window open in the next compartment." I let him guide me through the little window. It was a tight fit, and I thought I'd go out of it in exactly the same was as the dead man. But I held on hard to the window frame, and kicked about till I felt my feet touch on a ledge of some kind. We must have been moving no faster than twenty miles an hour. From inside, it had seemed as if we were creeping along. As I clung to the outside of the carriage, the cold wind hitting me like a hurricane, it was as if we were back on the magnetised line and were going at full speed. Inside the compartment, there was another shot—I don't know whose.

"Go now!" Pakeshi shouted. He jammed a hand against my chest, and pushed with a force that dislodged both hands from the window frame. I fell backwards into what seemed an infinite void. Then, I hit the ground. I landed on both feet, but went straight over to my right. I'd twisted round as I fell, and landed on my back. I felt myself lifted up again and went head over heels. I tried to curl into a ball, but felt a sharp pain in my back, and then I bounced on something hard. I rolled again and again, and then bounced off what might have been a little mound. My last clear recollection is of the railway train rumbling further and further into the distance, and of a burst of light in my head as I hit against something very hard.

CHAPTER SIXTEEN

The leaden skies of England out of the summer months don't easily tell what time of day it is. But I opened my eyes in what seemed to be the late morning. I was on my side and half out of my overcoat in a thorn bush. I'd had the impression, after I was pushed, of having bounced alongside the railway line. In fact, I'd come to rest a good twenty yards away from the line. How I'd avoided the broken down fence and the line of stumps of the cut down telephone and power distribution poles that lay between me and the line was a miracle I wasn't able to explain. To be sure, if I'd hit against them, I'd have been killed at once.

As it was, I lay covered in scratches everywhere my bare flesh had made contact with the ground, and bruised and bruised and bruised. There was a bump come up on the back of my head that would make wearing a hat painful for days. But I was alive. And apart from a stiffness in my right leg, I wasn't even much injured beyond the superficial. I rolled myself into a seated position, and pulled ineffectually to get my overcoat free of the thorns. It was raining steadily, and I was soaked through.

"Courage, old boy, and shuffle the cards," I called out in a surprisingly clear voice. Carefully, I got onto all fours and then tried very slowly to stand up. My right leg gave way under me at first, and I found myself sitting again. But I made another effort, and now was able to stand and look about me. About a mile further back along the line, I could see a couple of low buildings. Otherwise, the line cut through a countryside of fields separated by clumps of trees. I took an uncertain step forward. My leg hurt, but wasn't now giving way. Slowly, and still searching for evidence of substantial injury, I walked over to one of the telephone pole stumps and sat down. As you might imagine, my cigarette packet was crumpled and a little damp. But the matches were dry enough. After much striking in hands cupped against the steady breeze, I got a flame going and lit a cigarette. Something to eat or drink would have been nice. But the tobacco would do, and perhaps more than do. I blew out a cloud of smoke that dispersed immediately in the breeze, and tried to put my thoughts into some kind of order.

Where was Pakeshi? I looked vaguely round. I couldn't say where I'd come off the railway train. It might have been a few dozen yards back along the line. It might have been a hundred. Let's suppose Pakeshi had jumped a few seconds after he'd pushed me—I turned and looked in the other direction. There was a patch of scrub that went right up to the line and continued for thirty or forty yards in the direction of Lincoln. Had he landed there? I tried and failed to imagine Pakeshi in that lot with his neck broken. A man like that was surely reserved for a more significant end. But inability to imagine something isn't proof of its impossibility. I'd be sorry if he were dead. That aside, there was the matter of the Churchill Memorandum. If I were to take myself back to Sleaford Police Station, I might as well go with all relevant materials.

If he was in that lot, however, Pakeshi would need to have rolled into the most impenetrable undergrowth. I must have spent an hour picking my way through the bushes, looking about and calling his name. The rain was coming on heavier, and the sky was turning a still more depressing grey. I could easily spend all day rummaging about here. I'd probably find nothing, even if there were anything to find. I pulled out a damp handkerchief and rubbed as much of the brown makeup as I could feel from my face. It had served it purpose, and I saw no point now in shambling about like a nigger minstrel. I buried my head deeper into the collar of my soaked overcoat and turned myself back in the direction of Sleaford. There was no point hanging about. The sooner the police could take over the search, the better it would be for everyone.

I'd been in Lincolnshire many years before. That was when I was still a schoolboy, and the whole class had been packed off for a camping holiday to toughen us up. It was the year when we and the Germans had finally pressured the Japanese to halt their advance into Russia and consent to a League of Nations administration of Canton. Then, the sunny skies overhead had been filled with military airships and small aeroplanes. We'd all lain for hours on the grass, counting the airships and trying to write down their numbers. We'd made one trip to Sleaford, to look at the water mill and at the Wren altar rail in St Denys Church. It was before the ending of the agriculture subsidies, and had then been a prosperous little country town. Cheap food from Germany's Eastern Territories might have dented its cheerful bustle. But I wasn't going there today as a tourist. I picked my way across muddy but unploughed fields. Eventually, I came to a road that still had a few patches of tar from the old days. If I turned right along it, I might find myself in Sleaford. If not there, I'd find myself soon in some other place of habitation.

I'd have felt better with the Churchill Memorandum in my pocket. Without it, I was really just a wanted man with a tall story. I thought of the look on Pakeshi's face when I'd insisted on the good faith of the authorities. I couldn't feel the same conviction now as I had in that heated argument. Why were they after me? Were they really that separate from the men who were trying to kill me? What had Pakeshi jeered about a propensity to impose patterns on disparate events? All I really knew was that I'd been used to get a document into the country that simply shouldn't have existed. Why I'd been used, and why I was now being pursued, were things that I hadn't the information—or the spiritual peace—to think properly through.

I'd walked about two miles when I heard the motor car engine. It was an old-fashioned sound, long since abolished from the streets of London. I'd heard it many times in Chicago, when it had invariably heralded a peremptory shepherding by the police of every pedestrian off the streets. I heard the car several minutes before I could have seen it. I didn't bother trying to see it, but continued forward with my head down. The sound was from behind me. I did think to get myself off the road and try hiding. But this stretch had neither hedge nor ditches. If I did turn off, it would only be onto bare fields. I walked slowly forward until the car was right behind me. I went through the motions of getting out of its way. But there was no intention of passing me. The engine idling loudly, it came to a halt not more than a few yards behind me.

"Dr Markham?" It was a polite, well-spoken voice. It might be the police. It probably wasn't anyone wanting to spread me in the muddy track of the road and push a gun against the back of my head. I turned. "Dr Anthony Richard Markham?" I turned. I was looking at a young man, perhaps a few years younger than me. He was leaning out of the front passenger window of a very large, very shiny car. It was one of those hand-built luxury vehicles that last had a ready market in the late '40s, before electrification had got properly under way in the towns. Diesel engines were still occasionally used in the country. But, except for export markets, petrol-powered vehicles nowadays were always much smaller or more decidedly for use than display.

"And if I am, what might you be wanting?" I asked. The young man still didn't reach for a gun. Instead, he grinned and put his head back inside the window. A moment later, the door opened, and he got carefully out.

"Well, we're certainly glad to have caught up with you," he said. He looked up at the sky and put his hat on. "You've really been as elusive as any number of Pimpernels." He grinned again and turned to open one of the back doors of the car. "We're glad we've found you. I think you can count yourself lucky we've found you before—before anyone else could think to come out looking." He waved into the interior of the car. It must have been warmer than where I was standing. It couldn't have been wetter. "Do please get in, Dr Markham," he said again. "If we have to run into any of our competitors for your company, I'd rather have a car chase than a gun battle."

Since the end of tar spraying, English roads haven't been much good for long journeys by car. This was, as I said, a luxury vehicle, and its suspension was good for anything. Still, we made slow progress until we reached a wider paved road. We continued somewhat faster along this, though still had to slow down or swerve to avoid the inevitable potholes. For about half a mile, we found ourselves stuck behind a line of horse-drawn carts, all carrying sealed bags of something. Once or twice, we passed cars that had run out of electricity, and the drivers were in the rain, slowly cranking up charges from the emergency generators. Once, we passed a signpost that said Nottingham was twenty miles away. We didn't go to Nottingham, however, but turned off onto another muddy road. The next signpost I saw said we were heading towards Northampton. Another told me we were approaching Oxford. Another said Newbury. After this, the light faded. Except we were still headed south and south east, we might have been going anywhere. We avoided every main town. Even on the main roads, there weren't now more than a dozen other vehicles in any one hour.

There was no point plying the young man or the driver with questions. Though polite enough, and even sympathetic as I described my encounters on the railway train, he was letting nothing slip about who he was or where we were going. We stopped once for a late lunch. This was at a pub somewhere between Buckingham and Aylesbury. The driver came back with sandwiches and beer, and we lunched in the car. After this, we were off again. There was another stop just after dark in a village somewhere. There was no lighting, and I missed the village name as we swept in. We stopped by a Church of Saint Cuthbert, where the driver got out and made a short call from the village telephone box. Then it was off again on our endless journey through England. Rather than keep asking questions that wouldn't be answered, or try to find something else to talk about that didn't sound too contrived, I eventually pretended to sleep. After a while, I even did sleep. Still in wet clothes, now increasingly stiff and uncomfortable from the battering of my fall from the railway train, I swayed gently along roads that, even in my late boyhood, had still been smooth conduits for the traffic of a future that never came. I dozed. I slept fitfully. I dreamed on and off—disconnected fragments of dreams they were, involving railway trains and Pakeshi and second class carriages filled with grim-faced old men, all smoking cannabis in Germanic pipes.

I woke as we were driving over a smoother road. We were in another village. I saw a church in the car headlamps. I thought we'd pass through here as we had everywhere else. But we turned off the mainish road onto another that was also well-maintained. We stopped at some iron gates. There was a brief sound of the car horn, and the gates opened. As the headlamps went out, I felt the crunch of rubber on gravel. A dark building loomed ahead, dim lights in some of its windows. We were set down by the main entrance.

"Do you feel the need of a helping hand, Dr Markham?" the young man asked with a return of his friendly manner. I took his hand and stepped down onto the gravel. Someone deferential in a black coat met us in the main hall. I looked about me. If the main hall was any indication of the rest, this was an impressive building. The lighting was too dim for me to see any details of the paintings that covered the walls, and lined the grand staircase that led to the upper floors. But the smell of wax polish, and the ticking of the hallway clock, and the hushed, deferential tone of the butler who took my ruined coat—and didn't once look at my ruined and decidedly cheap shoes—told me nearly everything I could reasonably have asked about where I was.

"I'll leave you now," the young man said with one of his reassuring smiles. "But I'm sure we'll meet again tomorrow." I remembered to thank him. I even remembered myself not to gawp around as if I'd just paid half a crown for a guided tour of the house.

"If Sir would care to come this way," the butler said. He motioned me towards a closed door in the panelling just to the right of the staircase. We went through into a narrow corridor, also panelled. At the end of this, we turned left and went though another door. We were now in a high, darkened room with what looked like a billiard table in its centre. The butler opened another door, and I stepped through into a room where the lighting was average, but that dazzled me after so long in darkness and semi-darkness. I was in a small study. Books lined every wall beneath the pictures. I thought for a moment I was to be left alone here. But there were a couple of armchairs over by the fire, their backs to me. As the butler politely coughed, a man got nimbly out of one of the chairs and stepped across the room.

"My dear young fellow," he said, holding out a hand. "You will not credit how relieved I am to see you, alive and in one piece. Ever since you vanished from your flat yesterday morning, we've been turning the country upside down to get to you first." He stopped and looked at me. "Poor Anthony," he said with a weary smile. "For a man who normally takes such care with his appearance, you really do look ghastly. Have you been shopping in Marks & Spencer?"

I took the limp right hand of the Foreign Secretary, Harold Macmillan.

CHAPTER SEVENTEEN

As the plates were cleared away from the last course, I lit a Capstan Super Strength and looked at the glass of very red port the young footman had poured for me. A bath, a shave, two hours of dinner in a warm room, and dressed in a suit of my own clothes, and I was feeling more my usual self. I felt like a man who has been swept overboard from a liner into stormy seas, and who now, unaccountably, feels solid ground beneath his feet. Macmillan nodded at the footman, who bowed and left the room. As he closed the door behind him and we were alone, the Foreign Secretary smiled at me from across the table.

"I do think, young Anthony, you deserve some kind of an explanation for what has been happening," he said reassuringly. I took a sip of port and smiled nervously back. He paused and looked at me awhile in silence. "You may recall that, when we met a few months ago to discuss your Churchill biography, my people made you sign the Official Secrets Act. Do you consider yourself still bound by that?" He laughed softly. "Oh, the officials would tell you that signing the Act is rather like losing your virginity—you're never unbound by it! However, it would be helpful to me if you could confirm that whatever I say to you in this room will not turn up again somewhere in print." I nodded.

"Excellent," he said. "That really makes everything easier. All I have to do now is try and gather my thoughts to tell you in a few words what a whole volume might not exhaust." He stopped again and reached for his port. I took what I hoped was a delicate puff of my cigarette and waited. "There is a conspiracy we have known about since before Christmas," he said. "In the past few days, since you—unwittingly, of course—became one of its tools, it has begun to move at great and unexpected speed.

"You know, dear boy, my first lesson on becoming Foreign

Secretary was to learn that the relatively smooth face of international events covers some wild and very nasty currents. You may have noticed how old Halifax has grown of late. The real surprise, I'll tell you, is how long he's been able to hold things together. In the five years since he delegated everything to me, *I've* grown perceptibly older! The apparently massy gold of the *Pax Britannica* is, in many places nothing more than a coat of the thinnest gold leaf over nothing at all. We may be in a stronger position than at the time about which you are writing—the late '30's were dangerous days. Even so, an increased pressure at any one point may be enough to knock large holes in the structure that will encourage further attacks at all other points."

"So, how was the Churchill Memorandum allowed to fall into American hands?" I asked in the long pause that followed. Macmillan gave weary smile and waved his good hand vaguely at the ceiling.

"Don't ask me that, Anthony," he said. "Everything about Winston was chaotic towards the end. The family assured us that anything dodgy would be sifted out before the whole archive was shipped off. We did have someone go through it for our own assurance. But there was so much of it, and it was so jumbled, I don't blame anyone if something got overlooked. I suppose we should be grateful the American authorities took no special interest in it. But it is a shame that, of all the papers destroyed in the fire bombing of Harvard, parts of this one had to survive.

"There is some philosopher woman in America—her name slips my mind. She's presently in one of Anslinger's more salubrious concentration camps. Her followers somehow got wind of the Memorandum, and decided it might be a useful weapon for making trouble on her behalf. Naturally, our people in Canada overheard their plotting. Their plot, by the way, was to smuggle the document out and get it to the Germans. They couldn't try for a direct route to Germany—that would have alerted the intelligence wing of the Republican Guard. So they took advantage of your visit to get it into your luggage. You'd then be followed back to England and your flat would be robbed. From here to Germany seemed an easier hop than from there to Germany."

"So you sent Major Stanhope to make sure they got it out of

America," I said. "But why didn't he simply get it from me the moment we were in Croydon?" Macmillan raised his eyebrows quizzically. "Major Stanhope," I said. "He—he…." I trailed off, then explained what had happened in New York and subsequently. Macmillan looked at the tobacco pouch that had been left beside his pipe, but reached instead for the port decanter.

"Anthony," he said with heavy emphasis, "I want you to know that I have never heard of this 'Major Stanhope'. Certainly, our own agent in New York was taken by the Republican Guard. That's where we lost track of things." I sagged in my chair. Greenspan had been our man in New York. But if Stanhope had been anything to do with the Rand people or the Germans, why had he then killed those raiders? I wanted to try thinking this one through, but Macmillan was continuing.

"Anthony," he said, "I want you to promise that, if this man ever approaches you again, you will find me and tell me directly." I nodded. There was no point thinking too hard about this. For the moment, it was best simply to listen, and then try later to put some shape on it all. I lit another cigarette and watched the cloud of smoke writhe and disperse above the candle flames.

"The Germans, you can be sure," he went on, "are not passive watchers in this game. Even without any approach from these American lunatics, they learned about the Memorandum about the same time as we did. The moment they can lay hands on it, they'll publish it to our considerable and perhaps irreparable embarrassment." He now repeated and amplified on the points I'd covered with Pakeshi.

"But, surely," I objected, "the Germans are a satisfied power. They may use their Jewish and Turkish proxies to mess up the Arab oil markets. But they have no interest in any return to general instability?" Macmillan smiled and filled and lit his pipe..

"Anthony," he said very gently, "we are talking here about the *Boche*—the Beastly Hun, the Germans! Do you suppose they've ever forgiven us for the Great War?" Rather like Stanhope in New York—recollections of the pipe only added to the sensation—he held up his injured right arm. "Dear boy, I was there in 1918. Whatever they said afterwards about the 'stab in the back', we defeated them in the field. We looked them in the face in the summer of 1918, and they ran. We chased them all the way to Cologne. You know this as well as I do. And they know it too. It's very nice for the Jews if the treason charges have been buried. All it's done for the Germans is to remind them how fifty years of goose-stepping left them utterly smashed by the despised nation of shopkeepers.

"Oh, they've simmered down no end since their Austrian corporal had his accident in Prague. Goebbels is Rector of Heidelberg. Himmler's been pushing up the daisies since his failed *putsch* against Goering. Now Hayek and von Mises are running things, the apparently more civilised Danube has been flowing strongly through Berlin. But, if they go about in funny uniforms speaking of blood and soil, or if they wear shiny hats and talk Manchester economics, a Hun is still a Hun." He got up and went over to stand by the fire. Stooping, his moustache drooping down in its usual sad way, he looked older than his sixty five years—older, yet still very much in charge of all about him. He looked back at me, glass in one hand, pipe in the other.

"The time we spoke about Winston," he took up again, "we touched on our immense economic progress since 1931. And, whatever measurement you care to use, that great burst of prosperity compares well with anything even in Victorian times. Indeed let us be frank about it—most of our people have never had it so good. But the Germans have hardly been standing still all this time. Even before the present lot took over, they were doing very nicely. A decade of their own sound money, plus even lower taxes than we've been able to manage, and they're more than running level with us.

"Don't you see how that puts them back in the same relative position of 1914? They're ready for another crack at getting their place in the sun. Eastern Europe was nice. But it really was only their first course. If they don't feel ready yet to carve out Hitler's *Lebensraum* in Russia, they've got their eyes on a formal protectorate over the whole Near East. Getting us into renewed difficulties with America is exactly what they need to move us out of their way.

"And there are other things—though I really can't tell you about these. It isn't a matter of distrust. It's just that these are things known at the moment only to me and Halifax. If Butler and all the others are still in the dark, you can hardly complain if I don't tell you about them." He laughed and, with his foot, carefully moved a log back into the centre of the grate. He turned back to me with a broader smile.

"Now, Anthony, I've been as frank with you as I can possibly be. If you will now hand over the Churchill Memorandum, I can have you taken off to a nice warm bed for the night. Of course, you'll be my guest in the house until such time as it's safe for you to be taken back to your own flat in London. You can take it as read that we'll fix things with the press. If you'll just leave it to a spot of shadow boxing between the lawyers, I think you can even look forward to some nice libel damages."

The damages sounded nice. But I'd already frozen in my chair. A half inch away from my lips, the cigarette glowed between fingers that seemed about to go limp, but were somehow fixed in position.

"I don't have it," I said. Macmillan's face took on a look of pure nothingness. He came forward from the fire grate and stood by his place at the table. I explained about Pakeshi and his idea of getting himself and the Memorandum on the next available ferry out of Hull.

"I see," he said at last. His pipe had burned out, and he covered whatever was in his mind by a minute of fussing to get the thing refilled and alight. He looked up at me, now smiling again. "Of course, all this puts things in a different light." He looked steadily at me. I could feel sweat beginning to break out all over my back. "It puts things in a very different light. Of course, we still have to look after you. But we'll now need your active help in tracking down this Dr Pakeshi. We can't have him on the loose with that document in his pocket. Perhaps the worst thing about all this is that he probably knows that he's a walking atom bomb." He laughed bleakly and went across to the room to pull on a bell cord.

"Naturally, Harold," I said, clearing my throat, "I'll give your people a full description of Pakeshi. But Inspector O'Brien already has all that. I'm sure he can be waiting on the docks at Hull."

"This is not one for the police, Anthony," came the firm reply. He pulled again on the bell cord. "Your Inspector O'Brien may be a most splendid fellow. But we are talking affairs of state. We have our own people for that.

"Now, we'll need the fullest description you can provide. We really do need to head him off before he gets too far…."

CHAPTER EIGHTEEN

I groaned and turned over in bed. It was a firm if elderly feather mattress. It wasn't my own bed. But it was a fair substitute when it came to comfort. I reached over and looked at the luminous dial on the alarm clock. It was just gone 3am. After the endless questions regarding Pakeshi's appearance and likely response to being stopped, I'd been brought up here by Macmillan himself. "Anything you want dear boy—anything at all," he'd said before turning the light off and closing the door, "do just pull on the bell cord. It's what I pay the servants to provide, and you are my honoured guest.

"Yes, yes," he'd repeated with a strange chuckle—"my *most honoured* guest."

Nice to be treated like this by the second or third most important man in the country. I'd lain awhile, thinking over his brief remark about libel actions. What those newspapers had said about me was vicious beyond normal imagination. Even if it was to be a stitch-up between the Government and the proprietors, I was looking forward to the apology and the out of court settlement—oh, the settlement: I could do with that. I remembered the case, a few years before, where some pianist refugee from America—as obvious a degenerate as you could ever wish to see—had got £8,000 from *The Daily Mirror* for much less than had been said about me. £8,000—you could buy half a terrace with that. And I'd surely get more, even in an out of court settlement. It might even put me back where I had been. This time, to be sure, I'd not stuff it down any gold mines.

Thoughts of that had got me off to sleep a first time. Tired as I was, I was awake within half an hour, and looking at the glow on the ceiling from the dying embers of the fire that had been laid out in the room for me. Outside, it was raining hard again, and I could hear the patter on the window panes whenever the wind blew harder. *Why* had all these horrid tales about me been given in the first place to the newspapers? *What* was all this nonsense about the murder of Pakeshi? And, if we were drifting to war with Germany, *why* had we just signed that agreement in which the Germans would share all their rocket advances with us so that, before 1980, we could put a man jointly into space? Some of these questions I'd wanted to ask of Macmillan. Some were only coming to me now I was in bed. Perhaps I'd be able to raise these and other matters over breakfast. But, the more I thought about it, the more dinner seemed a lost opportunity.

For sure, I hadn't raised the possibility of switching publishers. Macmillan was a much bigger house than Richardson. It could pay higher advances. It had more clout with the reviewers. I hadn't raised this at our first meeting at the Foreign Office. Back then, it had been a matter of getting through a long list of questions about Churchill and the general debate over the first Munich Settlement. This evening, though, might have been a good time to discuss the possibility of switching publisher. Since being brought back into government, Harold himself had given up day to day management of the family business. But he could surely put in a word for me. Another point to raise over breakfast, perhaps. Or, since it looked as if I'd be a guest for at least several days, while this plot was foiled, I could raise it at another dinner….

I'd now had about three full hours of sleep. I might have dreamed, though I couldn't remember. I also couldn't remember what it was that had got me awake again. Was it the stiffness in my neck? Or the continued throbbing of my sore head. If I was lucky to have landed from that railway train in one piece, it was plain that I'd hurt for days and days to come.

Then I heard the quiet breathing of someone else in the room. Yes—that was it. I'd woken with a strong sense of not being alone. *And there was someone else in the room.* I resisted the urge to pull the blankets over my head and pretend to be asleep again. Trying not to make any sound, I reached for the bedside lamp. The fire now had burned right down, and the room was very dark.

"Not so fast, Professor Markham!" someone young said, speaking low in a faintly American accent. A hand closed on my wrist and gently moved me away from the switch.

"Come with me if you want to stay alive."

***

"What do you mean?" I asked again. I was fast getting over the shock, and I think my voice sounded pretty normal. His face showing dimly in the reflected light of the torch he put on, Macmillan's footman sat very still beside my bed. Even before the torch had gone on, I'd guessed it was him. Though a touch Hebraic in some of his features, he looked very young. And I hadn't been able to avoid noticing him as he served at dinner. Whatever first thoughts may have passed through my mind, I was now simply curious about his meaning.

"If I tell you that I'm here to save you," he said, "I need you to give me a fair trial." I sat fully up in the bed and pressed soft pillows back against the headboard.

"Saved?" I said with an invisible smile. "Saved indeed! Who are you?"

"These Limeys call me Edward," he said. "My real name, though, is Aaron P. Krellburger—Aaron P. Krellburger," he added with a touch of pride, "from the once fair city of St Louis." I looked at him a little longer in the darkness, then reached for my cigarettes. I looked at him in the flare of the match—he was *very* young, and he was here to "save" me! Perhaps he was mad. But I had no reason whatever to suppose he'd come into my bedroom to kill me.

"As you please, Mr Krellburger," I said drily. "But it would please me very much to know how and from what you are proposing to save me." I laughed and blew a stream of smoke into the air above my head.

"You can't have fallen for Big Mac's lies?" he sneered. He could see more of me in his torchlight than I of him. I put a quizzical look onto my face and flicked ash into the tray beside my bed. "Don't you see?" he went on, an impatient tone coming into his voice. "If he gets his hands on that document, he'll use it to destroy all civilisation in England and the world. He's been scheming to get it for months. He's getting a meeting arranged here at the weekend, where he'll read the whole document out and start his revolution. You'll be the one who authenticates it. Can't you see how everything he said to you over dinner was a lie? There is no German plot. The only danger to your national security is Big Mac himself."

"My dear young fellow," I said, stretching my arms out and putting on a voice of patronising contempt, "are you expecting me to believe that Her Majesty's Secretary of State for Foreign Affairs—'Big Mac' as you call him!—is engaged in some act of treason?"

"Yeah," came the instant reply. "And if you think he's gonna stay Foreign Secretary much longer, you haven't been reading your newspapers. You've gotta come with me now. You've gotta help us get to that document before his people do." I pushed the blankets aside and swung round to sit on the bed. I could see that my patterned silk pyjamas were shimmering softly in the torchlight.

"And how, Aaron P. Krellburger," I asked, "have you discovered a dastardly plot that no one else appears to have noticed?" The answer was an impatient snarl. I reached for the cigarette I'd parked in the ashtray. But the young man was on his feet and standing over me.

"Because I'm his—I'm his *special friend*," he hissed into my face. "I'm able to overhear things when he doesn't know he's being watched."

"I hope you don't intend by those words what I understand them to mean," I said grandly. "I'll have you know that Harold Macmillan is a happily married man with children." The answer to this may have been another snarl. It may have been a suppressed laugh. But further conversation was stopped by a sudden glare of car headlights through the window. My bedroom overlooked the front driveway of the house, and I could hear the soft purr of a petrol engine and the crunch of tyres on gravel.

Krellburger jumped up and went to the window. He looked carefully through the drawn curtains and turned back to face me.

"OK, *Professor* Markham," he jeered, "if you don't believe me, I think I can show you something that even you might understand. It'll save us the trouble of discussing what I was sent here to do with you." He pointed at the clothes one of Macmillan's servants had laid out for me. "Get dressed," he snapped. "Bring your shoes, but don't put them on."

***

Birch Grove isn't a big house as these places go. Even so, its many changes over the years to suit each successive owner, and the arrangement of its fourteen bedrooms, make it labyrinthine in the dark. But Krellburger knew his way about. We padded our way noiselessly along a corridor hung with photographs of what looked like Scotch grouse moors. Before reaching the top of the main staircase, he opened a door in the wall and we continued down some narrow spiral stairs that I supposed were there for the servants to come and go without bumping into the above stairs household. About half way down was another door. This took us onto an internal balcony that looked over the billiard room I'd seen on my arrival. Another door took us into another part of the balcony that had been closed off except for a wideish downward slit where the panelling on the other side had shrunk back. Through this came a dim light. Krellburger poked me from behind and indicated I should get on my knees to look through the slit. One of his elbows sticking into my back, he took his own viewing position above me.

I looked down over the study where Macmillan had first received me. The fire had now burned down to its last embers. With only a table lamp turned on, the paintings showed only as large areas of blackness on the dark panelling of the walls. The room was empty. I twisted round to whisper something at Krellburger. But he pushed his elbow sharper into my back and pushed his free hand against my ribcage. His own added weight pressing down on me was making my knees hurt on the bare wood of the balcony, and I was bent at a most unnatural angle. But I kept still and waited.

How long we waited there I can't say. It might have been ten minutes. It might have been a quarter of an hour. I was debating whether to get up and laugh into Krellburger's face, when I heard the soft click of the door handle and a burst of whispered conversation. Above me, I felt Krellburger suddenly tense. He jabbed a finger into my ribs to keep quiet. I pressed my face harder against the slit to try and see more of the room.

Directly underneath me, there were two men in the study.

CHAPTER NINETEEN

"I really don't see why you had to come straight down from London," Macmillan was saying, a slight nervousness in his voice. "Everything is pretty much under control again." I heard a soft click as the door was closed again. Then a key turned in the lock. "I imagine you took the usual precautions?" he asked. "But, really, everything is under control."

"If it's that much under control, Harold, I'd like to know when I can hold Winston's minute *in its entirety*," someone else said. He cleared his throat, and there was the sound of something heavy dropped onto the carpet—a bag, perhaps? "More to the point, though, I'd like to know what the fuck is going on with this little squirt Markham. If the newspaper reports are even half correct, it looks as if you gave those Americans a right homicidal maniac."

The other man was speaking low, but there was a certain familiarity about the voice. I pressed harder still against the inside of the panelling. But the two men were directly below me, and I couldn't see them.

"A little local difficulty," Macmillan replied in a tone that was surely accompanied by one of his dismissive waves. "I'll be in a better position to tell you about the police involvement tomorrow. I've had F.A. sodding Hayek all day—half an hour on Goering's state of mind, the rest on Hayek's new book on Edmund Burke and David Hume. Unless you've met the man, you can't imagine how he loves the sound of his own voice.

"Whisky, old boy?" There was an amused snort, then the sound of a match striking against a box. "Oh, God," Macmillan cried now, though still speaking soft, "not another of those ghastly things! I've had Markham smoking like a bloody trooper all evening. Do you know how long it takes to get the smell out of the carpets?" There was another snort. A moment later, I smelled what might, but for the touches of Player's Navy Cut about it, have been a Woodbine.

"Now that I'm here," the other man said, "you might as well fill me in on our good Dr Markham. The newspaper reports put me in a better mind about him. His Churchill biography, though, was a farrago of the most revolting nonsense. I got as far as his take on the July Crisis, and then threw the book away."

"Oh, come now, Michael," Macmillan protested. "He's not that bad. "He's just naively patriotic, and, for a half-*babu*, he doesn't write a bad sentence. Why not just admit you're jealous, Michael. After all, his sales, I think, are three or four times those of your Stalin hagiography—and he doesn't have your advantage of a captive market!"

There was a grunted response to this. But I didn't hear it for my own sudden sharp inward breath. This brought a savage jab from Krellburger, and I had to stop myself from yelping. But, now it was no longer needed for identification, the two men drifted over towards the fireplace. As Macmillan filled two tumblers from a decanter and topped both up with water, I found myself looking from behind at the long, unkempt hair of what could only be Michael Foot—since his colleagues had disappeared in Moscow, sole leader of the Communist Party of Great Britain.

Foot stubbed his cigarette out with vicious energy and threw himself into the one armchair beside the fire. Ignoring the whisky Macmillan was holding out, he lit another cigarette and stretched out both legs.

"Your call wasn't exactly convenient," he snapped. "We've a demonstration planned for Monday against the fascist octopus. I should be working on my speech. Still, since I surmised that our joint and several interests might best be served by coming straight down here, I'll be glad to know what went wrong in New York, and what has gone worse ever since. You did assure me it would all go like clockwork. From what I gather of the resulting triumph, I see I should have put my own people in charge." He now took the offered tumbler and sipped at its contents. Macmillan pulled up another chair and sat opposite.

"So far as I can tell," he opened in the mournful voice he used for putting off awkward questions, "the agent put in place by the Rand people was betrayed. Instead, Markham was taken through New York by someone else. This someone else was then able to get the airship to use up its entire fuel on a faster crossing. That meant Markham and his boxes couldn't be nabbed in Croydon. As for the people you lent me, they made a mess of things at his flat—twice, I might add! And I won't mention the idiot who followed him onto the train. I have no idea what instructions they were given. But, if that's a fair sample of what your men can do, I nearly wish I'd gone looking for my own heavy muscle.

"All this, however, is by the bye. What matters is that our Winston sheets are currently being taken off to Germany by a darkie with a bag of money. All very unsatisfactory, you'll agree. But I can't think how anyone with that colour face would get far in England without being spotted by your people."

"But Harold, don't be shy," Foot sneered, "Do tell me who is this *Someone Else*. Since you and Heath control the security services, I was given to suppose we might be reasonably safe. Or is Butler already getting his feet under the table?"

"My guess it's one of young Powell's men at the India Office," came the muttered reply. "What I still don't understand is how they've got the police dancing to their tune."

"So Enoch Powell is on to us?" Foot cried, jumping up. "Well, that *does* explain the manhunt! I should have known not to listen to your lunatic scheme. Can you imagine what credit I've used up in Moscow to push things along? We're already riding piggy back on an American fascist conspiracy, and using a courier who, for all he's a pisspoor historian, has shown a remarkable capacity for staying alive. Now you tell me that spies from the India Office are crawling all over us. If you'll pardon the vulgarity, Harold, this is a right fucking disaster. I'm more than three quarters inclined to get straight back in that car and get myself *tout* bloody *suite* to Moscow. Even in that snake pit, I'll be better off than with Powell on my back."

"Come, come, old boy," Macmillan said in his reassuring voice. "Come, come, dearest Michael. I won't try glossing over the unfortunate turn that events appear to have taken. But all we have to do is bring the plan forward a little. I know it was agreed for a May detonation. But can things be got ready at your end for next Monday? With Halifax still pottering about in Africa, even Powell can't move that quickly. For my part, I'm already getting my own people together for Saturday evening."

"I'm not happy about this," Foot replied. "It's plain that everyone is spying on everybody else, and the result stinks." He gave a bitter laugh. "I should be jumping ship while I can. Then again, what more should I have expected? I believe it was in his *The Possessed* that Dostoyevsky wrote how, in any conspiracy of three or more people, there would be at least one fanatic, one fool, and one informer. I know what I am. I hope I know what you are. For the rest, I can only trust that you really will be able to work too fast, and under too much protection, for your enemies to put a stop to your little game."

There was a long silence. Foot lit another cigarette. Macmillan fiddled nervously with his tobacco pouch. I could hear my own breathing. I could almost smell the triumph that Krellburger must have been enjoying, now I couldn't deny the awful truth about his employer. If he wasn't lying now to Michael Foot—and I didn't think he was—everything he'd told me over dinner was a lie. There was no German plot. That Jew Greenspan, who'd been shot in New York, wasn't working for us. Stanhope, on the other hand, was probably with the Indian Secret Service. It had been Macmillan and Foot who were trying to kill me in my flat and on the railway train.

But why hadn't Stanhope just taken the Churchill Memorandum when he'd had the chance? What was going on? Who was Krellburger?

Put me behind a desk with a mountain of paper, and I'd make sense of it. Fanciful secondary sources, lying memoirs, bought newspaper stories, speeches, letters, and all the rest—I could sort through these and get at something like the truth. Looking through that slit at the conversation below, and it all just crowded in on me. What was it that Macmillan needed so badly of Foot? It was beyond me. But I tried to clear my mind and turn myself to the immediate conversation. It might make sense later. For the moment, I knew that I had to listen and try to remember all that was said.

Below me, the silence went on and on. Suddenly, Foot laughed. He laughed until his body shook. Macmillan lit his pipe and looked over at the decanters. Still laughing. Foot stretched forward and pushed a poker in the still glowing embers of the fire. He only stopped for a long coughing fit that made me almost think he'd bring up one of his lungs.

"For the past three months," he gasped, "you've been dragging things out. First, it was more time needed to infiltrate and control the Rand people. Then you were insisting on more time once we'd reassembled the document." He coughed again and clutched his side. "But, if you think you can bring Halifax down next week and get yourself in his shoes, I think I can see to our side of the bargain." There was now a long coughing fit. "I suppose we can kill the *babu* once we've laid hands on his friend? Unless Powell has given a tissue of lies to the press, he doesn't sound the sort of creature one should leave hanging about."

"Dear me, no, Michael!" Macmillan said with a horror that might have sounded more convincing if he hadn't been waving his glass about. "You told me yourself when we were hatching this plot that provenance and verification were everything. Tucked safely away upstairs, we've now got the world's leading expert on Churchill. And he really is timid as a mouse. If you wheel him out at the right moment, no one will doubt the genuineness of what you get your friends to publish. I'm certainly planning to use him in my Saturday evening pep talk."

"And you think you can get some hyper-patriot to do that?" came Foot's rather obvious question. "Timid or not, you'll be asking rather a lot of someone whose political writings make Billy Bunter sound like Machiavelli!" Macmillan laughed now, and stood fully up. The slightly dotty old Edwardian gent had vanished. In his place stood someone taller and younger and much, much more ruthless. He cackled and rubbed his hands.

"Leave that one to me, old chum," he said. "I think I have already effected an introduction for our repressed young Indian that will turn him about very smartly—yes, very smartly indeed. A night of young Edward's embraces, and I might have him singing *The Internationale*!

"Now, would I be mistaken if I thought you had a message for me from Comrade Beria himself?" Foot laughed again and began walking back towards the door—wasn't that where he'd dumped his bag. Before he could get there, though, Macmillan began to laugh again. He caught hold of Foot by the hands, and they began a slow, capering dance about the room. Gasping and laughing, they danced together, looking out only to avoid crashing into the furniture.

"My darling Harold," Foot croaked on their second circuit of the room, "it will be a marriage made in heaven. Even if he couldn't himself see the shining future just ahead, old Winston himself would surely have approved."

I'd registered without fully noticing that Krellburger had been prodding my neck with increasing urgency. Now he began pulling on the hair above my left temple. I relaxed my whole body and looked up.

"You've seen enough," he whispered. "It's time to get out of here." I wanted to go away somewhere and cry at the horror of it all. But I also knew I couldn't stay under this roof another five minutes. Whatever happened to me, I had to get to the authorities. I didn't know the nature of this "bargain" between them. Even so, treason was treason, and we had days at the most to stop it. I got up and followed Krellburger noiselessly back to my room.

CHAPTER TWENTY

Our shoes crunched on the gravel as we walked from a side door of the house into the grounds. It had left off raining, and the night air had about it the fresh, silent chill of late winter. As I'd been told, I took shelter behind some bushes, and Krellburger continued forward towards the car that had brought both me and Foot to the house.

"The Master requires your immediate presence in the kitchen," he said in a surprisingly stately English accent. "There will be much driving shortly after dawn, and he would have you refreshed for it." The driver looked up from his newspaper and nodded. He switched off his reading light, and I heard the heavy thud of the car door closing. This was followed by the diminishing sound of the driver's own progress across the gravel. Once he was round the corner of the house, Krellburger jumped into the driving seat. I got in beside him and closed the door. The key turned twice in the lock before the engine started. It was the same soft, expensive purr as I'd known on the way here. Now, with Krellburger driving, its movements were jerkier. Still, he got the car turned and then accelerated through the open gates of Birch Grove into the silent darkness beyond.

I turned and looked back at the house. All was still in darkness. Krellburger had assured me that even Macmillan could only run a single car. Would he dare report the car to the police as stolen? Probably not. Since he couldn't follow us, we'd surely have all the head start we needed. So far, this had been a remarkably easy escape. I hugged myself as I thought of the bitter argument that would break out once my bed was found empty.

"There will be a police station in Haywards Heath," I said firmly. "From there, we can get in touch with Inspector O'Brien—I think at Scotland Yard. He can arrest the pair of them. A search of the house will give him all the evidence he needs to stop this plot, whatever it is."

Krellburger ignored me, and gripped the wheel tightly as he drove quickly along a stretch of reasonably smooth road.

"I think Haywards Heath is to the south," I added with greater firmness. "You seem to have got us onto the London Road." With a crunch of gears, Krellburger slowed the car and then stopped. He rummaged about in the glove compartment and pulled out a book of maps.

"We aren't going to the police," he said shortly. I opened my mouth to protest. But he turned and pulled a sour face.

"Give me one of your cigarettes," he demanded. Automatically, I reached into my breast pocket and took out my silver case. Whoever had collected stuff from my flat had made sure to refill it with Capstan Super Strength. There were ten left. They would last me and even someone else for any reasonable car journey. I offered one to him and took one for myself. He held the paper tube between forefinger and thumb and took no notice of the lighter I held up. I lit my own and relaxed in the car seat.

"I like to think of fire held in a man's hand," he said as if quoting from memory. "Fire, a dangerous force, tamed at his fingertips. I often wonder about the hours when a man sits alone, watching the smoke of a cigarette, thinking. I wonder what great things have come from such hours. When a man thinks, there is a spot of fire alive in his mind—and it is proper that he should have the burning point of a cigarette as his one expression."

I remained silent. But whoever's words those were had spoken pretty well. Krellburger looked out of the driver's window. Far over in the east, the pale light of the dawn showing behind, I could see the five great towers of the Colemans Hatch power station. It had been finished just as distributed power began to go out of fashion, and its nuclear reactor had never been fully brought into service. But great clouds of steam rose still white from the two central towers. He turned back and smiled at some inner joke. I lit his cigarette and prepared to urge him again to make for Haywards Heath.

I was unprepared for the coughing fit the moment he breathed in. Michael Foot's own attack had nothing on this. He coughed and spluttered until tears ran down his face. Indeed, his face went pale and then a darker shade that, in better lighting, might have shown as green. He leaned forward and clutched desperately at his chest. I patted hard on his back, and bent down to recover the cigarette from where it had fallen beside the pedal. I thought he'd even vomit, and reached back to get his hat ready. But it was only severe coughing.

"How old are you?" I asked once the main fit was passed.

"Sixteen," he groaned. I nodded wisely and put his hat back on the seat behind us.

"Well, at your age," I advised, "you'll be better off with Passing Clouds, or something with a filter. I started with Samovar Smooth Blend—but those really are for boys," He nodded and looked suspiciously at the still lit cigarette I held out to him. He took it and sucked the smoke gently into his mouth before spitting it out again. I rolled my own window down and took another long draw on my cigarette. I blew the smoke out into the gathering light and watched it disperse in the gentle breeze. I turned and looked back along the road. As expected, it was empty. If there was to be a problem, it would come from ahead.

"We aren't gonna go to the police," Krellburger said once he felt confident to speak again. "Nathaniel Branden has a bedsitting room in Catford. He's the only man who can stop them. He'll know what to do."

"And who is Nathaniel Branden?" I asked. I got a funny look.

"Branden is the second greatest philosophical genius the world has ever known," came the assured answer. I shrugged and took another deep draw on the cigarette.

"If he's only the second greatest," I said at length, "who might be the first?" I got another funny look. Then Krellburger laughed.

"I thought Englishmen were better educated than that," he said. I sniffed and flicked ash out of the window. "The greatest philosopher, of course, is Ayn Rand. You've heard of her?" I nodded. Even before that poor fool Greenspan had called it out, I'd heard that name. Who hadn't? When I was in Chicago, she'd been denounced every day in the American newspapers. According to them, she was, among much else, a traitor, a lesbian, a German spy, a corruptor of youth. One of the taxi drivers had assured me she was a Jewish nymphomaniac and a poisoner of reservoirs. Someone else had blamed her for the new strain of locusts that was resistant to all but German pesticides. Before then, I'd read the generally shrill letters of denunciation she sent three times a week from Montreal to *The Daily Telegraph*. Before starting work for Richardson on that vast hymn of praise to the *Fuhrer*, she'd published an equally vast cycle of plays about the trial of Anslinger after some future American uprising. A cut down version had been played at the Old Vic, with Kenneth Williams as Anslinger. The critical derision it received had only made her *Telegraph* philippics more demented. Of course, I knew about Ayn Rand. If I hadn't paid much attention to her books, I was in good company. And being told by some juvenile footman that she topped a list containing Plato and Aristotle put me in no mind to look further.

I changed the subject.

"Your people got me to bring in the Churchill Memorandum," I said, because you thought I was the man to validate it when you used it against Anslinger." He nodded. "So why don't you just work openly with Macmillan and Foot? Letting them think they've infiltrated your movement, when you've actually infiltrated theirs seems a somewhat roundabout way of securing what you both obviously want." I'd had some time to think matters through. It was worth taking the time now to clarify some of the more bizarre twists in whatever was going on.

"But we don't wanna *publish* that document," Krellburger insisted. "That would only provoke Anslinger to kill Miss Rand. All we want is to pressure him into releasing her so she can carry on her work. Big Mac wants to give the whole document to the papers. He's sure it will bring Lord Halifax down and discredit everyone except him. *He's gotta be stopped!*"

"So what's in the rest of the document?" I asked. "Even if I were to swear on a stack of Bibles that it was in his handwriting—and no one would deny that it was—those parts I've seen of the Churchill Memorandum say nothing beyond the mildly embarrassing. All Halifax has to do is say there was no meeting, and that Churchill wrote the whole thing in a drunken haze. What makes it worth killing and dying for?" The answer was a shrug. From the longer reply that followed, I guessed Krellburger didn't even know what was in the pages that I'd read with Pakeshi. He knew that Macmillan had the rest of it, but hadn't caught sight of it.

I asked what could be in it for Michael Foot and the Russians. Another vague answer. I turned to asking who might be attending the meeting Macmillan had mentioned. He tapped his head and tried to look smug. Even so, he couldn't keep the uncertainty from his face. So much for his claim to be Macmillan's catamite. Either Macmillan was a great deal more reserved than he was supposed to be, or this part of the story was the fabrication that I suspected it to be.

"Well, I sighed, hoping for something in the way of hard information, "do I guess right that the raid on my flat was supposed to be foiled by armed policemen, who'd then bring me down here, bubbling with gratitude to Macmillan? That would explain why those two jokers who broke in didn't know what they were supposed to take from me. Were the other two dead men working directly for Foot?"

It struck me as an entirely credible theory—my first unaided effort to understand what was happening. All I got, though, was another noncommittal shrug. Krellburger started the car and eased it through the lower gears. Sooner or later, we'd join one of the trunk roads to London. That would be in good shape, and we'd be in Catford perhaps shortly after lunch. I'd listen to this Nathaniel Branden. But I had no faith in American exiles. What little I'd read of them told me they were as loudmouthed and ineffectual as all the other refugee groups you saw raving away at Speaker's Corner every Sunday morning.

I remembered what Stanhope had said to me outside Boots.

"Doesn't your Ayn Rand preach that all sacrifice for others is evil?" I asked. "*The man who lets a leader prescribe his course is a wreck being towed to the scrap heap*," I recited primly from one of Rand's *Telegraph* letters. "*I swear, by my life and my love of it, that I will never live for the sake of another man, nor ask another man to live for mine*," I added with a laugh.

There was a loud protest from the engine as Krellburger changed gear again. I glanced forward and to my left. It was raining softly and continuously. Even so, a couple of men were digging hard in a field. There was a horse-drawn cart pulled off the road near them. The horse looked up from nibbling at the grass as we bumped over another pothole on our journey past. Krellburger found the gear he was seeking and a look of intense concentration spread over his face.

"A man lives by values that he has freely chosen," he said, evidently not quoting. "Freely chosen values are what distinguish a man from a slave. A man lives by these values, and that mean he may have to die for them." He changed into top gear and leaned forward against the wheel to see more clearly ahead. "I believe in liberty," he added. "I believe in America and the dream that inspired those brave, brave men so long ago in Philadelphia." He prosed on enthusiastically about Jefferson and Franklin and the other rebels. I could have asked how many of the men who'd signed that Declaration had staggered out of the room for refreshments served by negro slaves. But I didn't. It would have made for better conversation if I'd asked instead where he'd learned to drive. It wasn't a skill you expected in one so young—especially not for a car of the older design. But I fell silent and lit another cigarette. As we drove on, he spoke with rising passion about how limited government and free enterprise were the only natural state for mankind. Though without the calm intensity of delivery, he sounded rather like Enoch Powell.

The road improved after East Grinstead. It even widened to four lanes, and there was a steady stream of electric and internal combustion traffic in both directions. We moved up to ninety, and then to a hundred, and I watched as the fast lane in front of us emptied of all the slower electric vehicles.

"Do you mind?" I asked, pointing at the car wireless. It was pushing midday, and I wanted to hear the news. Krellburger nodded. We swerved to avoid a police car that had unwisely moved out of the slow lane a hundred yards ahead. For a moment, I hoped it would flash us down. But its back lights went on instead, and it moved out of our way. I switched on the wireless and twiddled the running dial until I caught the last of the pips for the Home Service news.

The main item, as I listened through bursts of rhythmical interference, was the consecration of the new altar in Coventry Cathedral. The Queen and Prince-Consort were there, and about half the bulletin was taken up with the proceedings. The next main item was about the standing down of Japanese troops from the Russian border. I supposed the Russians were already pulling back, though nothing was said here. Then it was the Indian rioting, where nothing seemed to have worsened or improved. The only other home item was about the proposed shifting of the August Bank Holiday and the creation of another one in October. There was nothing about me or my supposed crimes. I didn't know whether to feel pleased or slighted.

"We've gotta get some gas," Krellburger said about twenty miles outside the suburbs. Luckily, my wallet had also been recovered from my flat. I opened it and found a five pound note and some gold. I looked at the crisp, white banknote, and wondered how much this would buy of a liquid more precious, ounce for ounce, than the better Scotch whiskies. I'd never bought petrol, but supposed £5 should get us at least to Catford. We pulled into a filling station and drove past the long queue of cars for the charging points. An old man grunted at the banknote and unscrewed the filling cap. I tried not to wonder how many more banknotes like this I might have to my name. Five minutes later, we were back on the road.

We were now well within range of the general network of charging points, and the road was crowded with traffic. Here and there, it was slowed to a crawl. We came off the main road near Croydon and plunged into the teeming suburbs. First was the outer ring of detached and semi-detached properties. After another mile of so, we hit the immense inner ring of Victorian terraces, grander or meaner, where worked, slept and lived the bulk of the Imperial City's ten million people. As we passed slowly by the shell of the new Crystal Palace, Krellburger knocked the cigarette from my mouth with a sudden hand signal, and pulled left into the car park of one of the larger self-service food markets. I thought for a moment he'd start one of his recitations from Ayn Rand for or against this loving, if slow, recreation of Paxton's green house. But he didn't bother looking at it.

"I've gotta make a 'phone call," he said shortly. "Nathaniel's gotta call the Council together." I smiled weakly. He opened the door. "Listen," he said, looking in, "if you see anybody suspicious, just keep your head low. I'll be back in five minutes." I nodded. I watched him thread his way through the parked vehicles towards the big building where, as sign above the entrance shouted, all that a modern household might require could be found. Even in his travelling clothes, he had a pleasing shape, and it rested my mind to see his confident stride. Once he was gone out of sight, I took out my wallet again and began counting the change.

"Anthony!" A voice sounded urgently from all round me. I looked behind. Of course, the back seats were empty. "Anthony, I will say this only once. You have to listen to me and do exactly as I say." I swallowed and dropped my wallet. Was I going mad? Had Macmillan fed me some slow-acting drug at dinner? But no—there was a voice. It came from the wireless speakers buried in the upholstery of the doors. And it was Vicky Richardson speaking to me.

CHAPTER TWENTY ONE

"Don't try speaking back to me," Vicky continued. "Just listen very carefully." I looked about me. Outside, the rain had cleared, and a watery sun was low in the sky. We were in a car park crowded with electric vehicles. Women with children were supervising uniformed boys as they unloaded metal trolleys filled with bags into the boots of the cars. Some of the boys were pointing at the very grand vehicle where I was sitting. But I couldn't see anyone who seemed interested in me. For sure, I couldn't see Vicky Richardson anywhere.

"Anthony," she said again, now urgent, "I want you to get out of that car at once. In just a few minutes, men with guns will surround it and take you prisoner again. If you try to resist, they will shoot you. I want you to get yourself to Daddy's office. You will be safe there, and all will be explained."

"Where are you?" I shouted. "What is going on?" But she'd told me not to try speaking back. Either she couldn't hear me, or she wasn't interested in conversation. The wireless went silent. Then, through more static, I heard the measured tones of the Home Service presenter as he read out the sermon Archbishop Lewis had earlier delivered on the new altar. There was a note of relish in his voice at those clear and balanced sentences. Normally, I'd have given my whole attention. But I turned the wireless off and unlocked the car door. I got out and stretched my legs. I was stiff all over from the long drive, and I could feel another headache coming on. I reached back in to get my overcoat and hat. As I put them on, I thought of waiting for Krellburger. Or I could follow him into the shop, where he was making his telephone call.

But now I saw the black van pull into the car park. It was one of those fancy models that had been popular back when diesel was still a viable fuel. This one hadn't been converted to some other fuel, and I could hear the loud throbbing of its engine from fifty yards away. Its way was blocked by a couple of cars that were waiting to get out into the stream of traffic in the main road. Looking through the windscreen of the van, I could see two big men. The one who wasn't driving was looking carefully about. I stepped back behind the cover of one of the higher electric cars. I crouched down and made my way under cover to the far side of the car park. There was a brick wall, rather low on my side, but with an eight foot drop on the other. I swung myself over and dropped into a road lined with small houses that dated, by the look of them, from the early 1940s. I looked left and right. About a hundred yards to my left, brisk traffic was moving up and down Westwood Hill. I didn't know Catford terribly well. All considered, I didn't really want to see Catford today. But I knew that going down in that direction would take me into an impenetrable maze of streets and alleys where no one would be able to track me.

I broke into a limping run along the road. At the junction with Westwood Hill, I looked left, back up towards the shopping market car park. There was no sight of the van or of anyone suspicious. I darted across the road and turned right down the hill. Running would have drawn attention to me. So I walked as briskly as I could, keeping myself away from the kerb. In the summer months, the gardens of the fine, detached houses I was passing would be in full bloom, and the trees and bushes of their front gardens would have given plenty of cover where they overhung the pavement. But, even if some had their garden heating on for the early shrubs, this was March, and there was no cover. Still, I hoped I could keep myself inconspicuous. Even if my pursuers were still poking about the car park, I was a wanted man. If I was to give myself in, it wouldn't be to the local plod. I pulled my hat down and pushed my chin into the collar of my overcoat. Once or twice, I looked round. There were people behind me. But no one looked as if he was following me.

At the junction with Kirkdale, I managed to catch a trolley bus. This hadn't gone past where I'd started, and—nervous as I was still feeling—I couldn't imagine that the women and schoolchildren who filled the seats were in the service of Harold Macmillan or Michael Foot. We trundled rapidly along the whole length of Kirkdale, and turned right when we came to Horniman Museum. From here, it was downhill through a small but respectable shopping street, and then into a series of bends that took me into another wide road lined with detached older properties. I got off at the junction with Brockley Rise and walked quickly past a parade of shops that were mostly selling second hand furniture and second hand books. It was the bookshops that had, in better days, brought me this far out into the suburbs of South East London. I stopped for a moment beside a council school and looked across the road at the window of Mortimer's Fine Antiquarian Books. It took up the less broken down half of some storage building that had gone up when, all about, there was nothing but fields and a few muddy lanes. Such warm and jolly times I'd had in there. Most of the books, I'd soon discovered, weren't so old as the proprietor. But Mortimer always claimed he'd once carried proofs for Oscar Wilde, and was a source of entertaining, if somewhat unlikely, anecdotes about life in the fabled days before the Great War. I thought of going in a throwing myself on his mercy. "Never speak to the rozzers about anything!" was the favourite text on which he preached to his younger admirers. "Never give them anything. Never ask for anything." Would he believe me if I told him I was being hunted by the Foreign Secretary and the Leader of the Communist Party? He probably would, and he'd gladly shut me away in one of his basements until such time as all danger had passed and I was tired of his recollections of an astonishingly scandalous youth.

But today was Friday, and he would be spending all afternoon holding court in a pub beside the Catford Dog Stadium. Jowls wobbling above a grimy wing collar, his partner scowled back at me through the dusty window of the shop. If he too wouldn't call the police, he'd not welcome me inside either. The sky had darkened again, and a thin drizzle was starting. A bit of warmth would have been welcome—a touch of mist even more so. But Brockley Rise was far beyond the outermost reach of the pavement heating, and no good was likely to be served by dithering here in full view of anyone who might be inclined to look in my direction.

I smiled at Mortimer's partner and walked on. I looked briefly left through the bars of the school playground. It was afternoon break, and about a hundred children ran about, playing and shouting in the rain. Hooded or bareheaded, they all had the pale faces of those whose skin hadn't been touched by sun since the previous October.

I passed a greengrocer's. Two old women came out as I went by. They were carrying string bags filled with onions and cabbages, and were talking about some neighbour who'd had a child out of wedlock. It was the most normal conversation I'd heard in days. Just beyond, at the entrance to some mews, about a dozen boys in short trousers were smoking and arguing about the football. One of them gave me a suspicious look—though, more, I suspected, from fear of the truancy man than out of any desire to lay violent hands on me. It was all reassuringly normal.

I stepped into a sweetshop and bought fifty cigarettes. I'd pushed my hat back, and my face was on the front page of two of the daily newspapers. But the middle aged woman who served me was more concerned with counting the change of the shilling I'd given her. She muttered about the growing lack of silver since the fall in gold, and loaded me up with coppers.

I stepped out into the chilly breeze and lit a cigarette. I looked briefly at the boys. They were all rather willowy. One had the most disgusting spots I'd seen since America. I wondered if Krellburger had made his way to the bedsitting room in Catford, and how he'd explain himself to the second greatest mind of the past eight thousand years. I smiled and looked left along Brockley Rise. About a mile on, and I'd come to Crofton Road Railway Station. From there, I could get myself up to Blackfriars. No one would find me in the warren of alleys and courts that surrounded St Paul's. There, I could sit down and think about all that had happened and what I might most safely do next. Vicky had told me to get to the offices of Richardson & Co. There, she's said, I'd be safe. She'd also mentioned an explanation. That would be very handy. The more I thought about it, though, the more attractive seemed a quick dash to Scotland Yard—or perhaps the India Office. If Macmillan and Foot were scared of Powell, the good offices of that slithery book on legs were surely my own best hope.

I looked right at the telephone box I'd hurried past on my way to buy the cigarettes. A halfpenny would buy me all the time I needed to call O'Brien, or anyone else—this was assuming I'd made up my mind. Perhaps, though, I should get myself up into Town. More time for thinking would do no harm at all. I was still looking at the telephone box when I heard the loud click beyond. At the junction where I'd got off the trolley bus, the lights had changed. My stomach turned over as I saw that black van stopped behind another trolley bus. It was indicating to turn left and come in my direction.

I turned and hurried up the road beside a church yard. Because I was continually twisting round to look behind, I nearly bumped into a woman dressed in a plastic mackintosh. She was pushing a heated pram and impatiently watching a duffle-coated boy as he jumped in and out of a puddle. I croaked an apology and hurried on. After a few yards, my nerve snapped and I broke into a panicky trot. It's astonishing what speed fear can give to a bruised, aching body. I hadn't run so fast since a whole mob of youths had once mistaken a friendly nod. I must have covered fifty yards before drawing breath. I knew the only way out from the end of the road beyond this one was an alley where no wheeled vehicle could follow. I was a little hazy about the streets that lay beyond. But I could probably skirt round and get myself to a railway station or to a convenient bus stop. Or I might risk a telephone call.

I looked back from the other end of the alley and clutched at myself with terror. The van was now parked at the end of the road I'd just left, and men were tramping about. I couldn't hear what they were saying, but it sounded pretty confident. An hour earlier, I'd thought any pursuit must be hours behind me. A few minutes before, I'd thought it was at least several miles back. It was now a few dozen yards. There comes a moment when the firmest common sense begins to break down. Tracking devices were things you read about in novels where the author was running out of plot development, or saw in the more lurid spy films. But, as I'd already heard the impossible, when Vicky Richardson spoke to me through a car wireless, why doubt the merely unlikely? I went quickly through my pockets and ran hands over the lining of my overcoat. Nothing. Was it worth taking off my overcoat and hat? What if it was in my trousers of shirt collar? I'd have to do something pretty soon if I wasn't to be tracked through London like a wounded stag. But I had somehow to get a little more distance between me and these pursuers.

"Give me that bicycle!" I demanded of a boy who'd dismounted to shelter under the cover of a doorway. With cold and shaking fingers, I managed to get a sovereign out of my wallet. I pushed it at him, and snatched at the handlebars. Before he could even look at the coin and realise the bargain was well on his side, I'd swung myself onto the saddle and was peddling off as fast as my legs would push.

I hurried along the straight, quiet streets—all terraced houses of red brick and fronted by little gardens. Some of these gardens had their heating on at full pelt, and there was already blossom on a few of the bushes. After a few minutes, I found myself at Honor Oak Park Railway Station. I hadn't known about this one, and didn't know where it went. Also, there were no trains in sight. I could carry on up a hill to somewhere else I didn't know. Or I could continue towards Crofton Park. I knew there was a Blackfriars service at 3:57. Assuming the clock above one of the shops was correct, I could just make that. I might not go all the way into London. But, if I got off at Peckham or Denmark Hill, I didn't see how anyone would have the foresight to be waiting for me there. I turned down the gentle incline that led back to Brockley Rise. Then I thought better of that idea and took a left into another terraced road. The top gear of the bicycle didn't work. But peddling fast in third gear got me to a reasonable speed. *If* I was being tracked, that van couldn't be far behind. It was a question of keeping out of sight and hoping for alleys or parks where I couldn't be followed by anything on four wheels. The rain had now stopped again, and the light was fading. I could hear my breath coming in ragged gasps as I pedalled like a maniac and hoped I was going in the right direction.

As luck would have it, I got to the railway station just as the 3:57 was rolling in. I darted past the ticket inspector and down the stairs. I opened the door of one of the middle carriages and bundled myself and the bicycle into the bright warmth of an almost empty commuter service. I ignored the faint disapproval of a couple of young women, who'd squeezed themselves into fashionable, though unseasonable, running shorts, and pulled the window down. I looked out along the platform. I'd half-expected to see men in dark hats running down the stairs and chasing after me as the train moved steadily out of the station. Except for a very angry ticket inspector, who was already turning to go back up the stairs, the platform was empty.

I closed the window and steadied the bicycle. For reasons I couldn't recall, the South London lines hadn't yet been magnetised, and this was a slow and bumpy ride. But the road junctions we passed all looked reassuringly jammed up. Surely the van wouldn't be able to follow me along the line? The young women had given up on looking at me and were again singing snatches to each other of something that had been popular last season in the Blackpool Electrodomes. The words were hardly Noel Coward, but the tune had a cheap Dago lilt that doubtless commended itself to these off-duty shop girls.

Next stop was Nunhead. I didn't know this, so stayed on. A couple of people got off here, but no one got on. I closed the window again, and now sat down and lit a cigarette. I could stay on all the way to Blackfriars and ignore the renewed attentions of the shopgirls as I stripped off and examined my clothes. But every minute on the railway train magnified the chances that someone would eventually get on or be waiting for me. The next stop would be Peckham. I didn't know this place very well. But I knew there was a big street market. It would soon be dark, and I could disappear within that great expanse of lighted stalls and look for a coffee shop or somewhere else with a toilet, where I could examine myself at reasonable leisure.

Coming out of the other carriages, about a dozen people got off with me at Peckham. None of them showed any interest in me. I gave a silver threepence to a guard, who didn't ask for a ticket and helped carry the bicycle down the stairs. In the street outside the station, there were the expected crowds of shouting, jostling people. I was about to throw myself among them, when two men stepped out of the waiting room.

"We're so glad you could make it, Sir," one of them said, removing his hat. "We weren't at all sure the message had got through that we were starting early." He looked closely into my face.

"Weren't you on the television a few nights ago?" he asked.

CHAPTER TWENTY TWO

I looked down from the raised platform at the rows of expectant faces. I'd been too busy smoking and racking my brains to bother listening to what the man who'd spoken to me at the railway station was now saying. I was feeling thoroughly stupid for having gone along with them. But they'd guided me with firm deference into an elderly car that had been converted to run on methane, and had then pushed through the crowds deep into an area of crumbling properties that all looked as if they'd been cut up into bedsitting rooms. We'd got out at what might have been an old chapel, and I'd been allowed ten minutes to lock myself into the toilet and hunt feverishly through every shred of clothing I had on. Now, washed and brushed—and no wiser about how I'd been so easily tracked through England—I sat in the middle place at a trestle table while the man beside me was now droning on about the rise of the single old age pension to 19s.9d.

"But this brings me to the main business of our meeting," he said finally with a change of tone. He kicked my right foot and looked down at me. "We are both pleased and honoured to have with us Arthur Nobbing, who has come down from London at very short notice to speak about the Future of Britain after the Next General Election." He stopped and everyone in the audience clapped politely.

Now, of course, would have been a good time to make my excuses and run for the door. My bicycle had been propped up just inside the main door. If I got back on it, I might be able to make it to a bus stop before any of my pursuers was able to home in on me. But my legs were aching from the previous bicycle ride. Here was as good a place as any for demanding a call to the police. Besides, I was in a large crowd. Surely no one would dare move against me in front of all these witnesses?

"Ladies and Gentlemen," I said as I stood up. I spoke in my best lecturing voice and wished I'd paid a little more attention to the details of who I was supposed to be and what I was expected to say. But I'd at least caught the theme of my speech, and I might as well play along with things before I asked if there was a telephone in the building.

"Ladies and Gentlemen," I repeated. I suddenly noticed that, with one possible exception at the back, my whole audience was male. They were mostly of the South London working classes. A few still had their cloth caps on. I glared at one old man who sat in the front row. He was picking wax out of his ears with a matchstick. He grinned toothlessly back and put the matchstick behind one of his ears. They he took off his cap. I pressed my brain to the task in hand and took another deep breath.

"I wish to thank the good people of this association for having taken the trouble to invite me down from London. And I'd like to thank you all personally for having had the goodness to come out on this rather inclement afternoon to listen to me." I paused. A youngish man near the back of the hall shouted at me to get on with things. The man beside me stood up and pointed. My heckler fell silent and shook his head. He continued staring insolently back at me. The old man at the front had now begun picking his nose and inspecting the results through one lens of a pair of reading spectacles. I swallowed and pressed on.

"You will have noticed," I went on, now ignoring everyone in the audience, "that, of all the great European powers—indeed, of all the powers in the world—our own England has escaped the opposing but equal horrors of revolution and tyranny. We alone have passed beyond the middle years of our century with our historic institutions and our historic liberties intact.

"No—more than this," I added, warming to my theme: this might, after all, be one of the asides in volume two of Churchill—"we have not emerged into the present with our institutions and liberties merely intact. We have even renewed and strengthened them. Which of you who had arrived at manhood twenty five or twenty years ago, would that thought that we could now be looking back on a generation of profound and unbroken peace, and that we should be looking forward to a general election where the will of the people would be honestly consulted and fully respected? Which of you would have expected the Bill of Rights Act? Or the reforms to Church and State that, even had our neighbours enjoyed average fortune, would have renewed our claim to be the classic home of civil liberty?"

Someone coughed loudly. My heckler said nothing, but now made a most vulgar gesture with his left hand. I stared him down and continued:

"England is a country where the people are free to live as they please. We do not fear, in this country, to open our doors to a policeman. We are not stopped as we go about our business and made to show proof of identity, or to persuade the authorities that we are behaving as they would wish us. We can read and speak as our wills direct us. We are free men in a free country, living in plenty under the Queen's Peace.

"Nor do we confine our happy state to England alone. In every corner of the world where our own have settled, our Dominions are also advancing in peace and liberty and the most perfect external security. Yes, look at the Empire—that groups of states, all independent in their own local concerns, but all united for the defence of their common interests and the defence of a common civilisation, united not in an alliance, for alliances can be made and unmade, but in a *permanent and organic union.*

"Look at our common future as it might have seemed in the March of 1939. Look at our future as it so reasonably seems twenty years later—a future of longer and richer lives, of weather control and space flight, of electrical devices almost unimaginable just ten years ago, but soon to be in every home. Look at this contrast, and let us all be grateful for the Providence that has enabled England alone—England and all her dependencies—so successfully to negotiate the rapids of the past half century."

I drew another breath, and was about to launch into an encomium on the gold standard and the removal of the food taxes, when I felt a sharp kick from the man sitting next to me.

"You are from the *Labour* Headquarters?" he hissed, an anxious look on his face.

"Er, yes," I said. I looked about the room. Now I thought about it, everyone was looking rather common—and there was an omnipresent smell of unwashed clothes and stale tobacco. Even otherwise, this was Peckham—and I surely ought to have noticed the trade union banner on the wall behind me, and the framed picture of Dennis Healey. Silly me, I told myself. Of course, this had to be the Labour Party! I had come into the room with other concerns in my head. But I should perhaps have asked which party I was supposed to be representing. Still, no one had actually started a slow hand clap. The heckler aside, no one was even looking very put out. But I put myself into a change of mental gears that Krellburger himself might have thought sudden and went on:

"But, if all this must be appreciated, Brothers, are we to think it enough?" There was a gratifying shout of "No, never!" from the heckler. I flashed a brilliant smile in his direction, and wondered what might presently be on Labour-thinking minds. "Oh, there is the Health Insurance Act that relieves the poorest among us from fear of sickness. There is the Higher Education Act that awards bursaries to the young and able poor to study at university. But no one should be deceived that this is the limit to what a country as wealthy as ours has become may afford. Where are the co-operative associations that the Tories promised at the last election? Have they supplemented the work of the private friendly societies and of state subsidy? I tell you, Brothers, they were allowed to fall stillborn from the womb of Parliament." I slapped the table for emphasis, and thought its trestles would give way under the sudden shock. I stared defiantly about. "Where is the strict enforcement of the Imperial Immigration Act? Is it not notorious that whole streets of our cities have been allowed to fill with persons of alien and inferior race?"

I now got my first cheer of the entire speech. There was a long burst of applause, and several men got up to wave their cloth caps in the air. I was thinking to explain the laws of supply and demand as they operated in labour markets, when I suddenly noticed that the audience had increased by three. Large men, still wearing their hats and overcoats, they stood at the back of the hall beside the only known exit. I slumped forward and leaned on both hands.

"Is there a telephone here?" I asked from the corner of my mouth. The chairman of the meeting shook his head and asked if I could explain Labour's policy on colonial birth control. If I'd known what it was, I'd now have been hard put to string more than a dozen words together. I thought desperately. "I need to use the toilet again," I said. The chairman looked alarmed. I swallowed and looked once more at the back of the hall. The three men had now multiplied to six, and they were edging forward. Right at the back, framed in the doorway, I got a quick flash of a familiar, moustached face—its usual melancholy look replaced by a glare of blazing and malevolent triumph.

"But Brothers," I shouted. I banged very hard on the table, not caring now if it did collapse. That got everyone's attention. "Brothers, let it never be said that the Labour Party was at all exclusive in its welcome to speakers. You've heard me put the socialist case for our national future. If you want to hear the other side, be aware that our Foreign Secretary—Harold Macmillan himself—is standing just outside this room, and is waiting to answer all your questions in person."

There was a sound of disbelieving laughter. Then someone at the back forced his way through the door and jumped back in, nodding and waving his arms. There was a deafening scrape of chairs and a cheerful shout of "Big Mac! Big Mac!" as sixty people got to their feet and formed a chaotic, jostling mob at the exit. I could see one of the big men trying to struggle forward. For the moment, the others had simply vanished into the crowd.

Even before the chairman could get in his obvious question, I had my hat and coat and was off the stage and rushing for one of the side doors. I threw myself into the little cubicle and shot the bolt. The window was painted shut. But I stepped onto the seat and smashed it open with both fists protected by my hat. It was only a couple of feet square, and my shoulders would only go out diagonally. But it's astonishing what acrobatics a man can achieve when he's in a blind terror. It couldn't have been thirty seconds between jumping down from the stage and my rolling about on an overgrown gravelled path outside the hall. There was a high wall in front of me, and a rusted wire mesh gate a few yards along on my left that might well have been locked. I crept right along the path to the main street. No one had yet bubbled out of the hall. Perhaps the door was being kept shut while Macmillan's men fought their way through the crowd in search of me. The methane car was still parked outside. The only other parked vehicle, I realised with a shock, was the one in which Krellburger and I had made our escape from Birch Grove. I dodged back behind the high wall and looked carefully out at the car. It was dark now, and many of the street lights were broken or hadn't yet come on. But the reading light was on in the front of the big car. Was that Krellburger sat in the driving seat? I stared hard. It was. No point asking what he was doing here. It was either make an ineffectual dash either way along a street where I couldn't recall any openings or turnings off, or resign myself to a delayed meeting with the great Nathaniel Branden.

Hesitantly, I approached the car. The street was otherwise still empty, I pulled at the handle on the passenger's side. The door opened and I got in.

"I won't ask what you're doing here, old boy," I said, trying to sound cheerful through my fit of the shakes. "But you are, beyond all doubt, a sight for sore eyes."

No answer.

I looked at Krellburger. Now I was beside him, I could see that he was slumped forward against the wheel. I reached slowly out and patted his arm. Like a thing disturbed from some unstable equilibrium, he fell heavily towards me. As his hat fell off onto my lap, I saw his blank, staring eyes, and the exposed, darkened flesh of his throat.

I heard a noise from the seat directly behind me.

"It helps with these old cars, Dr Markham, if you have the keys ready."

Michael Foot sniggered and tossed the keys onto the top of the dashboard. Then he clamped his bony, murdering hands about the dead boy's throat and pulled him back into a sitting position.

CHAPTER TWENTY THREE

So far as I could tell without my watch, it was about midnight. Following a short though scary helicopter flight, we were back at Birch Grove—now in one of the deeper cellars. A man held me by each of my arms. I stood handcuffed. About eight feet from me stood a ceramic vat of some dark liquid.

"It really was silly of you, Anthony, to try escaping," Macmillan said with a pitying leer. "I'm sure you'll agree that no good came of it." I gritted my teeth and looked back into his face.

"I'll see you hang for this," I snarled. Macmillan smiled and walked over to a wooden chair. He pulled the handkerchief from his breast pocket and carefully dusted the chair before sitting down.

"I don't think, my dear young fellow," he said in his most reassuring voice, "you are in a position to see anyone hanged." He shook the dust from the handkerchief and blew his nose.

"Pick it up and bring it over here," Foot barked at two other men. "Then just leave it. I can do all the rest myself." He licked his lips as the small, naked corpse was carried across the room. I squeezed my eyes shut and tried to pray. But Foot was now standing before me.

"Don't try to imagine this is a dream, Dr Markham," he said with soft delight. "This is reality. Everything else in your stupid life—the time you spent as a day boy in your minor public school, your furtive buggeries, your posing as an historian of petty note—all that and more was the dream. And you've just woken from it. Welcome to the real world."

I looked past him to the pathetic young body. The boy had told me he was only sixteen. He'd read too many silly books. He'd believed too much in a country that never was what he thought it might become again. *But he'd only been sixteen.* I thought of his enthusiasm, his courage, the open, trusting look he'd given me when he asked for one of my cigarettes. I couldn't think of any reason that would stand up in writing, but I felt a sudden wave sweep over me of self-loathing. If I couldn't be blamed for his death, I was the cause. He might have thought he was dying for Ayn Rand. All I could think was how I should have sent him back to bed after he'd woken me, and waited, unaware of the truth, for what the morning would bring.

Suddenly—for all the world as if I'd been looking at things through the eyes of the narrator in a novel, I pushed myself closer to Foot and spat in his face. Shocked he stepped back. He put up a hand and wiped the gob from his chin.

"You murdering bastard!" I shouted. "When they come to hanging *you*, I'll beg to be the one who pulls the lever." Foot held up his wet fingers and smiled. Then, without seeming to move, he stood closer and brought a knee up hard into my groin. As I gasped and sagged forward, he took hold of me and pulled upright. He punched me viciously in the stomach, and then landed a blow on my left cheek. I would have gone down, but for the two men, who now held me tighter. Foot raised his fist again and looked ready to set about me in earnest.

"No violence, Michael—please!" Macmillan cried. He was back on his feet and was pulling Foot away from me. "We've had enough of that for one day, I'm sure you'll agree. I really do want us all to think that we are—or can be—friends in this room." He smiled at me and led Foot away. Foot looked down at the body and a horrid gloat spread over his face.

"Bring the Indian boy forward," he said to the men. "I want him to watch this. There's nothing that a true historian wouldn't want to see—*once*." He turned and picked up a leather apron from a bench against the wall of the little room. He pulled it over his head, and reached for a pair of goggles, and next for a pair of gloves that covered his forearms. He stopped and thought, then took off the goggles and put his own wired spectacles back on. He stopped again and grinned. Beneath the apron had been a small box, about the size and shape of a self-charging television battery. Foot went back and stroked this. He looked shiftily at Macmillan, who was looking away. He covered the box with some sacking and turned his attention back to his apron.

He pointed at the men. "Hold him back a few feet," he ordered. "When I say, bring him right forward." His next words were covered with an involuntary giggle. "Take a few deep breaths, *Dr* Anthony Markham of the LSE," he now sneered. "I'll tell you when to hold your breath. You don't have to, of course. But I'll advise you to hold your breath when I say."

He giggled again and bent down. He put his arms about the body and lifted it upright. Eyes still open, though dull in the light from the single overhead bulb, the head lolled sideways. The arms hung limply down. With surprising strength, Foot lifted the body high in what looked a parody of a lover's embrace. Bending carefully forward, and now moving slowly, so as not to disturb the dark surface of its contents, he lowered the body into the vat. Pulled by its own weight, the body slid down into the liquid until all was hidden up to the chest. He put a hand on each shoulder and pushed down. The body now disappeared but for the neatly cropped hair and the very pale forehead.

"Sulphuric acid is ever such a wonderful substance," Foot crooned at me. "But come forward, and look in while you can. In a moment, fumes will start to gather above the surface. After a few minutes, I regret we shall have to leave the room. But do look while you can. You can't see it properly? Oh, that's a shame, *Dr* Markham—Dr *Anthony* Markham—such a terrible shame. Still, shall I describe the acid's action on a human body? It's been in hardly a few seconds, but just look at this –" He took hold of the short hair and pulled the head up and let it fall onto the other shoulder. I nearly retched at the hissing, bubbling transformation of what had been clear skin.

"Yes, isn't it beautiful?" he continued. "All over the body, skin will be shrivelling and splitting. In just a minute or two, the outer layers of skin will begin to slough off. Soon, the stomach muscles will sag and dissolve, and intestines will spool out to almost immediate dissolution. Give it another hour, and the bones themselves will come apart at their thinnest points. This head will then sink under its own weight into the depths of our forty gallon container.

"By morning, there will be nothing left—nothing identifiable, that is. There will be a few of the larger teeth and one or two fatty lumps that you'll find floating on the cold surface of the now exhausted acid. Come the dawn, my men will decant what remains into smaller containers and take them up for pouring into the drains.

"Are you aware, my pisspoor biographer of Winston Churchill," he asked with another giggle, "of the Latin phrase *corpus delecti*?" He paused for another giggle, then repeated the phrase, still in the unreformed pronunciation. "It means 'body of evidence for the crime'. In bourgeois jurisprudence, a man cannot easily be found guilty of murder without a body. In this case there will be no body.

"Yes, *Dr* Anthony Richard Markham, First Class Honours from the LSE—a little acid rids us of this deed!" He stared up from the vat and looked straight at me. As he did so, the light caught the lenses of his spectacles and turned them to blank disks. It was as if there were no eyes behind them. But it was the impression of barely a moment. The fumes had now overspread the liquid, and a stray snake of the fumes had found its way close by Foot. He fell back in his most ghastly coughing fit yet. One of his men bent down and helped him to his feet, and then over to the chair where Macmillan had been sitting. Macmillan put his handkerchief up to his face and pointed with his free hand to have me led back from the overboiling vat. The visible fumes didn't reach me. But the stink of bad eggs was unendurable. My captors let go of me, and a cloth was put in my hands. I reached up and pressed it over my mouth and nose. I thought I'd be led out of the cellar, but Michael Foot was up again and standing triumphantly before me.

"Get away from me," I shouted through the cloth. "You're fucking mad."

"Mad?" he cried with mock astonishment. "Mad? Yes, I suppose I am mad. But Anthony, Anthony, you've seen nothing here to shock the firmer sensibility. Can you imagine the effect of my burning bath on a *living* body?" He laughed maniacally. "Yes, think of that. How else do you think Jones and Rutherford disappeared in Moscow without trace? Do you suppose that, all by themselves, the Russians would have been so daring with British subjects? Oh, you should have been with me in the main office of our Party Legation in Moscow. I led them in, claiming I needed help with the wording of a manifesto. I was so deferential—that class enemy I've just cleansed from the world had nothing on my manner then! Jones was in up to his waist before he realised what was happening. He splashed about and screamed a little. But he was dead almost before he knew he was suffering.

"It was Rutherford who was forced slowly and knowingly into the bath of pain. You should have seen the clothing dissolve from his body. You should have heard his squeals and then bellows of pain. You should have heard his desperate and prolonged attempts to negotiate. Even as his stomach burst, he was offering me sole leadership of the Party."

Foot broke off for another long coughing attack. Now Macmillan took charge.

"Get everyone upstairs," he snapped at the men as he walked past me to the door.

***

I drained the brandy glass in two gulps and reached for my cigarettes. The butler leaned forward to light it for me, then straightened again.

"Will that be all, Sir?" he asked.

"Yes, Bellamy, that will be all," Macmillan said, reaching for the decanter. "Thank you for waiting up. It is much appreciated."

"Am I to understand, Sir," the butler asked again, "that young Edward will not be rejoining us?" I looked at the man. Was this some elaborate game? If so, was it for my benefit or theirs? Hard to say. Macmillan shook his head sadly and sipped at his brandy.

"Tell the other servants that young Edward has left us," he said. "It was not what I should have wished, and I am sure he will be missed below stairs as much as above. But he will not be rejoining us." The butler nodded. He went over to the fire and put on another log. He looked about the room and straightened a rug that I'd kicked aside as I was brought into the room. He walked slowly over to the door and closed it behind him. I was now alone with Macmillan in his study.

"Look, Anthony," he said, "I know that our relationship has not developed as I might have wished it. But I would urge you with all passion to put aside any conceptions you may have formed of me since our last conversation. Indeed, I'd even ask for some indulgence of dear Michael. I'll not deny that, since his break with the Labour Party, he's fallen into a set of rather unpleasant people. But he was a most distinguished President of the Oxford Union. And all those lost elections to Parliament—why, they'd sour anyone of his background."

"Young Edward will not be rejoining us," I said in a mocking impersonation of his own voice. "Is that how you write off one of your bum boys? 'Young Edward will not be rejoining us'? Is that how you write off all your servants when Foot takes it into his mind to strangle one?"

"Dear me, Anthony, of course not," came the smiled answer. "'Bum boys', as you well know, can be picked up for 7s.6d a go. A proper servant is much harder to find—especially in these modern days of prosperity.

"By the way, dear boy, I heard most of your speech to those Labour chappies. Would you care for a safe seat at the next election? I'll need all the eloquent young men I can find once I'm in Downing Street.

"That assumes, I hardly need clarify, that I don't let Michael murder you first."

CHAPTER TWENTY FOUR

I rubbed my uncuffed wrists. I'll not say the cellar horrors had faded. But the return to an outward semblance of normality had steadied my nerves and allowed me to do a little thinking. I pushed my glass across the desk and waited for Macmillan to refill it. I dropped my cigarette end into the ashtray his butler had provided, and lit another. I looked over at Macmillan and smiled.

"Let's not argue about the details, Harold," I said with what I hoped was bright insolence. "We can simply agree that every word you said to me last night was a lie. You do know that I heard everything you and Foot discussed in this room when I was supposed to be in bed." He raised his eyebrows. I twisted round and pointed up at the cracked panelling just below the ceiling. He pursed his lips and nodded wisely. "So why don't you tell me what you're really up to—and what my Churchill Memorandum does to advance it?" I took another mouthful of brandy, and then a more delicate sip. It's surprising how calm a man can feel when he knows he probably can't escape death in one form or another in the next few days. Even the most cowardly murderers, I'm told, walk to the gallows with a firm tread. I was resigned to death. And, if I can't say exactly how I felt, Krellburger's end had filled me with a righteous anger that still flattened any native tendency towards gibbering terror.

"I did say to you last night," Macmillan began, "that it can be hard to summarise whole volumes into a few words. This is really hard when the volumes are real and the words need to be true. But I'll do my best by starting with a little background." He lit his pipe and watched contentedly as its smoke rose in a slow and aromatic column.

"There is an apparently pleasing symmetry about the balance of world power," he said. "Since 1917, the country everyone has most wanted to check has been Soviet Russia. This is effectively checked in the West by Germany and in the East by Japan. The Germans and the Japanese have better, though smaller, armed forces. What might be Germany's decisive advantage in the atom bomb is effectively nullified by the terror they share with us of the effects of ever using it. Germany and Japan have a formal alliance against Russia, though they are separated by half the world.

"Each relies on our vague support in its own sphere of resistance. At the same time, while each relies on our vague support, each has its own disputes with us. The Germans would like us to get out of their way in the Middle East. The Japanese would dearly love to set hands on the Dutch colonies.

"This system, as it has evolved, is inherently unstable. It relies on the fact that Halifax will not make any commitments that might allow a repeat of the crisis that got us into the Great War—and on the continuation in power of some ageing and very cautious men in Berlin and Tokyo, and in Russia itself. As required, Halifax will even give the occasional support to Russia.

"We ride the system as a man does a bicycle. Though, in relative terms, we are far weaker than in the golden days of Queen Victoria, we remain the hegemonic power, and, so long as we do not push our luck, can usually get our way against any one other power. Of course, any two of the other powers would sink us in no time if they dared combine against us. But they won't, because we give them no reason, and because they fear the support we could bribe out of the one other uncommitted power. If it was first envisioned by Chamberlain, the system has been perfected by Halifax, and he is openly pleased with himself that it has lasted so long as it has."

"And, all considered," I broke in, "it's surely the best anyone could have wished for. But I suppose you want another big war."

"No, Anthony," he replied, "I *don't* want a big war. I just think that one may ultimately be necessary. But look at your phrasing—'all considered', 'the best anyone could have wished for'! This is the language that has guided our foreign policy since the War. It's always a matter of 'safety first', or 'appeasement', or 'muddling through to the other side of the storm'. There is no imagination here—no long term vision for our race and our civilisation.

"Twenty years ago, there did seem to be an alternative system on offer. This involved a close and equal friendship between the two great Anglo-Saxon powers. We could then have smashed both Germany and Japan. Had we chosen that system—and I am really only following your own reasoning here in those articles you wrote for Beaverbrook—we might not have ended up as the world's hegemonic power on sufferance. We might not have sat like some inwardly rotting fruit, waiting for everyone else to wake up to the fact that we couldn't really defend our position. Together with the Americans, we could have stamped our dominion on the world, unshakable forever."

"But the Americans are out of it," I said in the pause that resulted. I lit another cigarette and looked defiantly across the desk. "Talking of fruit, America was like the tamarind—it went rotten before it was ripe." Macmillan smiled and took a key from his waistcoat pocket. With this, he unlocked a drawer in his desk and stared down at what was in it.

"You talk, dear boy, of how the Americans 'went' rotten," he said, still looking down. "Everyone thinks the Roosevelt assassination, and then Lindbergh's, and all the other troubles that America has had since 1940, were sad accidents. And it is terrible to think how all that dynamic force, that should have been turned outward on the world, for its control and improvement—indeed, for its *salvation*—should instead have been turned against itself. Even today, if you look at fundamentals like coal and steel and grain production, America remains the richest nation in the world. But, after those troubles, and under the demented sway of Harry Anslinger, America might as well not exist.

"But supposing I could show that America's troubles *were not accidental*—supposing I could show evidence of a meeting between Chamberlain and Halifax and Goering, in which the settlement of all main disputes between Britain and Germany was sealed in American blood?" He now reached into the drawer and pulled out perhaps a dozen sheets of white foolscap. Except they were uncharred and unfolded, I saw, by the writing that covered every sheet, that they were the continuation sheets of the Churchill Memorandum. Macmillan held them up and grinned at me.

"The Pressburg Accords!" I said softly. "To show that he was aware of them, Anslinger summarised them at his meeting with Halifax—and Churchill faithfully recorded what was said. I suppose we and the Germans agreed to intervene in American politics to destroy the country. So long as America remained our potential ally, the Germans would never agree to put themselves at the disadvantage we were demanding. Therefore, the public treaty signed at Pressburg was accompanied by a secret protocol."

"Got it in one, my dear, young friend," Macmillan purred. He raised his glass in a mock toast, and went back to inspecting the stack of Churchill writings. "I won't give you more than a distant sight of these, Anthony. Your uncharacteristic firmness of mind might extend to an impulsiveness of action. And, though I'll not be so vulgar as to produce it, be assured that I do have a gun in my pocket. But you've really hit the nail on the head about what was agreed at Pressburg. We jointly put up the cash and trained and armed the assassination squad that bombed Roosevelt and his Cabinet, and the entire Congress assembled to hear him. What the continuation sheets also show is that, when Anslinger refused our initial offer, we added the further assassination of Lindbergh and then a private subsidy to Anslinger of a million a year in gold to enable his own takeover. It's all terribly sordid, you'll agree. And, since he was in up to his neck with both deals—Goering at Pressburg, later with Anslinger in Chartwell—you'll also agree that it won't look too good with Halifax when it's all published in *The Daily Worker* and then discussed on Michael's television show.

"Oh, and in case you're wondering, we do need the whole document if the world is to be fully persuaded of what happened. These few pages in my hand don't say that Churchill is the author, and don't actually say who is speaking. I haven't seen the opening of the Memorandum, but I imagine dear Winston was rather more collected in his account at the beginning that he was towards the end."

"But why all this plotting to get an account of the Protocols given at second or third hand by a drink-sodden manic depressive?" I asked. "Why not just leak the original text?"

"Oh, Anthony," he laughed, "you really are stuck in the past. You remember all that fuss after the Great War about secret treaties? Well, the modern rule is that the full text of every treaty must be published, in full and at the time of signing. And so, when you want to make a secret treaty, you just don't write anything down. The reason Halifax went with Chamberlain to Pressburg wasn't just out of regard for his status as Foreign Secretary. It was because Chamberlain knew that, this time, his cancer really was fatal. When he and Goering sat down in private and settled their unwritten Protocols to the Treaty of Pressburg, there had to be someone on our side who'd live long enough to carry our part into effect.

"How Anslinger got wind of the agreement is a bit of a mystery. But, so far as I can tell, our Churchill Memorandum is the only documentary evidence for the Protocols. I wish we had more than that. But, so long as the text is properly authenticated, it fits in well enough with what everyone already knows to be accepted.

"Therefore, we'll publish old Winston's Memorandum. My part in the matter will be to show the uttermost shock and horror—and to be the only man left in the upper reaches of government with clean hands.

"The Americans will think ill of us, we can have no doubt. But, when all the dust is settled from the explosion I have arranged, and America has shaken Anslinger off, I also have no doubt that his successors will see the logic of their position and embrace the hand of renewed friendship."

I suddenly recalled those women outside the toilet on the railway train. "It's the children I feel sorry for," one of them had said. "They just don't know which side they're on." Like Churchill, Macmillan himself was half-American. If I was only half-English, I was at least all Empire. I lit another cigarette and looked up at one of Macmillan's ancestors—or at someone in a wig whose picture had stayed on the wall when the Macmillan family had got enough cash from publishing to put on the airs and graces of aristocracy.

But Macmillan's immediate and distant ancestry was a side issue. For days, I'd been trying to rack my brains to make sense of what was going on about me. Now, it was all making sense. As if I were safe and snug in the Public Records Office, the elements of the puzzle were falling neatly into place. If Macmillan thought the Americans would come round to what he called the "logic of their position", he knew more about them than I did. But it was plain that what he was aiming at was the unsettling of the entire world order as it had come out of that conference in Pressburg. This was his only chance of smashing up Butler and getting himself into Downing Street. He'd do all this—and doubtless much more—to make sure it was his lips brushing the Royal Hand once Halifax was out of the way.

"And what's in all this for Michael Foot?" I jeered. "Don't tell me you've offered him a seat in the Lords. That may be the only way he'll ever get into Parliament. But I doubt if he'd give you the full weight of the Communist Party—not to mention whatever you've been promised by Moscow—just to get himself called Lord Foot of the Lubyanka."

Macmillan scowled and dropped his part of the Churchill Memorandum back into the drawer. He locked it again. He began a muttered claim that "dear old Footie" could be dispensed with when the time was right. But he was interrupted by Foot's own sudden appearance in the room.

"Glorious news!" he crowed. He laughed and began a little dance of triumph. "My people have called to say Dr Markham's friend is dead. They got the rest of the document from him, and will be here in your car within the hour."

"Well, that is absolutely splendid, Michael dear," Macmillan beamed at him. He got up for another glass and handed it, brimful of clear liquid to Foot. He then refilled his own glass and mine also. "All our little local difficulties are neatly solved. I am, of course, deeply embarrassed that young Edward's people weren't so *naïve* as we thought them. But we managed to cut off his telephone call before he could say anything. And we can be sure that neither young Markham nor his friend has been in touch with the authorities. We simply need to press on with redoubled speed. Before Halifax can get back to England on Monday, everything can and will be in place. I think the time has come to break out the vodka and wish everyone a most sincere *nastrovje*!"

They both drained their glasses. As Foot plainly speculated on whether he could get away with dashing his empty glass into the fireplace, I sipped cautiously on what smelled rather like one of the cheaper brands of generator reagent.

"One thing, I suppose does remain," Macmillan said after an appreciative suck on his pipe. "Young Markham has been kept alive so he can authenticate the reunited Churchill Memorandum. Before we all turn in, I think we can go through some of the questions and responses we shall need for my own little gathering, and then for the interview Michael will conduct on his television programme."

"Than help either of you bastards," I said, trying to control the shaking of my hands, "I'd rather step into one of Foot's acid baths."

"That can easily be arranged, Dr Markham," came the gloating response.

"No it *can't*, Michael!" Macmillan said impatiently. "This is *my* conspiracy, and I'm the one who decides on who gets killed, and by who."

"Isn't it 'by *whom*', darling Harold?" Foot asked with silken charm. "We are only proposing to reshape the world. Or have you revolutionary designs as well on the rules of grammar?" Macmillan's response was a flash of what seemed his first genuine anger in the time I'd known him. He dropped the idea of rehearsing my own contribution to his dastardly treason. Foot also said nothing more about his acid baths.

In ill-natured silence, we sat smoking and drinking for what may have been an hour. The log in the fire grate burned through and finally collapsed upon itself. Once or twice, Macmillan seemed about to pull himself back in order and start a new conversation. Foot gave me the occasional speculative leer—perhaps wondering what volume barrel he might need for getting me up to my chest in acid. My own spark of courage, that had burned so unexpectedly bright and for so unexpectedly long, was burning down faster than that log in the grate. I wondered, with an increasingly chilly stomach, if my end, when it came, would involve one of Macmillan's bullets, or if he'd give me over to Foot.

At last, a light flashed on the telephone beside Macmillan. He looked at it a moment, then over at where Foot was sitting. The flashing went on until I thought the caller would lose patience. But Foot heaved himself up and grabbed at the receiver. He grunted his name and listened awhile, and made a few noncommittal replies. He looked once at me and said a firm "yes." After perhaps thirty seconds, he put the receiver down and smiled.

"I am given to understand, Dr Markham, that we have another body," he said. This is sad for your brown friend, though—since I shall then be short of sulphuric acid—good news for you." He got up and bowed ironically. "I trust you will forgive my leaving you for a couple of minutes."

He got up and hurried from the room. Macmillan took the key from his pocket and looked nervously down at the drawer. He looked at me and raised his eyebrows. Once again, I thought he was about to begin another conversation.

But now the door opened behind me. I saw Macmillan's eyes open wide with surprise.

"Goodness gracious me!" a familiar voice burbled from the doorway. "I should have gone easier on the beast I tortured. It really is Mr Harold Macmillan himself I'm beholding!"

Was there a faint smell of curry in the room?

CHAPTER TWENTY FIVE

"Look out—he's got a gun in his pocket," I managed eventually to blurt out. Pakeshi tightened his arm about Michael Foot's throat and pulled him up to give better cover. He pushed his own gun harder into Foot's right temple.

"My dear fellow," Macmillan said calmly at Pakeshi, "this is a peaceful house. We need no trouble here. If you'll only sit down and have a little drinkie, I'm sure we can reach an agreement to our complete mutual satisfaction."

"Open that drawer," I shouted at him. "I want all those pages."

"In the name of God, do as he tells you!" Foot squealed from behind me. "Please, Harold—don't let him hurt me." Macmillan smiled and relaxed.

"If you try opening my drawer, Anthony," he drawled, "I'll go for my gun. It's hard to say who'll get killed in the resulting fire. But you'll certainly wake the house, and that will be an end to any chance of a smooth escape." He patted the key in his pocket and then blew a kiss at Pakeshi, or at Foot. Then he leaned back in his chair and smiled.

"Though we haven't bothered so far with introductions," he said, still smiling, "I do assure you that I've made my enquiries. I know exactly who you are, Dr Pakeshi, and what you're about. Why the authorities have insisted so that you died at poor Anthony's hands is a bit of a mystery at present. But I'm sure you can see its convenient side. Now, Srindomar, supposing I were to promise not only continued death, but also a new identity and a one way trip to somewhere like Brazil—might that persuade you to unclamp your left forearm from Michael's windpipe and join me in a glass of this superb single malt?"

Pakeshi remained silent for just a moment longer than I'd have liked. Then, Foot still held firm, he was backing towards the open door.

"We must go at once, Anthony," he said. "I think I saw your hat and coat laid out in the hall." Macmillan took up his glass and grinned at me.

"The word the Frenchies use, I think, is *adieu*," he said. "Do leave Michael in the drive. I'll come out and see if he's alive once I've heard you drive off into the night."

I looked back from the billiard room. He was sucking complacently on his pipe.

***

Out in the drive, there were armed men stood between us and the usual car. It took every breath in his half-strangled body for Foot to make them stand aside. Pakeshi pulled him into the back seat of the car. That left me to do the driving.

Dear me! The last time I'd sat behind the wheel of this sort of car was in 1943, just before petrol went through the roof and my father switched over to horse and buggy. I looked at the dashboard and felt for the pedals. I tried to think what I'd seen earlier of poor Krellburger's driving. Fortunately, the engine was already ticking over. It was just a matter of getting into gear and then of steering the thing….

I managed an uncontrollable lurch backwards, followed by a sickening stop as we backed into a little fountain. I heard Foot scream on the back seat and something obscene from Pakeshi. Outside, in the drive, Foot's men were fanning out with drawn guns. Holding his gun out in both hands, one of them was now aiming straight at me. I shoved the correct pedal into the floor and pulled on the gear handle. The car shot forward half a dozen yards. I saw two men jump hurriedly out of the way. The one who'd been aiming wasn't to be seen. We were still pointing at the front door of the house. I saw Macmillan just inside the door. He'd straightened his tie and refilled his glass. He put up his free hand for shade as the headlamps shone fully on him. I eased off the brake and went forward again, now slowly. I twisted the appallingly heavy steering wheel, and the car began to turn. I felt a scrape of leafless branches on the passenger's side of the car, and we were looking at the open gates. I stepped again on the accelerator, and we sped forward through the opening. There was a crunch as one of the mirrors on the front bonnet hit against something and came away. But we were through the gates, and I pushed harder on the accelerator. I heard the back door open and Foot's horrified wail as Pakeshi kicked him out of the car. The door slammed shut again, and we were speeding down the smooth road towards the village of Horsted Keynes.

Once we were out of the village, we stopped so Pakeshi could take over the wheel.

"They've got a helicopter," I gasped. Even as I spoke, I heard its loud clatter somewhere behind us. Pakeshi swore loudly in Hindi, and then in English. He flipped off the lights, and we drove for a couple of seconds in total darkness. We went over a bump, and then another, as we joined one of the main roads. He swore again and turned the lights back on. He reached into his pocket and got out his gun.

"Ever used one of these?" he asked. I had. My headmaster had given out pistols to everyone in the Upper Sixth, and we'd all had weeks of fun with the local wildlife—weeks of fun, that is, until the letters of complaint began flooding in from everyone whose cats had been shot or windows broken. Since then, I'd had only slightly more experience of shooting than of driving. But I nodded and took the heavy gun. I balanced it in my hand and felt for the safety catch. Pakeshi slowed the car and I wound the window down. I looked out and up. The helicopter sounded as if it were directly above us. As I wondered how many bullets Pakeshi had, its spotlight went on and showed that it was really about a hundred yards behind us. I pulled my head back in and closed the window. I climbed over the seat into the back of the car, and wound down the window on the driver's side. Pakeshi was doing about twenty, and the helicopter was soon almost overhead.

Aiming from a moving car at a moving target is something you see in films, and it generally allows an effective battle. But even holding the gun in the right direction was a job in itself. Judging when to shoot was something else. I looked ahead. There was something large and solid looming over the road perhaps three hundred yards ahead.

Until then, the road was straight and clear on both sides. I swallowed and pushed my whole upper body out of the window. I twisted round, and, holding the gun in both hands, let off a single shot in the right direction. I thought I'd snapped my spine with the recoil, but got myself back into the car before we could pass under what may have been a railway bridge.

I don't think the pilot had even noticed the gunshot. When I'd travelled down from London, the noise of the rotor blades was deafening. The helicopter rose far overhead as we passed under the railway bridge. Then it was back, now travelling faster and pressing closer to us. I think the idea was to knock us off the road. Or it might have been to jump ahead and block the road as it landed before us. But Pakeshi had slowed the car still more. I pushed myself out again and fired straight up. It would have been nice to think I'd got the helicopter, and that we'd soon hear its impact and explosion far behind. But if the rotor blades kept up their loud clatter, the searchlight was suddenly switched off, and the clatter itself began to come from further and further overhead. I looked out again into the darkness. Far above, there were two red lights. For a few seconds, they seemed to keep pace with the car. Then, as we accelerated, it turned back, and it sound grew steadily more distant.

"They can still track us." I said in Pakeshi's left ear. "There's some kind of transmitter on me."

"Great minds indeed think alike," he replied. We were passing over the brow of a low hill. As we looked down, the headlamps revealed a road straight as the eye could see. Pakeshi played with a lever beneath the steering wheel, and the headlamps dipped to show more of the road immediately before us. The good roads were still at least twenty miles ahead. For the moment, it would never do to break an axle in one of the inevitable potholes.

"How did you get off the train?" I asked.

"I didn't" he said shortly. There was a long pause, then a gentle laugh. "I'd already guessed you were tagged," he added. "Once you were out of the carriage, all I had to do was get myself and my dear, sweet little bag onto the roof. You can be sure that I arrived in York both frozen and very, very dirty." He laughed again. I tried to get myself into the mood for plying him with questions. If hardly talkative, Pakeshi had the good cheer about him of one who's just tried something clever and has totally succeeded. In little dribs and drabs, and accompanied by an increasingly sub-Continental whine of laughter, he told me how he'd jumped on Foot's men as they thought they lay in wait for him outside the docks in Hull. He'd killed one of them, and then performed some unspeakable surgery on the two he'd left alive until he had as much as the need-to-know status of his "patients" allowed.

"But why did you come looking for me?" I asked once I'd finished giving my side of the story.

"Oh, dearest and most learned and brave Anthony," he smiled in the darkness. "I came back because we were neighbours and fellow countrymen of a sort—and, I suppose, because there was no way out of England for me. If I had to present myself eventually to Inspector O'Brien, it might as well be with you under my arm."

Now might have been a good moment to ask what Macmillan's offer had been about—what was all that about new identities in Brazil? But, even as I thought of the words, I heard the renewed clatter of the helicopter. To be sure, it was now keeping its distance. From a few hundred feet up, though, we'd have been easily visible—even without whatever device had somehow been secreted about me. We came to a junction. Pakeshi slowed and looked carefully out at some road signs I couldn't see from where I sat. He dithered a moment, then reversed back into the junction and took the left turn.

In silence, we bumped gently on through the darkness of South East England by night. Pakeshi had mentioned O'Brien. Yes—we probably should go and see him. On the other hand, Vicky had been specific about going to her. Or there was always Enoch Powell at the India Office. So many choices. But they could wait until morning. I might even let Pakeshi decide. I still didn't know his own agenda. What had been said earlier was playing on my mind, if not to much effect. So far as keeping me alive was concerned, his current agenda appeared to overlap with mine. He might even find it convenient to pay some regard to the safety of England and the Empire.

I sank back into the leather upholstery and stubbed out my

cigarette. Pakeshi was a better driver than I or Krellburger. All the hard drink I'd downed in Burch Grove was finally having a soporific effect. If I didn't catch up now on what felt like a month of missed sleep, I wasn't sure when the next chance would present itself.

CHAPTER TWENTY SIX

It was astonishingly late in the morning when the need for a pee forced me awake. We were still moving, though now it was through the dumpier streets of a small town.

"I'm glad you've woken at last," Pakeshi said in a weary voice. What I could see of his face looked as baggy and lined as an unironed shirt. Parts of it were red from continual nervous plucking.

"No helicopter?" I asked. I listened and heard nothing. Had we somehow managed to outrun them?

"No helicopter since the dawn," he said. He sniffed and took a swig from a half bottle of gin he'd somehow acquired. "But do take a look behind you," he added with an effort to sound brighter than he appeared. I glanced through the back window of the car. The same van I'd seen the day before in Crystal Palace was following us at a longish distance. "It's been following us at least since the helicopter vanished," he explained. "I think the strategy is to follow us until we run out of petrol." He pointed at one of the dials set into the gleaming wood of the dash board. "This is something that we shall face within the hour. I was hoping you'd wake soon, as I supposed I should consult you on our next move. We could stop outside a police station and throw ourselves on the mercy of the authorities. Otherwise, unless we can shut down the Markham Broadcasting Corporation, I fear we must make a stand or to give in to whatever is intended for us."

"Where are we?" I asked. I thought quickly of the police station idea. Almost certainly, that would send the van packing. On the other hand, I was a wanted man, and how would the average provincial plod take the claim that I was also being hunted by a Foreign Secretary engaged in some treasonous conspiracy with the leader of the Communist Party?

"Welcome to Basingstoke," Pakeshi said once he was finished with one of those hard to reach bristles that poked from a roll of fat beneath his chin. "I practised here for a few months after my arrival in the Imperial motherland. If you're as reluctant to face the police as you look, its industrial area provides us with a chance that, if it were not our only one, would seem absurdly slender."

We drove on for another five minutes. I'd never seen Basingstoke. But the place was crowded with factories. Most of these were the small, modern buildings of yellow brick you see everywhere. They might have been turning out computers or other electrical products. Bearing in mind the slow, electric lorries that cracked and sputtered about with the names of shipping companies on their sides, the factories were closely tied to the export market, and might have been producing machine tools. It was hard to say. But they all looked rather busy, and were mostly surrounded with wire mesh fences. What chance Pakeshi thought they might provide was beyond my guess.

Any tendency to a fit of nerves was held at bay by the rising urgency of my bladder. Whatever our need for petrol, we really would need to stop soon. Or might there be a handy container somewhere in the car? As I was thinking of the right suggestion, Pakeshi turned a corner with a sudden and most painful swerve. He accelerated along the now empty road. After a few hundred yards, he did what amounted to an emergency stop that nearly pitched me over the front seats and through the windscreen. Looking closely at the crumbling and mostly abandoned factory buildings of the much older district we'd now entered, he turned again, and then again. For the moment at least, the black van was vanished from behind us.

"Haven't we been down this road before?" I gasped. Pakeshi nodded, and, without warning, pushed his foot down even harder on the accelerator. I fell backwards onto the seat. When I managed to get myself upright, I turned and looked through the back window. There was still nothing behind us—though I'd seen the day before in South London how little chance there was of true escape. With another apparently impulsive turn of the wheel, Pakeshi turned sharp left through some gates that had been removed or had rusted open. He turned again and, out of sight from the road, parked in the loading yard of what might once have been a flour mill.

"Time to get out, Dr Markham," he said. Before I could make any reply, he was out of the car and pulling at the back door on his own side. I fell out into his arms and prepared to stagger over into a corner of the yard. "Not so fast, Anthony," he called. He reached back into the car for his big leather bag. He looked at it for a moment and put it into the boot, and then locked all the doors. "Come on," he urged. "If we have more than a few minutes for this, we'll be lucky." He dragged me towards the gate and into the road. As we crossed to the other side, and went through another, smaller, gate, I looked about. There wasn't another human being in sight. A thin drizzle had started again, and a solitary cat had taken shelter beneath some crumpled metal sheeting. It paused from licking itself dry and gave us an unpleasant look. We hurried past towards the main building.

Pakeshi almost danced with his own fit of the nerves as we pushed an old crate against the wall, and I then climbed slowly through a broken window into the large, empty space within. I felt what I'd thought were solid boards crumble beneath my feet. One of them smashed as Pakeshi's much heavier bulk landed beside me. In the dim light that reached through the dirty or boarded up other windows, I could see that we were in a very large space indeed. This might once have been filled with steam-powered machinery, and hundreds or even thousands of workers would have teemed about. But the tide of prosperity that must have carried this place into the 1920s had first ebbed, and then, on its mighty return, had flowed in new channels. Now, its roof covered eight or nine floors of mournful dereliction, each one half the size of a football pitch.

Pakeshi looked sharply about the abandoned factory building. He pointed at a staircase in the middle of the floor that led down. He pulled me across the rot-spoiled floor. At the head of the staircase, he stopped and looked up for a brief and alien prayer to whatever deity he thought it worth hoping to exist. I looked back to the window and nearly lost control of my bladder. I could hear the distant throbbing of the van as it drove along those deserted streets. If it chose to park outside the gates of this factory, we'd never get back to Macmillan's car. And I could see two damp sets of footprints in the dust that covered the floor between the window and where we now stood.

Pakeshi led me hurriedly down the stairs into a basement. We raced along a darkened corridor towards the light of another staircase. There was an old lift shaft beside. Pakeshi looked into this and then up. He muttered another prayer and now dashed up the stairs. We hurried upwards, our shoes rasping loud on the cluttered iron and concrete of the stairs. On every floor Pakeshi looked at the closed doors of the lift. I think it was on the third floor that he stopped. Through one of the broken window panes that threw light onto the stairs, I could hear the sound of shouted orders in the yard outside.

There was a loud swish and Pakeshi pulled open the lift doors. I looked into the bleak iron mesh of a goods lift. He pushed me in and forced the door shut behind us.

"What are you doing?" I cried. I looked with horror at the sweaty brown face. Did he suppose there'd be any electricity in this building after so long? Even if there was, where did he think the lift would take us?

"Shut up and get your clothes off," he snarled. I put a hand automatically on the top button of my overcoat, then let it fall again. I tried to begin an argument.

"Shut the fuck up!" he hissed through gritted teeth. "Have you never heard of a Faraday Cage?" I thought back fifteen years to Science lessons with Mr Davis. If I remembered correctly, it was all about blocking the progress of electromagnetic radiation. There was a formula that related the distance between the wires of the mesh and the wavelength of the radiation that needed to be blocked. You could have searched me for the formula. All I wanted was a good long pee through the rusty mesh that surrounded the lift. "We've got ten minutes at the most," Pakeshi cried, pulling his hat off and twisting it desperately in his hands. "Make that five. Get those clothes off and spread your legs."

I did as I was told and stripped. We might have been in a cold store when I stood naked before Pakeshi. With cold but expert fingers, he began prodding at me. He started on the fleshy areas under my arms. He moved slowly down, prodding and poking with steady urgency. I heard him mutter over and again that he was mad—mad, utterly mad.

But still he continued.

With a yelp of joy, he reached my left buttock. I let out my own little yelp of pain as he pressed hard with his fingers.

"Well, well, Dr Markham," he asked with a relieved gloat, "how did it get in *there*?" On his knees behind me, he jammed a fingernail into what I'd thought must be a boil.

"It may have been on the railway train from Chicago," I babbled without caring what I might reveal. "I—I fell asleep, and…." I pulled myself together. "It isn't what you may think it is," I added lamely.

"And as you fell, I suppose your dressing gown swung open?" he tittered. I felt him rummage through one of his breast pockets. I turned and looked down at a small leather case, about twice the size of a cigarette case. He opened it and looked at the neat row of surgical instruments, each of them gleaming in the suffused light of where we were. "Get your fingers into those meshes and hold on," he commanded. "If it hurts—and it will—just think of England."

I don't know what instrument he chose for thrusting into me—a nail file, a pocket knife, a cold chisel? All I can say is that, as I tried to hold back the screams of agony from an operation that seemed to go on and on, I lost control of my bladder.

"Dry yourself with this and get dressed," Pakeshi said finally. He unwound his scarf and dropped it onto my back. As the hideous probing had ceased, I'd fallen down and was now sobbing uncontrollably on my hands and knees. I could hear the splatter of urine as it continued running off the inclined floor of the lift into the shaft.

"Did you get it?" I gasped. Pakeshi's answer was a sharp kick to my stomach and a pointed finger to the one dry area of the floor where, mercifully, I'd piled all my clothes. I got up and dabbed at myself with his scarf. I reach for my underpants. As I put them on, I looked at the very small sliver of metal he held in the palm of its hand. About a quarter of an inch long, it had the shape and appearance of a cut down matchstick. The little bulb at its end even had the red colour of a Swan Vesta. I thought it was glowing gently, but couldn't tell for sure. Pakeshi passed me my shirt and bent to pick up my trousers.

"It must have required just a little prick to get that thing into you," he sneered softly. "I've no doubt you'd just had a much larger one. Mrs Dale did bet ten shillings you'd not be able to contain yourself for a whole month in America. I said you'd never dare. But she was firm that even the risk of public castration wouldn't keep you to the straight and narrow!" He laughed and wiped his bloodied instrument on the lining of my jacket.

I said nothing, but hurried about my dressing. There were quiet voices on one of the lower floors. Their owners might have been arguing. They might have been discussing how most effectively to search this immense space. Taking care to make as little noise as possible, Pakeshi turned to sliding the lift door open an inch at a time. The crash of getting it open had echoed round the empty building. Now, it was a few barely perceptible grinding noises. He picked up his soaked scarf and rolled it into a tight ball. He pushed the transmitter into it and dropped both into the shaft. Below us, there was a sudden shout of "I've got a reading—he's below us!" I heard a crunch of shoe leather on the stairs. They were going down into the basement.

CHAPTER TWENTY SEVEN

We rushed as noiselessly as we could down the stairs to the ground floor, and back across the crumbling boards. Below us, I could hear a rising babble of argument. As we reached the window, I heard another shout from below, this time of rage. Now, there was a renewed scraping of shoes on the stairs. I saw that Pakeshi had his gun out and was looking round with an intense and rapid calm.

"Help me up," he whispered, pointing at the window. The floor within was about a foot higher than the ground outside. Here, though, we had nothing to put against the wall. The window was at the height of my nose, which meant the top of Pakeshi's head barely reached it. "Come on," he hissed. "help me up. I need to see what's outside. I'll then pull you up behind me." I got down on all fours and took the whole of Pakeshi's sixteen or seventeen stone between my shoulder blades. I was about to moan something up at him, when I heard a shout from far across the floor:

"Remember, we take the white one alive!" This was followed by a shouted challenge. I jumped up and looked across the floor. About fifty yards away, there were two men in the doorway that led to the main stairs. Both were armed. I heard an immensely loud crash from overhead as Pakeshi took a shot at them. Another stone or so was added to the already immense weight on my shoulders as he braced himself against the recoil. When I was able to look round again, the men had dodged back within the safety of the stair well.

"Come on, Anthony," Pakeshi gasped, holding down a hand. Gun still in hand, his right arm hooked round the metal frame, he pulled me straight up beside him and swung me onto the crate on the outside of the building.

"Put the gun down!" another man said. Hat pulled down against the drizzle, he was standing in the yard. Gun in hand, he stood between us and the gate back into the street. As he took a step towards us, Pakeshi jumped heavily down beside me and pulled me to the ground. Just as he had with Michael Foot, he got himself behind me, his gun pushed against my temple.

"Shoot at me if you dare," the man jeered. "If I don't get you, it'll be the acid bath for you!" I tried for a strangled protest as Pakeshi pushed me rapidly across the yard. All of a sudden, he spun round, and I was now looking back at the window. The other two men were now climbing out. One of them stood on the crate and took careful aim at us. Pakeshi dragged me up so that I covered about as much of him as he could manage. He took a shot at the man who was aiming, and I watched him spin round and fall. Pakeshi laughed maniacally and continued backing out into the street. He jabbed a knee into my left buttock and relaxed his grip on my throat so I could scream at the sudden flash of agony that, but for the continued hold on me, would have had me rolling about on the ground.

Fifty yards away on our right, a man was walking a dog. Pakeshi laughed again at the two men who remained. As they darted for cover within the loading yard, we turned and raced across the road towards where our own car was still hidden. We were no sooner in when the men were now aiming at us from the cover of either side of the gate.

Pakeshi pushed the gun into my hand and started the car.

"Shoot at them!" he shouted. I fiddled ineffectually with the side window handle. "Shoot through the windscreen!" he shouted again. "Just shoot at them!" I pulled the trigger and saw the windscreen explode outwards. The recoil pushed me deep into the upholstery of the chair. As we sped through the gate and into the street, I fired through my side window. I didn't hit the man, who shrank back only six feet from me. But, with a squeal of rubber on cobblestones, Pakeshi turned the car and pressed like a lunatic on the accelerator pedal. By the time I was able to twist myself round, the men were vanishing into the distance. Their van was nowhere to be seen. His dog jumping about uncontrollably on its lead, the one other man in the street had frozen where he stood.

"That was a close run thing," I said, trying to sound nonchalant, though my words came out as a dry croak. Now I had time to register the pain, my left buttock seemed to be on fire. Pakeshi screamed something back at me in Hindi and raised his foot from the pedal.

"It was fucking brill!" he screamed, now in English. "Fucking brill! Sometimes—sometimes, I amaze even myself!" He breathed hard and laughed. As we approached a junction, he looked in the mirror and did a sudden stop. He took the gun from my trembling hands and used it as a hammer to smash out what was left of the windscreen. When we set off again, it was at a more sedate pace. A few pedestrians in a shopping street looked at the unusual sight of a petrol car—a petrol car that must by now appear to have survived a head on collision. We drove past a policeman. Through the bonnet mirror on my side, I watched him stop his slow patrol of the street and take out his notebook. I supposed he was taking our number, and that this would, in due course, be passed to one of the mobile patrols.

"Where do we go now?" I asked.

"We still need petrol," came the triumphant reply. "We can take this where the trunk road starts. After that, there is a small hotel outside Hungerford where you may choose to help me consider our next move.

"But goodness gracious me," he laughed in his Indian voice. "Did you not see the look on their faces as we drove straight past them? Unless he has more subtle management skills than you have indicated, Mr Michael Foot will surely need to make a wholesale purchase of sulphuric acid!"

"Do you think you killed that man when you shot him?" I asked. Pakeshi shrugged.

"Probably not," he said. He brushed some cubes of laminated glass from the top of the dashboard and put his gun away. "When I have time to aim, I generally try for headshots. On this occasion, I might have got the creature's left arm." He giggled and plucked a bristle from his upper lip.

I fumbled for my cigarettes and began to wonder about the next move Pakeshi had mentioned.

***

"It all sounds so perfectly beastly," Vicky Richardson said again. She took the cigarette holder from her mouth and blew smoke up at the ceiling. Major Stanhope grunted something noncommittal and stabbed a giant forefinger at a line on the lunch menu.

"The man isn't Indian, you say?" he barked at Pakeshi.

"He was in charge for many years in the officer's mess at Tombola," came the helpful and surprisingly polite reply. "I think you'll find his cuisine exactly as you would wish." Stanhope gave a wolfish grin and looked up and down the list of probably vile foreign dishes. Once I'd got past Gwen's obscene greeting, we'd waited no more than half an hour in the bridal suite of the King's Garter outside Hungerford before Vicky and Stanhope had arrived together. Though I'd heard nothing as I sat in my bath, they must have come down from London by helicopter. Now, we were seated in one of the private dining rooms, and I'd finished the best report I could make of all the horrors I'd experienced since Thursday morning.

Thursday morning! It was now Saturday afternoon. It seemed as if a gulf of months or even years lay between me as I sat here and me as I'd watched the morning news in my flat and waited for O'Brien to turn up for those boxes. I'd given my side of the story. I'd made some effort to try to find out what Vicky was doing with Stanhope—and, of course, what she'd been about when her voice was beamed to the wireless in Macmillan's car. For all the answers I'd got, I might have addressed my questions to the ugly, many-armed statue of the Indian goddess that leered at me from the corner of the dining room.

Stanhope pushed the menu aside and took up one of the cracked pages of the Churchill Memorandum. Even Pakeshi had been alarmed at the look Stanhope gave him on its production. Certainly, I'd expected at least a pat on the head for having kept it out of Macmillan's hands. Instead, Stanhope's face was like thunder as he pushed the two halves of the sheet together and peered at the faded ink.

"The man didn't even see this?" he muttered. I shook my head. Pakeshi looked as if he was about to start another argument. But Stanhope ignored him. He sighed and put our whole fragment of the Memorandum beneath the menu.

There was a polite knock on the door, and all tension vanished from the room as we made our orders. As the waiter withdrew, Stanhope rammed a plug of cannabis tobacco into his pipe and put a match to the bowl. He took a thoughtful puff, and then, as if it had been a cigarette, sucked hard and held the smoke in his lungs. As he breathed out, he smiled for the first time since we'd met. He fastened his pipe to the claw which was serving today in place of his dark glove, and stared at me.

"You've been looking hard at the Goddess Shambleeta," he said—"she of the hundred wombs." He paused and uttered something rhythmical in one of the Indian languages. Pakeshi giggled nervously. "I see you're of the modern opinion," Stanhope growled at him. "For all your political activities, you're one of Macaulay's children." He laughed unpleasantly, and bent his head down to get at the stem of his pipe. "Well, there are still many out East who believe that, for those of a certain age, the regular embrace of her statue is necessary to the care and maintenance of the *lingam*." He recited more of his Indian poem and twisted round to look at the wanton ugliness of the statue's face. For the first time, I noticed the hideous red gashes that covered its lower belly and thighs. I swallowed and looked away.

"But we foiled the plot," I said, trying not to sound like a schoolboy accused of some unstated offence. "Macmillan doesn't have the whole Memorandum. All you have to do is hurry down to Birch Grove and arrest him and Foot, and the plot is over. If you really hurry, you might even catch all the friends he's invited for this evening." Stanhope turned back from his inspection of the Goddess Shambleeta. The look of faint veneration vanished from his face, and he glowered at me.

"On the contrary, dear boy," he said, "you've complicated everything. By now, we were rather expecting that our pair of villains would be activating their entire network in readiness for their Monday *coup*. Instead of that, they could well be burning every sheet of paper in the house preparatory for an escape to Moscow." He took another lungful of smoke. For all it was mellowing him, the additive in his tobacco might have been coca leaf.

"But, Vicky," I cried in soft despair, "why did you tell me to get away if you wanted Macmillan to succeed?" She took the holder from her lips and smiled coldly at me. Beside me, Pakeshi looked silently down at the tablecloth.

"Darling Anthony," she said in an almost pitying voice, "when we picked up the boy's call to Nathaniel Branden, we guessed you were alone in the car. I told you to get out and run because we didn't want poor silly Aaron to be with you when you were caught again. I really don't know what possessed the boy to try rescuing you. But you must understand that I was trying to save his life, not yours." She had the nerve to dab at an eye as she expatiated on Krellburger's youthful charms, and how I'd surely not been able to keep my eyes or hands off the boy. "I did *so* want you to get yourself away from gorgeous young Aaron. He could then have got himself down to Catford to take further instructions from Nathaniel. But it all ended so—so *very* badly!" She broke off for a sob into a handkerchief that Stanhope had pulled out in readiness.

CHAPTER TWENTY EIGHT

I finished my glass of red and reached for the bottle. My hand shook uncontrollably as I refilled my glass.

"Don't be a fool, man!" Stanhope snarled at my snivelled protest. "We weren't expecting you to *die* in their hands. The idea was for you to hand over the rest of that bloody Memorandum. Bearing in mind the trouble I'd made for them, they'd then be bringing all their plans forward—which is exactly what you say I have achieved. They'd get you on side to authenticate the entire document, and everyone else would start to break cover. The purpose of getting the police on your back—not to mention the frighteners I put on you in the street last Wednesday—was to get you out of sorts with us, and make you cooperate all the more willingly. You weren't expected to blunder about like Richard Hannay on benzedrine. Nor would you have without that slimy troublemaker you have living next door to you—Dr Srindomar bleeding Pakeshi, MD (failed)!" He glared across the table at Pakeshi, who tried without much success for a self-deprecatory smile.

"You tell me that Foot mentioned Heath as one of the other conspirators?" he demanded. I nodded. Stanhope smiled bleakly. "Well, that's of some value. Even the India Office can't spy intensively on the Home Secretary. But we've known for years that Heath used to take money from the Germans—they photographed his antics in one of their spa towns in about 1941, and only stopped waving the pictures under his nose when Chamberlain and Goering settled everything in Pressburg. It's news to us that he's now in up to his neck in some other act of treason.

"But there are dozens of others in on the plot. Some of them we think we know about. Most are hidden. Macmillan's got a whole bloody conspiracy going. Even if only Heath, one of his co-conspirators is in the Cabinet. The others are studded through the middle reaches of our national life. The purpose of all that's been going on in the past week was to flush them out. Thanks to you, it's all gone tits bloody up!"

He had to break off his lecture as the door opened again, and waiters began wheeling in trolleys loaded with food. He stared appreciatively at the dishes placed on the table before him. Still bubbling from the spirit burners on the trolley, they looked and smelled as if they'd come from both ends of an overfed cat. Stanhope tucked a napkin into his collar and tore off a chunk of unleavened bread. He dipped it into one of the pots and pushed it into his mouth. He grunted out something approving in Hindi. Pakeshi smiled nervously, and gave a little seated bow.

I turned my attention to the beans on toast I'd ordered, and we all ate in a silence that was variously angry and miserable. Afterwards, I reached for another wine bottle and lit a cigarette. I was getting ready for a speech on angry defiance when Stanhope pulled out his napkin and wiped his hands clean.

"I've decided," he said. "You've got to go back." He flattened my horrified objections and pointed at the door. "There's a telephone in your room," he went on. "You can call Macmillan from there. You'll tell him that you escaped from our Indian National Party man." He scowled at Pakeshi, who looked silently away. "Yes, you'll tell him that you had an argument with the good Dr Pakeshi, and that you're now alone in this hotel, where you've had time to consider all you were told and to agree with it."

"And you suppose he'll believe that?" I cried. I got up from the table, knocking a bottle of red all over the carpet. "If I go back there, I'll be murdered."

"That's possible," Stanhope conceded. "But, if that boy—who wasn't even British—was willing to give his life to stop them, you can't ask less of yourself. Besides," he added, now with a reassuring smile, "from what we know, and from what you say, they'll *want* to believe you. Believing you gets their conspiracy back on course. What time was it you say Pakeshi dug that radio from your arse?" He looked at his watch and counted under his breath. "There's still time," he grunted. "You just travel obediently back down to

Macmillan's house, and you do whatever he and Foot ask of you."

"And if I don't?" I shouted—"if I don't do you think it'll be any worse if I give myself up to the police?" I took a step towards the door. Stanhope smiled wolfishly.

"If you don't do exactly as your Queen and Country ask of you," he gloated straight back at me, "Inspector O'Brien is waiting downstairs with two plainclothes officers. If you try leaving this hotel, he'll arrest you for murder. We can sort out whom you've murdered in due course. But we'll certainly make sure you hang for whatever charges we do make. And every day, during your trial, the evidence will be read out to a crowded press gallery of your sodomitical propensities, and of the vicious sadism with which you satisfied them. The jurymen will faint as the Crown produces your whips and dildoes, samples of the hideous pornography recovered from your flat—Japanese pornography, you'll be pleased to know, specially imported by me and involving raped and murdered children. Don't suppose anyone will believe a word of some cock and bull story about me or about conspiracies involving the Foreign Secretary. Oh, we'll have to content ourselves with giving Macmillan a warning. He'll look suitably annoyed as he gets up before the cameras and dismisses you as a fantasist as well as a murderer.

"You'll hang for sure, and the mob outside your prison will cheer as the bell strikes eight. You'll hang, and every respectable man and woman in the Empire will breathe a sigh of relief that the world has been thereby made a safer place. Oh, Dr Markham, by the time we've finished with you, your own mother would spit on you if she were still alive."

Stanhope grinned and sat back in his chair. Vicky lit another cigarette and wrinkled her nose. I hovered a moment between the table and the door. Then I sat down.

"Since I'm to be hung for three murders," I sneered, "I suppose that means curtains for Pakeshi. You wouldn't want one of my victims turning up in future, alive and well." Stanhope shrugged and looked at Pakeshi.

"My dear, young fellow," he said back, very smooth, "I don't think we need any more bodies on our hands than is absolutely necessary."

He looked across the table at Pakeshi, who was now very still and silent. "We'll have no trouble here from Srindomar—will we?" Pakeshi looked down at the dessert menu. "No trouble at all," Stanhope went on, "from the good 'Dr Pakeshi' here." He gave a sniff of disgust and relit his pipe.

"Be aware, Anthony," he continued, "that, ever since the big famine, the Indian struggle for independence has been divided between a few local nutters, who can raise a mob and little more, and the Indian National Party, based in London. This Party, with Labour support, has so far managed to get a single Member elected to Parliament. For the most part, it works through propaganda campaigns. Its funding comes overwhelmingly from the Indian masses. Think of them—millions of the poor buggers—all getting by on a handful of rice a day. Yet, when the collection box goes round the villages, they can still pull out a few annas here, a rupee there. It builds up to a tidy sum, and they go dinnerless to bed, warm in the knowledge that their self-sacrifice is being put to use in bringing reason to bear on the *sahibs* in London.

"And so it was until, one day, a worthless charmer turned up and managed to embezzle an inconceivable sum of money out of the INP. Knowing what I do of the trusting fools who manage the Party's business, it's more of a surprise that it took so long to part them from their money. But it was done. And, the person who now calls himself Srindomar Pakeshi must consider how most efficiently to disappear with the proceeds of his crime. Such a shame that he seems to have forgotten his passport when he bundled you out of his flat. Not such a shame for you, though, Anthony. Since it became part of his interest to keep you alive, you didn't share the fate of those others who tried to get in his way." Still hugging the dessert menu, Pakeshi smiled feebly back at me.

"Yes, your friend Pakeshi has no interest whatever in contradicting whatever case we care to make up against you. He'll give back some of the money. Some of it, after all, we'll need to recover at the time of your arrest. We'll give that straight back, of course, to the INP. The loss of the rest will weaken the Party—but it will be able to function again as a counterweight to the less cautious nationalists. What we don't recover we'll tell the world was spent on your disgusting perversions. Pakeshi can then take it and get himself to some part of the world that doesn't have a Union Flag flying over it. Two birds with one stone—bah!"

"You wouldn't dare!" I said. "You're bluffing." I blew smoke into Stanhope's face. I even struck the flat of my hand onto the table so that all the glasses and dishes rattled. "You know I'd be believed in court. You couldn't pervert the course of British justice. This isn't some woggy place where everything can be fixed."

"Listen here, Markham," Stanhope growled with quiet menace. "And don't try telling me what we can and couldn't do. There is no limit to what we can and will do to keep chancers like Macmillan and Heath—and certainly Michael Foot—from directing the affairs of this country. You will obey, or the last you know of this world will be the knot of a hangman's rope. So help me God—but you'll obey!" I looked once into his red face. I'd have found more humanity looking at Shambleeta. I stared up at the ceiling and ran fingers through my hair.

"Oh, dearest, darling Anthony," Vicky now broke in, "I don't think Major Stanhope has told you everything. You see, if you appear in the slightest inclined to speak out in court, he'll just arrange a suicide for you in prison. You'll be found hanging one morning with the appropriate note beside you. I really do think you should consider playing along with us. All considered, Michael Foot's acid bath would be the lesser of two evils. And, if you do get out alive, Daddy and everyone else will be very, *very* grateful." She fluttered her eyelashes and inspected the tip of her cigarette.

"So what's in it for you?" I asked. Still wanting to void my bowels where I sat, I was moving back into my bravery-born-of-despair mood. "Are you in this out of patriotism? Or is it so you can puff up sales of your bastard Hitler biography?"

"Anything for Queen and Country," she crooned back at me. "But, of course, we'd not want Ayn to be electrocuted, when we have a signed contract for her complementary volume on Mussolini. You probably only know her writings from the play she had put on last year. She has a poor sense of the dramatic—and she did deserve all the critical scorn when she introduced Richard Nixon as a tap-dancing space lizard. But she's a fine biographer. It would be a loss to the world if Messrs Macmillan and Foot were to get her life cut prematurely short."

I fell back in my chair. I tried to think everything through. Stanhope and his people had got wind of what Macmillan was up to. They'd brought the Richardsons in to help set me up in America with the Churchill Memorandum, and quietly helped Macmillan and the Rand people get me back to England. Stanhope had then foiled the raid on my flat so that Macmillan could be panicked into early action. The shredding of my reputation had been to push me towards Macmillan. Now, they were trying to force me back into his clutches. I sat up and asked about the Jew Greenspan they'd sacrificed in New York. Or had they sacrificed him?

"Oh, darling Anthony," Vicky replied, "this isn't the last chapter of an Agatha Christie novel. We are still very much in the middle of things. Besides, not everything fits that neatly together in real life.

"But, since you haven't yet walked out of the room, can I take it that you'll make that telephone call? It really is your patriotic duty, you know."

CHAPTER TWENTY NINE

"Do have one of these Russian cigarettes, dear boy," Macmillan said with an easy smile. "Michael swears by them." He pushed the gold box across the table at me. Foot, sitting beside him, gave me one of his blank stares. "I was fully convinced you'd see the force of my reasoning. I would take you upstairs at once to film an interview that I have in mind. Sadly, Michael's acid has done something to our generators, and it will take a while to get them back up."

I lit the cigarette on one of the candles Macmillan's butler had placed all about the dining room. Since Pakeshi was supposed to have gone off in the big car, and the helicopter seemed to be otherwise engaged, I'd been eventually collected from Hungerford by an electric car that had taken much of the day to get me back down to Birch Grove. Whatever I'd thought as Vicky took her gushing leave of me before getting into Stanhope's own helicopter, and Pakeshi, crestfallen, had sloped off to his taxi—his bag much lighter than it had started—I now felt horribly like a fly who's gone willingly into a spider's web.

"I don't trust the little shit, Harold," Foot said with cold contempt. He twisted his face into a snarl, then winced as he stretched whatever injury was covered by the sticking plaster that covered his forehead. "I don't trust him one inch. I'll take a lot of convincing he's not made a full report to Powell." He reached down to the floor and brought up what looked rather like the remote control box for one of the toy boats that boys are given for Christmas. He pointed it at me and slowly twiddled the knobs. It bleeped and grated as Foot went up and down all the frequencies. Still suspicious, he put his radio box away. He got up and came round the table. "Give me your left wrist," he demanded. "Undo your cuff buttons." He took a plastic band from his pocket and put it about my wrist. It was one of those fastenings that close on themselves, but can't be opened without being cut.

"This will track you within a twenty mile radius," he explained, looking closely into my face. "If you cut it off, it will ooze a clear and subtle poison, one drop of which on your skin will kill in you terrible convulsions. I can, by sending out the appropriate signal, cause it to self-destruct—which, of course, will also kill you. It was perfected in Russia for use on class enemies when shown to the foreign press."

I swallowed and looked at the opaque, flexible band. It was fastened tightly enough to stretch slightly if I clenched my fist. In the light, I thought I could see a pattern of wires and circuitry just below the surface of the band. There was no point wondering how it worked. No doubt, Foot would be itching to press whatever button activated the thing. I took another drag on his cigarette and looked back at Macmillan.

"I would ask you, Anthony, not to upset Michael," he said with a slight glower at Foot. "The Russians may not be technically proficient in the all round sense. But they do know about killing."

"Correction, Harold," came the humourless reply. "The Workers' State knows all about the often profound implications of technical changes. It is not, for example, backwardness that causes it to rely on distributed power. I did warn you all ten years ago not to allow Hotpoint to bring its home generators to market. Not since before Hollywood was closed down has there been so powerful a force for raising false consciousness among the masses. The illusory independence that comes of being able to generate electricity in the home did not merely cause every Communist Member to lose his seat at the next election. It has also reinforced a most dangerous spirit of individualism among the people. They think that, because they do not need to rely on a central authority to provide or underwrite the delivery of energy to their homes, they are somehow free. You will take my advice when you come to power, and tax those generators out of existence. You will also forbid further importation of the German sun panels. You might also care to do something about the risible enforcement of the Firearms Acts."

"Quite so, Michael, quite so," Macmillan said with an apologetic smile in my direction. "But all that really matters right now is that Anthony has joined us of his own free will, and we can press ahead as planned.

"So, what exactly are you planning?" I tried to ask in a steady voice.

"You say a word to this piece of offal," Foot snarled, "and I'm walking straight out of the room. Whatever really prompted him to come back here, he's a prisoner. He does as he's told. He lives if he's lucky. We don't tell him *anything*!" He went and stood by the fireplace and lit one of his Russian cigarettes. Being half way through one myself, I was ready to admit they were rather nice. Even so, this one set him off on a mild coughing fit. He threw it at the fireplace. As Macmillan got hurriedly up to recover it from the carpet and drop it into the fire, I heard a chuckle from Foot.

"Behold your new leash, Dr Markham," he said with another cough. He'd produced a second radio box and was allowing his fingers to flutter lightly over its button. "I need but press the red and green buttons at the same time, and then flick this switch, and you will appreciate the technical proficiency of the Workers' State."

"Oh, do put that away, Michael!" Macmillan sighed. He looked at his watch and muttered something about a cold menu for his guests by candle light. There was suddenly a loud sputter that filled the house, and the lights came on. He got up and smiled. Foot twisted in his chair as if the burning sensation in my own bottom had been transferred to him. He licked dry lips and seemed about to say something. With equal suddenness, though, the lights went out. A few seconds later, they came back on. Another few seconds, and they'd gone back out again. We sat a while, staring at the candles. Foot relaxed and smoked steadily. It seemed his acid—whatever his men had been doing with it—had done for the generators until professional help could be brought in.

"The only telephone that currently works is in the servants' hall," Macmillan said with a hurt look at Foot. "I suppose I'd better make what calls I dare from below stairs. I do hope that, in my absence, you can find something more congenial to discuss than murder *à la mode* in Mother Russia." He finished his whisky and got up to leave the room.

I sat, looking at one of the candles. Except I was to do whatever Macmillan demanded, my instructions might as well not have been given. "The more I tell you, the more you're likely to bugger things up again if they torture you," Stanhope had barked in response to my terrified pleas for enlightenment. He had promised "help at the appropriate moment". If I believed that now, I'd have to be more stupid than I felt. I reached for the cigarette box.

"I don't suppose you saw last week's *Observer*," Foot struck up, an oddly friendly tone in his voice. "It carried a long and remarkably fine article of my own about the new Soviet penal code. However, what I most enjoyed reading was a symposium, led by A.J.P. Taylor, on what might have happened during the past forty four years if the world hadn't gone to war in 1914. The three contributions, including Taylor's, were fascinating. You haven't read any of them, of course. But would you care to give me your own take on the subject?" He smiled politely and lit a cigarette. I smiled back at him and reached for the decanter. Talking history with the man was an improvement on begging for mercy.

"The War broke out in 1914," I began. "We are now in 1959. With all respect to Alan Taylor, I suggest that it's too long now to say what would have happened if Princip's gun had misfired at Sarajevo. Oh, I can see it now. The boy gets up onto the Archduke's car and pulls the trigger. Nothing happens. He tries to fire again—but the guards have him firm. He's taken off into custody, and the Archduke and his wife continue about their business before getting on the railway train back to Vienna. The problem is that too many things have happened since then because of the war that *did* break out. Trying to disentangle these things from what else might have happened is too hard for getting anything sensible. The electronic people talk about white noise. There really is too much of that to see any clear picture.

"However"—I didn't like the hard look that was coming again over Foot—"however, let's take a shorter time. Let's not assume 1959, but 1934, which is twenty years after a Great War that never happened. What might we have seen then? Some things, no doubt, would have happened anyway, and were only accelerated or retarded by the War. Among these must be the emancipation of women, and universal suffrage, and Irish Home Rule, and the decline of France as a great power, and the rise of Japan. You can add to this the development of radio communications and the simplification of clothing. I think you can also add the greater devolution of power to the White

Dominions.

"We can be more certain about the things that *wouldn't* have happened. Obviously there wouldn't have been the violent death, by 1923, of between ten and twenty million people. There would still have been Imperial governments in Berlin and Vienna and probably Moscow. Turkey wouldn't have gone though the eclipse that ended with its reconquest of Syria and the Arabian Gulf, and its conquest of Persia. The American genie would not have been so abruptly summoned from its bottle—and then so brutally stuffed back in. There would have been no Great Depression. Music and the arts wouldn't have gone through that long descent into freakishness. We'd probably not have continued so long up the dead ends of the distributed power that you like so much, or of oil power, or of aeroplane development. Hitler would never have got his statues put up all over Germany and its Eastern Territories. Lenin"—I stared at Foot and flicked ash from my cigarette—"would have died in Switzerland of tertiary syphilis. Stalin would have been caught and hanged for bank robbery.

"Turning to what *might* have happened is rather hard, even just looking at 1934. But, if most of the millions who died in or because of the Great War would otherwise have passed unmemorable lives—and there's nothing bad about that!—there must have been other Beethovens and Pasteurs and Edisons who would have enriched mankind. Without their early deaths, we might, by 1934, have been roughly where we are now. The tuberculosis and polio vaccines might have been developed twenty or thirty years earlier. The development of the cancer vaccines might not have had to wait until now to be at the testing stage. The non-development of certain technologies would have been balanced by the earlier development of other technologies—and even by the development of some that are as yet unknown. But, as I've said, these are difficult conjectures to make. Think of the unfinished Mozart *Requiem*. We know what Mozart wrote. We can scrape away the additions that Süssmayr made to complete the work. Saying how Mozart *would* have completed it himself is as hard as saying how the world would have gone without the Great War.

"I suppose I should add that the non-occurrence of known evils does not mean that other evils would not have taken their place. Perhaps, without the Great War, all manner of other bad things would have happened in its place. It requires a leap of faith to say it—but I do believe that, but for the Great War, mankind would have been far better off by 1934 than it was."

I would have said more, but Foot was now twisting his face into the best sneer he could manage. He got up and went over to the dead wireless set. He played a moment with its buttons, then turned back to me.

"I really should have expected nothing more from you," he said with amusement and contempt. "The problem with all you bourgeois historians is your utter superficiality. I see you've changed your mind since your book about Churchill. Then, I recall, you were almost foaming at the mouth about the German naval challenge. But, if you've changed your mind, you've still seen no deeper into the nature of things. The Great War was historically inevitable. Lenin himself said that capitalism proceeds by its own natural unfolding through imperialism to world war. The Sarajevo assassinations may have been contingent. But there are no great contingencies. If Princip's gun had jammed, the War would only have been delayed. If the first breakthrough to socialism hadn't occurred in Russia, it would have done so in Germany or America."

"I rather think Lenin only discovered that capitalism leads to war," I said sweetly, "*after* the Great War had broken out. Nothing is inevitable until it's happened." Foot cut me off with a peal of scornful laughter. He lit another cigarette and blew smoke towards me. He picked up his remote control killing device and played again with the buttons. I lit another cigarette for myself and tried not to look worried.

"*A* Great War was inevitable," he said flatly. "*A* socialist revolution was inevitable. Equally, a second great war was inevitable after about 1930. If the crises at the end of that decade didn't end as Comrade Stalin infallibly predicted, it was a delay—nothing more. When a house is built on sand, it may not fall down at once. And its continuation from one year to the next will be taken by fools as evidence that foundations are not necessary. But fall down it inevitably must. There was no war in 1940. Believe me, Dr Markham, there *will* be a war in 1960."

"You seem very certain," I said.

"I know," he replied with a loving stare at his control box, "because I will help to start it."

CHAPTER THIRTY

One of the candles now began to splutter as it burned down. I turned away from Foot and watched as it dimmed and went out. There were a dozen other candles in the room. But its failure brought a perceptible darkening of Macmillan's study. I could no longer see the titles of the books in the case beside the fireplace. The faces in the paintings had faded from view. But I could still see Foot. A look of triumph on his face, he blew out a smoke ring and watched as it grew larger and dispersed.

"If you were to listen to his speeches as he heaved his obscene body about his empire," he continued, "you'd think Goering was a second Alexander or Napoleon. It is, of course, plain, after twenty years of this, that he's as terrified of war as any of the black-coated Ministers he's allowed to take power from him. The world since Hitler's death has been held in a calm that reflects only the cowardice of a few dozen ageing men. How long has this country and Germany had possession of the atom bomb? How typical of the German and British Governments that it has never—aside from a single controlled explosion deep underground—been tested. But I put it to you, Dr Markham, that whoever controls the power of the atom has the world in the palm of his hand.

"There is one country on this planet where the government is not made up of frightened old women. Let that country have the power of the atom, and the world will awake from its long slumber and rub its eyes in the brightness of the dawn that has been prepared for it."

"Oh," I said. I stretched my arms and smiled. "Oh—so your pay-off is that Russia gets the Bomb. If Stalin and Beria hadn't murdered all the scientists, Russia might have got it years ago. Now, it will be Big Mac who hands it over on a plate." Foot smiled and flicked ash with the theatrical gesture made famous by his television programme. "Can I ask against whom the Russians will use the Bomb? Surely, it won't be us or the Germans."

"It will be the Japanese, you fool," he replied. "Vicious, bandy-legged creatures, all of them," he spat. "It will be imported into Japan one piece at a time in the Soviet diplomatic bag. It will then be reassembled in Tokyo. Comrade Beria will declare war at the moment of his choosing. As the Soviet diplomatic mission looks back from the ship on which it departs, the flash of the explosion will light up the horizon. This will be their punishment for the fire-bombing of Pekin and their germ attacks, and for their abduction of Mongolia from the Socialist Family."

"I see," I said. I thought quickly. I thought back to the conversation I'd had in my flat with Pakeshi when the Memorandum had first come to sight. "If Japan is taken out by Russia, this unbalances the world. We and the Germans must then either consider nuclear war with Russia, or we must bring America out of retirement. I suppose that America will come out anyway once the Memorandum is published. That leaves us with the option of formal alliance with Germany against America, or Macmillan's understanding with America. But, with a nuclear Russia, and then eventually America, it's hard to see exactly how things would work out.

"Can I ask how Russia is to be equipped with atom bombs?" Foot smiled again.

"The reason Harold was unable to send his helicopter out to collect you this afternoon," he said, "is that it is already filled with microfilmed documents and sufficient nuclear materials for Russia to have its own Bomb before Christmas. You are wrong that every prominent scientist in Russia has been unmasked as a spy or other class enemy. The Socialist Homeland is richly provided with every variety of genius. If the secret of a chain reaction has so far eluded our scientists, everything is ready for the transfer of British technology to cut short the need for ten years of further development."

Finally, this part of the plot was making sense. Macmillan was making a gigantic gamble. Publishing the Churchill Memorandum might bring him to power. Foot's part in this was less to supply heavy muscle—useful as this might be—than to help release Macmillan from a diplomatic system that would otherwise have held him tight. Whether he would survive the multiple revolutions he was planning to unleash, and where these might leave England, were matters impossible to predict. It was like trying to give complete answers to Foot's question about the Great War. One thing, though, was certain. Behind that pipe and that carefully-designed mask of aged Edwardian fop, there lurked the world's most desperate and unprincipled gambler since the car accident in Prague twenty years before. To become Prime Minister, and to stamp his name into all the future history books, there was no limit to wickedness of Harold Macmillan.

"There are—or should be—two questions in your mind, Dr Markham," Foot continued after another cough. "The first is why, if I now have everything I need, I am still here. The answer to this is easy. Harold's helicopter has a range of sixty miles. This will not get me to Russia, but will get me to a Russian submarine that will surface five miles from Selsey at 1am.

"The second question is what the British authorities will do to stop me. Don't try telling me you aren't working for Enoch Powell, and that this house will not be raided the moment Harold's dinner party reaches its climax. With his present eminence, not to mention the time he spent at Eton, Harold seems to believe that he can't be touched by anyone short of Lord Halifax himself. We both know better than that—don't we, Anthony?" He paused dramatically. I said nothing, and waited for him to continue. He laughed and took a long drag on his cigarette. "It is because of this, not my acid, that Harold's generators are not working," he said, his laugh trailing off into a giggle that ended in the ghost of a cough.

"But Michael," I asked with what I desperately tried to make a knowing smile, "why are you telling me all this? You did insist earlier to Harold that I wasn't to be told a thing. Now, you're spouting away like a pantomime villain to his audience."

"Because, Anthony," he flashed right back at me, "I like you." My smile faded and I looked rather doubtfully at the insane scarecrow before me. It didn't look as if he'd washed his hair since his disposal of Jones and Rutherford. But Foot was now laughing with a semblance of good humour. "Oh, Anthony, Anthony, I can read your mind as if its contents were being shown on a computer display.

Harold, no doubt, fancies the arse off you. Since his whore of a wife went mad, he's been turning more and more into a proper old queen. As with Tiberius on Capri, foul urges long suppressed have shown through at last. Why else do you suppose he employed that American boy without even checking his references?

"My own interest is intellectual. You are a fool. But fools can be taught. I despise your whole view of the world. But Harold is right that you have a talent for words. Every Johnson needs his Boswell. You have been wasted on reactionary old Winston. Come with me to Russia, and I will make your name immortal."

I was saved the trouble of a reply when the door opened and Macmillan hurried in. Foot picked up his remote control and waved it at me with a quiet smile. Macmillan poured himself a whisky and perched on the side of his desk.

"The first guests have been sighted," he said. "There's thirty of them, which will mean a certain doubling up and more of sleeping arrangements. Michael, I hope you won't mind sharing your room with Edward Heath. Young Markham can sleep with me—er, I mean, he can share my room." He finished his whisky and put a trembling hand up to his moustache.

"You'll be pleased to know that Cook has got an old log stove working, which means we shall dine properly after all. I'm afraid dinner will be at ten. But we shall start our little revolution after the main course." He smiled nervously and looked at the decanter. "Yes, the Revolution will precede the dessert—and every mouthful has already been put on ministerial expenses."

He slid off his desk and reached out his left hand to me.

"Come along, Anthony," he urged. "One of these days, you will describe all this in the vivid tints you gave to the asides between Churchill and Lloyd George in those Cabinet discussions that took us to war. I wouldn't have you miss the arrival of the guests."

I took his hand and got to my feet. As we walked from the study, I noticed that Foot was carrying his radio box.

***

Because there was no electricity, the drive had been lit by filling the basin of its central fountain with something flammable. The fire coiled about and hissed in the thin drizzle of a March evening, and threw a doubtful light over the gravel. The three of us stood together just inside the main door. Macmillan's butler stood respectfully behind us. Behind him, the entire household was lined up in readiness. I looked out into the chill darkness. Macmillan had been sure the guests were arriving. How or when this would be I had no idea. Except for the sound of a gentle wind in the trees beyond the gate, all was silent.

I thought of the fissile materials and rolls of film loaded into the helicopter for Foot's departure. He'd said there would be a Russian submarine to collect him. The helicopter was somewhere above us on the darkened roof. Would it really be able to make the midnight *rendezvous*? Foot had been very confident. Somewhere out beyond the trees, Stanhope would be waiting with his men. There was no point calling out to them. The only working telephone was buried away below stairs. I really was like a fly stuck in a web. I shivered slightly and reached into my pocket for my own cigarettes.

"Can you hear them, Anthony?" Macmillan suddenly whispered. I strained. About half a mile away, I could hear what might have been the throbbing of a diesel engine. It grew insensibly louder. Then I saw, reflected on the higher branches of the trees, the glow of car headlamps.

First to arrive, in his official and diesel-powered car, was the Home Secretary. Even before the car had come fully to a halt, Heath had its back door open and was jumping out. He walked briskly across the gravel to us and took Macmillan's hand. He was polite to Foot, and gave me a long and thoughtful smile. Being the most wanted man in England, I'd expected some acknowledgement. I found Heath's stare a touch unsettling. He might have lingered out in the drive. But other cars—all these smaller and powered by electricity—were now arriving. They came through the gates, sometimes singly, sometimes in convoys of two or three. Only Heath had been grand enough for his own driver. The other guests had all driven themselves. It was difficult, in that central firelight, to see much of the cars. What I could see of them, though, told me that most were at least second hand, and several had holes in their glass fibre bodywork. Heath aside, it was unlikely to be a grand occasion. But, as if they'd all carried persons of a certain quality, the man Krellburger had sent back into the house two nights earlier waved and danced about as he guided each vehicle to its parking place in the majestic drive.

Macmillan made sure, as he greeted them, to introduce everyone to me. If it was his fancy that I should write the inside history of what he was planning, it made sense that I should know who else was to be in on the plot. To be honest, I'd never heard of half these people. I knew Kenneth Tynan, of course—who hadn't read those obscene, drink-fuelled tirades in the newspapers? But John Braine, Harold Wilson, the Reverend John Robinson, Hugh Carleton Greene, Roy Jenkins, Ian Gilmour, Leslie Scarman, Robin Day, and all the others—who on earth were these? I'd never heard of them. Foot knew some of them. I could see, though, that he was frequently as vacant as I was as Macmillan called out his effusive greeting and introductions. For their part, the guests were pretty well overawed. They fawned on Macmillan, of course. They treated Foot with all the respect due to a party leader and the presenter of an important television programme. They even ignored that I was a wanted sex murderer and were most deferential to Anthony Markham, the famous young historian.

Inside the house, all was uproar, as servants ran about with cases and stacks of paper and led the guests away to their rooms. Macmillan strode grandly about the hall, laughing and patting backs and cracking little jokes. Even though the lack of electricity had thrown it into still darker gloom, the house had come properly to life for the first time in my various stays there.

"I've had your dinner suit laid out in my room," Macmillan said to me. "I'm sure we've much to discuss while we change for the reception."

"And I'm sure I'd love to hear it all," Foot added with a civil leer. He took my left hand and stroked the bracelet about my wrist. "It will be so much more interesting than a lecture from Heath on the proper manner of conducting Britten's *Fourth Symphony*."

CHAPTER THIRTY ONE

"Is it true, Michael, that the death penalty has now been abolished in Russia?" Foot smiled back at the fat, greasy Welshman.

"It has indeed been abolished, Roy," he said. "More than that, however, the new penal code actually abolishes trials. What happens now is that suspects are interviewed in private about their crimes. Once they've confessed, they are consulted on the fit punishment. Many ask to be allowed to commit suicide. Some are persuaded to accept a period of re-education, accompanied by socially useful labour, in the bracing climate of the north."

The Welshman nodded eagerly and launched into a monologue about his own plans for law reform in England. They struck me as ludicrous, but were less tiresome than the lecture I'd just escaped on something called "child-centred"—or was it "comprehensive?"—education. Whatever it was called, this seemed to involve not teaching anyone to read or write at school, and carefully forcing all the cleverer children into the company of the most stupid. Macmillan had stood by me throughout this, nodding and smiling at every refinement of the scheme. He'd been jollying everyone along for about an hour now, and looked as if he were enjoying himself no end. For myself, the only compensation I'd found for attending this ghastly reception was the one or two bottles of champagne I'd been able to down.

The reception was being held in the billiard room. All the tables removed, and the carpets rolled back, this was filled with as dire a set of bores as you'll find outside a book launch. I grabbed another glass from the butler and inched my way through the crowd towards one of the lower candelabras where I could light another cigarette. Over in a corner, the Reverend Dr Robinson had finished what might have been his second rant on the impropriety of having made C.S. Lewis Archbishop of Canterbury. He'd now buttonholed Kenneth Tynan and was explaining the sacramental qualities to be found in the smuttier parts of D.H. Lawrence. Tynan looked in my direction and pulled a most lascivious face. I avoided his eye and made for a clear space over by the window. Foot was staring at me. I smiled back and shook my head. Under other circumstances, I'd have thrown myself head first through the opened window and tried making my way out of the grounds. But I could feel his bracelet chafing my wrist, and was neither drunk enough nor desperate enough to test exactly how far his new liking for me stretched.

"I do think, Dr Markham," someone small and intense and slightly foreign cried as he came over and breathed halitosis into my face, "that you have made a brave stand against racial hatred." I gave the creature a blank stare and looked into my glass to see how much of the twelve ounces of Krug might be left. He ran fingers through his wiry hair and struck a pose. "I have made a study of the guilt that is imposed upon those whose only 'crime' is diversity. It is not you who are guilty of murder. It is the society that has imposed a racial and sexual discourse that leaves people like you with no choice but to lash out." He rambled on for five minutes about the need for remodelling every police force in England into a centralised system where half of all the officers would be homosexuals and specially imported coloureds.

"Our task," he suddenly barked in no particular direction, "is to break down the false distinction between the so-called 'policeman' and the so-called 'criminal', in the first place by a programme of reciprocal role-playing in which the police are encouraged to engage in so-called 'criminal' acts while uniformed 'criminals' take over so-called 'police' duties. 'Police' and 'criminals' alike will then come to share a sense of social grievance, realising that they are equally victims of an unjust, class-oriented, racialist and consumerist society. They will gradually be enabled to become equal members of the fully caring society that all people of good will are trying to build."

I looked over at Foot and envied him. He'd only been grabbed by some bearded man in a caftan who was braying on about compulsory metrication and a decimal currency. But Macmillan was now beside me, a reassuring hand on my arm.

"Dear boy," he said, "I'd like you to meet Nicholas Kaldor, who wants to discuss your work on our recovery from the Great

Depression. His theory, that the time has come for taking Keynes seriously, might be of interest to you."

"Until we achieve this goal," the shrivelled foreigner was now raving at the top of his voice, "our society will remain a guilty society. But it is not only our society which is guilty…." Macmillan blenched and tightened his grip to lead me firmly back into the main scrum. Through the insulation of five bodies, I heard the demented scream of "WE ARE ALL GUILTY!" It sounded as if from all corners of the room at once, and silenced every other discussion for a few seconds. Then someone beside me struck up again about re-imposing excise duty on tobacco and using the proceeds for a government campaign against smoking, and the economist Macmillan had mentioned was into a smooth patter about how import controls and printing banknotes might double our rate of economic progress to fourteen or even twenty per cent.

I drank more and more champagne and smoked, and tried not to listen too hard to the drivelling opinions of everyone in the room. There was talk of censoring the press and locking up anyone who breathed the word "nigger". There was talk of lowering the income tax threshold to force married women out to work. Somebody who'd drunk far too much was shambling about and bellowing "Lovely, lovely lesbians" to anyone he could lean against. Once or twice, I heard Kenneth Tynan's shout of "Let it all hang out!" Someone had found a guitar, and was singing in a put-on Liverpool accent that all the world needed was love. Where Macmillan had found this lot was a mystery. Why he thought them worth bringing down to Birch Grove to share his revolution wasn't worth considering. All told, he'd gathered round himself a proper Academy of Projectors. Given half a chance, these nutters would turn England into something unrecognisable and distinctly scary. By comparison, Michael Foot was almost sane. All he wanted, after all, was an excuse to murder everyone with a decent coat on his back or who might dare give him and his friends a funny look.

And now Foot was beside me. Incongruous in a dinner suit, he flashed me a chilly smile.

"Don't tell me I wasn't right about you and Powell," he whispered. "My men have been scanning the darkness beyond the gates. They've now detected heat patterns all about the house that can only be human." I tried to focus on him and see only one face instead of the two that simply couldn't be.

"Well, Michael," I giggled tipsily, "I suppose you'll have to miss dinner. Do you suppose your Russian friends might surface a few hours early?" He shook his head and laughed.

"Harold may think publication to this lot is the same as unstoppable publication to the whole world," he said. "Or he may have something else up his sleeve. You can be sure I'm still working to Plan A."

I caught hold of a mantelpiece and steadied myself against the urge to sit down on the floor and bury my head in my hands. I tried to think of something witty. But this part of the nightmare was finally over, and the dinner bell was ringing. Macmillan had broken away from what may still have been a lecture on the need to abolish juries in civil cases and allow majority verdicts in the criminal courts, and was ushering us towards the big dining room.

I staggered out into the hall, and tried to get myself in order. But Foot was still beside me. He put his right arm about me and led me towards the servants' staircase that led to the upper floors. I'd last been this way with Krellburger. The champagne allowed me to think I should feel disquiet as I went there again—but didn't let me feel more than dizzy.

***

"They really are out there, Anthony," Foot said, pushing the night binoculars back into my hands. We stood on the flat roof that covered the new extension to Birch Grove. One of his big men stood behind us with an umbrella to shelter us from the rain that now fell in cold, steady sheets. "It may be that one of Harold's 'friends' will give the signal when the card has been played. It may be that the half dozen we've so far spotted are waiting for reinforcements. Whatever the case, they are out there, I assure you. And they don't intend anyone to get out of here on four wheels or two legs without being arrested."

"It doesn't seem to worry you," I said. I looked again into the binoculars. A smoke out here in the cold, and Foot's bony fingers clutching at my arm, had sobered me pretty well. Now, I could see the white shapes he'd mentioned, moving purposefully about against a dappled background that reminded me of an overexposed negative. They must have been half a mile away. Mostly, they kept behind the trees and bushes. I thought of the helicopter behind me. It was a darker blur in the general darkness. The pilot was nowhere to be seen. "Have you been laying mines round the house?" I asked with a sudden thought.

"Not exactly," came the laughed reply. "The military arts have moved on since the Japanese attack on Mongolia." He leaned closer and switched into German. "But let me tell you something of what I've been planning ever since I was called down here last Thursday and Harold broke the news about Powell's interest in his plot. The reason there is no electricity in this house is because we've abstracted it to our own use. There are trigger points all about this house. The moment they are crossed, beams of invisible but concentrated light will flash out in an elaborate pattern that no one can pass without being cut into halves or quarters."

"I see," I said in a more halting German than his own. I'd read about these the year before as possible air defences. I didn't know anyone had yet been able to get them to work. Perhaps the Russians weren't as far behind as everyone said they were. If so, it would explain—caution aside—why the Germans hadn't attacked. I took in a deep breath of the cold, damp air, and waited for my head to clear a little more.

"Macmillan and his document and all his friends are the cheese in a giant mousetrap," I went on, now in more confident German. "Once it's been sprung and there's no one left to sniff about, you can spread your wings and head for Mother Russia." Foot smiled. I had another thought. "Might I be correct in thinking your invisible beams are also directed into the sky—so that no one without the proper glasses can know where to fly safely?"

"Fools can indeed be taught," came the approving reply, now back in English. "Sometimes, they can even learn for themselves. A shame you'll not have time to pack an overnight bag. But do stay close if you want to get out of here alive."

"What on earth are you doing up here?" It was Macmillan. He'd poked his head through the hatch that led onto the roof, and was waving a pocket watch in our direction. "I've had the house searched from top to bottom. Everyone's been in his place at table for twenty minutes."

"Too much champagne for our Indian boy, dear Harold," Foot rasped easily. "Though it might be a natural reaction, you wouldn't want him vomiting all over your guests." I caught a look at Macmillan's impatient face as he stepped back to let us into the house. He looked at the night binoculars Foot was now carrying. Now, he smiled.

"Dear boys," he said, "Whoever's lurking out there will eventually come through the gates of Birch Grove. By then, however, it will be to take my instructions."

"Then, I do hope," Foot sneered, "that you'll be giving tonight's audience more undeniable truth than I've ever found in your speeches".

"Truth, dearest Michael, is what people believe," came the reply as Macmillan went back into his avuncular manner. "Undeniable truth is what everyone believes. Shall we make our way downstairs to dinner?"

CHAPTER THIRTY TWO

I once read a story about a man who invited people to dinner, and, for a joke, served them pictures of food. Macmillan's kitchen had managed better than this. But, for all his staff must have slaved away and screamed at each other, tastier dinners may have been eaten in the most minor public school. The game soup had tasted mostly of pepper. The mutton might have been pre-cooked on its journey from New Zealand and then kept cold for reheating. But no one could fault the wine, and plenty of this was served. Almost before the soup plates could be cleared away, an already well-lubricated gathering was swimming in drink.

Nor could anyone fault the silver and the fine china on which dinner was served and eaten, or the supreme hospitality with which Macmillan had made everyone at home in Birch Grove. If Dr Robinson's grace had turned into a strange, little sermon about how the Christian Faith—"in a *very real sense*"—required the abandonment of religion, no one seemed unhappy. This done, Macmillan had got up and made a short speech of his own that lasted until his own soup dish was filled.

Now, the plates of the main course were cleared away, and the room was filling with the dense smoke of several dozen pipes and cigars and cigarettes. One of the servants opened a window for air, and every candle fluttered in the sudden breeze. With a gentle crash, the window was pulled shut again, and the light and all the clouds of smoke steadied. There was another gust of air—this time internal, as the dining room door opened, and all the staff filed out.

I looked at my watch and thought again about timings. Foot had eaten nothing, but instead—and to the evident annoyance of those sat beside him—had chain-smoked throughout the dinner. Every so often, he'd darted knowing looks in my direction. I was beside Macmillan at the head of the long table. He'd jollied me along through both main courses with stories of his time as manager of the family business. Had I known less than I did, I'd have been angling like mad for him to buy me out of Richardson & Co. and to load me with lavish advances. As it was, I'd smiled politely and made the best of things with his wine. I was light-headed again. But, so long as no one expected me to get up and make a speech, I felt surprisingly cheerful.

"Please, gentlemen," Macmillan was saying, now on his feet, "if I might have your attention." He beat with the stem of his pipe on a wine glass. The hushed chatter died away from round the table, and every face was turned in our direction. Last of all to break off his conversation was Edward Heath. But even he smothered one of his ridiculous laughs and turned away from hectoring some smelly writer with spots who'd been introduced to me as Dennis Potter.

"Gentlemen, I'd like to thank you collectively for having had the goodness to drop everything at such short notice and come out into the middle of nowhere for what has turned out to be an unscheduled trip into the past." He waved at all the candles and paused for a ripple of subdued laughter to sweep round the table. "But, to be serious, there have been developments that place on us all a duty to go beyond the private conversations each of you has shared with me during the past year or so.

"Let me take up the main theme of our private conversations. This room, I do not think anyone will disagree, is filled with the finest and most original minds this country has to offer. Each one of you has shown outstanding ability in your chosen field. Each and every one of you deserves to fill the highest positions within your field. And yet, with one or two exceptions, you have failed to obtain the advancement that is your right, or it has been made plain that you will fail. What are you as things stand? I will tell you. You are nothing. Who, then, are the professors in our universities, the bishops of the Established Church, the newspaper editors and great men of broadcasting, the playwrights and novelists, the High Court Judges, the departmental heads, the Ministers of the Crown? They are all men of far lesser quality than yourselves.

"Indeed, gentlemen, even those of you who have, against every opposition, achieved a certain eminence—do you suppose that you will be suffered to advance beyond this? I do not think so. I will not mention my own example. You will surely have read the newspaper articles about what has supposedly been agreed between Lord Halifax and my Cabinet colleagues. But, as it is with me, so it is with Edward over there—yes, *you*, Edward, if you will kindly pay attention." There was more laughter. Heath blushed, and turned the stare he'd fixed on me back to the Foreign Secretary.

"If just one or two of you had been passed over, we might easily put this down to bad luck. Not everyone who is by nature of the first class can be expected to reach the first rank in fact. But, gentlemen, it really is as if each of you had been the victim of some overarching conspiracy. Now, let me say at once that I do not suggest that there has been a meeting in some smoke-filled room, where faceless men sat and marked each of your cards. Things do not work in that way in our country. Neither do they need to. I only say this—ever since the fall of the Lloyd George Ministry, far back in 1922, there has been a settled preference, in every walk of our national life, for original talent to be passed over in favour of dependable mediocrity. Even as you have distinguished yourselves, so you have marked your own cards.

"This close and foetid stillness of our national life has continued long enough. The time has come for a wind of change to blow though this country—a wind that will blow away every cobweb, and, with the light that accompanies it, will renew England as a young country. The forces of conservatism have held sway for too much of the present century. The moment has arrived for breaking the mould of how things have been done and to reforge Britain in the white heat that our minds alone can generate."

Macmillan turned and reached down for the foolscap envelope he'd placed against his chair. He straightened up, charred and fresh pages of the Churchill Memorandum now reunited. He looked down at me and raised his eyebrows. He glanced about the room. Every face but one was turned in his direction. Michael Foot alone looked at me. He had his hands together under the table. He smiled, and, as he did so, his spectacles once more caught the light and stopped me from seeing into his eyes.

"I have in my hand," Macmillan continued in a thrilling voice, "an account written by Winston Churchill of a meeting that will excite the same disgust and horror in your minds as it did in mine when Michael Foot first showed it to me. It is a long account, but you will surely forgive me if I now read it out to you in full." He looked down at the pages. Most of the charred sheets had now broken in half, and there was a brief pause as he made sure they were in the correct order. This done, he picked up the first of them and began to read. In a voice no longer old and avuncular, he read out the Memorandum in its entirety. He read it out to the complete silence of everyone else in the room. Some of the men lit cigarettes. A few looked nervously at each other. Listening to the parts I hadn't read over with Pakeshi, I found my own mouth falling open. Macmillan had been right that this later part made no sense without the pages I'd brought from America. Read in conjunction with what I'd supplied, it was hard to imagine that anything more scandalous had ever been agreed in the past by two great powers. The Partition Treaty that Swift had pilloried was nothing by comparison. The most cynical agreements made during the Great War, and published afterwards to universal condemnation, were, by comparison, open covenants, openly arrived at. If Foot ever got to read all this out on his television programme, it would have the emotional effect of an atom bomb.

As he dropped the final sheet onto the table before him and looked round, Macmillan smiled. He looked round the now troubled gathering.

"This is fucking dynamite, Harold," Kenneth Tynan slurred out of the surrounding silence. "But how can we know that any of this is genuine?" he turned and waved at Foot. "We've all heard Michael's whining about the Zinoviev Letter. How do we know this isn't another of them?" Nicholas Kaldor nodded eagerly. Sitting close by me, a certain Robin Day put up a hand to ask why Macmillan hadn't simply destroyed the document and bullied Foot into silence. Macmillan smiled ruefully and continued.

"Of course," he said, "whatever I might think of the men who govern this country, it would be my duty to suppress the evidence of their wrongdoing. The problem is that Michael has already shown this document, *and had it authenticated*, in too many places behind the scenes. There really is nothing I can do to stop the Monday morning newspapers, here and elsewhere, from publishing it in facsimile and with full authentication. My purpose in calling you all together at such short notice is to let us consider how—even at this late stage—we can ensure that some good comes out of evil.

"And, yes, I must expect a certain incredulity regarding what I have just read out. If true, it shows just what rotten foundations underlie the present order of things in this country and the world. And extraordinary claims require extraordinary proof. It is because of this that I have invited the eminent young historian, Anthony Markham, to join us this evening and repeat what he has done elsewhere for Michael. You will, no doubt, be aware that Dr Markham has been the subject of some alarming allegations. These are, I do assure you, quite untrue, and there will be full apologies and compensation paid in due course. For the time being, though, I would remind you that young Anthony is the world's leading authority on Winston Churchill. When he came here with Michael and showed me the original of this document, he told me of his certainty that it was truly in Churchill's handwriting. He also told me that there were good external reasons for believing in the truth of the document's contents.

"Dearest Anthony," he said, looking down at me, "would you care to repeat to this eminent company what you explained to me yesterday afternoon?" He stooped forward and pushed the now disordered heap of manuscript in front of me. I thought of standing up, but decided to remain seated. Everyone was looking at me. I doubted if I'd need to raise my voice. I took a last pull on my cigarette and propped it in the ashtray. It was burned half down. I picked it up again and stubbed it out. I took a sip from my wine glass and gathered my thoughts.

"When assessing whether a document is genuine," I began, "there are various matters to consider. Obviously, you must check that it really is in the handwriting of its alleged author. You must read the contents very closely, to see that there are no anachronisms—that is, no references to later events or to things not yet invented. The day and date need to match. If, as with this document, other people are said to be present, you need to know that they were indeed alive at the time, and either that they were or that they could have been in the place where they are said to be. There are many other tests that I will not for the moment describe.

"I like to think myself a modest man. But I suppose Mr Macmillan is right when he says that I am the leading Churchill scholar. Then again, bearing in mind Winston Churchill's current obscurity, it would have been less flattering, though more correct, to describe me as the *only* Churchill scholar." I paused, expecting at least a titter at the joke. I looked round a gathering that might as well have been turned to stone for all the response I got from it. I swallowed and picked up half of one of the charred sheets and one of the sheets that Macmillan had found in England.

"I must have read every surviving document in Churchill's hand," I went on. "I do believe that, if you showed me an undated sample of his handwriting, I could date it purely from the ways in which the formation of letters changed throughout his life. Applying this test, I cannot deny that this document is in the handwriting of Mr Churchill, and that it dates from the last five years of his life." I checked the murmur that now broke out round the table and smiled easily.

"No, gentlemen," I said, speaking firmly, "this does not in itself authenticate what our host has just read to you. We are all scholars of one kind or another. I think you have the right and obligation to hear all that I have to say before you reach your own conclusion. Perhaps the most preliminary test of authenticity is to examine the paper on which a document is written. Let me hand some of these good sheets about. Please, Mr Day, do have the kindness to take this one and pass the others on. Do please hold them up to the light to inspect the watermark." I waited for everyone to be settled again. I continued:

"These good sheets are all in standard foolscap of the sort that has been used for many years in England. It has been kept in a cool, dry place. The ink on it might have been applied yesterday. It might have been applied in 1920. Without ordering chemical tests of the ink itself and how it has aged, I am willing to allow that it dates from the April of 1948, which is the purported date of Mr Churchill's memorandum." I turned and smiled easily at Macmillan, who was fiddling with his pipe and looking complacent.

"But let us turn to the charred sheets. I will pass only the one entire sheet around, and ask you to look again at the watermark." I smiled again and swallowed. "You will notice at once that this sheet is of different manufacture. It is, in fact, Russian." I looked briefly over at

Foot. He was leaning forward, impatient to lay hands on the sheet that was passing from one tipsy but nervous hand to another. "This does not say anything in itself. People often use two different kinds of paper when writing a long document—especially if the document is written over several days and at more than one desk, which is what may have happened here. And, for the past fifteen years, Russian imports have supplied most of our cheaper paper. Nevertheless, if you look closely at the watermark, you will see three heads above the Hammer and Sickle emblem of the Soviet Federal Union. The large one in the centre is Lenin. The one to the left is Stalin. The one to the right is Beria, the present General Secretary of the Communist Party."

I looked about the Room. Heath looked as if he'd just had a stroke. Someone else was clutching at himself. Foot was smiling at me with cold interest, both hands on view as he drummed lightly on the tablecloth. I didn't look left at Macmillan, though I could hear the sudden change in his breathing. I took time to light a cigarette and watch the cloud of my own smoke merge in with the general fog above the table.

"I hope you will all remember," I went on, a slight tremor now in my voice. "that Stalin died of food poisoning in January 1950. Beria did not assume his present eminence for another nine months after that. This paper, therefore, could not have been in existence in the April of 1948. Since all the charred sheets—so far as I was able to tell on my brief inspection this afternoon—bear the same watermark, I can say, without any need for further tests, that those parts of this document that give the whole its alleged meaning must be a crude forgery.

"I will not say that there was no secret protocol to the Treaty of Pressburg. All I will say is that Mr Macmillan's document proves absolutely nothing."

CHAPTER THIRTY THREE

You could have heard mouse droppings fall in that dining room. It was a silence that couldn't have lasted more than a few seconds. But it seemed to last an age and a half beyond an age. Trying to keep my hands from shaking, I flicked ash from my cigarette and found myself looking at Kenneth Tynan. He looked back with a wolfish grin. If he were ever allowed to write this up for his newspaper, it wouldn't be the account Macmillan had been hoping for.

The silence was broken by a slow and derisive handclap from Michael Foot.

"Bravo, Dr Markham," he called scornfully, "bravo!" He lit a cigarette and blew smoke in my direction. With a strangled gasp beside me, Macmillan grabbed two of the half sheets and held them up together to the light. He dropped them so that one fell unregarded to the floor. With a mighty effort, he took control of his features and turned to Foot.

"Would I be right to suppose, Michael," he asked with a fair semblance of good humour, "that this is all one of your little jokes? If so, I can only observe that it has been in remarkably poor taste, and I look forward to hearing your explanation to Cook. She has"—he waved vaguely about the table—"done her very best for a party that wasn't really called for."

The door opened and one of Foot's men came in. He whispered in his master's ear. Foot scowled and whispered a question. There was a short conversation that left Foot as troubled as Macmillan had been. As the man nodded and made back for the door, there was a distant burst of machine gun fire. A man at the other end of the table screamed softly. Heath looked pleadingly at Macmillan. Foot smiled suddenly and got up.

"Gentlemen," he said with soft irony, "the Workers' State does not joke. If you feel at all upset that the authorities may soon be walking in to arrest the lot of you under the Conspiracy Act, you should address your complaints to Harold. He, after all, has had six hours to do what Markham has just done. Instead, he spent them counting chickens that will never hatch."

He looked about and bowed to the hushed, now terrified company. There was another burst of gunfire. Though still distant, it might have been closer than before.

"Dear me, Michael," I asked, "have Powell's men broken through your ring of invisible light?"

"Not exactly," he said with one of his madder smiles. "But they do seem to have found a way of blocking it on a narrow front. What you hear is my men preparing to die in the cause of working people everywhere as they enable my escape."

"Kill him, Michael," Macmillan grated with a sideways look at me. "Kill him now!" Foot smiled again and pulled out his remote control box. While my throat tightened to the point where I thought that alone would kill me, his fingers hovered over the buttons. He dropped the box lightly onto the table.

"No, Harold, I won't kill the Indian boy," he said. "I won't kill him because he only did tonight what someone else would surely have done on Monday. And I won't kill him because I may have a better use for him. This conspiracy is at an end, and so is your leadership. Remember what Dostoyevsky said about fanatics, fools and informers? I think I can be sure at last you weren't an informer. Neither were you a fanatic." He ignored Macmillan's attempt at a reply, and looked at me. "Let us see, Dr Markham, how much a fool can learn once he's set his mind to the task. How do you think I propose to get the pair of us safe out of here?"

"I think you have a bomb in the house," I said. Someone screamed softly at the other end of the table. From somewhere else, there was the smash of a dropped wine glass. I smiled. "It will go off at a fixed time, or when you press a button. Whatever the case, the house and everyone in it will be blown sky high, and that will take all attention away from you." Foot began his slow handclap again and smiled about the room. There was another explosion that rattled all the windows, and now the gunfire became continuous.

"There *is* a bomb in the house," Foot confirmed. Macmillan tried to get up, but fell back in a manner suggesting a stroke. No one paid attention. All attention was now on Foot. "Yes, there's a bomb. Even before that goes off, though, I'd like you lot to create a nice disturbance for me. Whatever Harold said, you're not up to much. But even you can, with a touch of prompting, create an impressive crowd scene." He pointed round the still, terrified gathering. I saw Ian Gilmour shrink down in his place. Others rubbed their eyes, doubtless trying to work out if this were a drunken hallucination. No one moved. Foot looked at his watch. "Come on, you stupid fuckers," he snarled—"or are you too pissy drunk on Harold's booze even for that?" He pulled a revolver from one of his trouser pockets. He cocked it and, having chosen a victim at random, took careful aim. Almost before I'd registered the noise of the shot, I saw Robin Day jerk backward in his place, his forehead smashed in as if it had been a boiled egg attacked at breakfast.

Even after this, there was another moment of silence. Foot took another shot, now at Kenneth Tynan. This time, he missed. But it was enough to begin the stampede. With a scraping of chairs and a collective wail of terror, everyone was on his feet and fighting to get out through the door. Foot let off another shot at the ceiling, and another that got someone in the back. Above the squeals and babbling of terror, I heard Foot's voice still raised, as he shouted his encouragement. He broke off for a cackle and then a cough. He hugged himself and climbed on the table to dance for joy. But I didn't wait about. He'd told us to get out of the room. Since I was sat pretty close to it, I was among the first half dozen to get out into the darkened main hall. Almost at once, I bumped into one of the servants. I think she'd been by the big front door to watch the gun battle outside.

"Get out of the house," I said. "There's a bomb in here!" In a long flash of whiteness that steamed through one of the fanlights above the door, I saw her face contort itself with fear. She said something I couldn't hear. I tried to speak to her again. But she grabbed up her white bonnet from where it had fallen on the wooden floor, and was running back to the doorway that led below stairs.

It was the head of some colonial mission society—Trevor Huddleston, I think his name—who got first out of the house. He jumped straight down the stairs onto the drive. He waited a moment, as he looked about to see what was happening. Someone had sent up a couple of flares into the sky, and all about was bright and sharp as noon in a black and white film. I heard the heavy crunch of Huddleston's feet on the gravel as he ran towards one of Foot's men, who stood beside the now extinguished fountain, a rifle in his hands.

"Peace be with you, my son," he cried, "Put down these sinful weapons. Let us ask what Jesus might have"—He got no further. From what may have been behind me, a single shot rang out. I saw Huddleston spin round as if in slow motion. His mouth opened in a silent scream, and what started as a little spot on his shirtfront grew larger and larger. I didn't see him fall. Instead, someone pushed me from behind and I went sprawling myself onto the gravel.

"Eeout of my way, you little shit!" I heard Edward Heath snarl. He stood over me and sniffed the air. I thought he was about to jump over me and try for the gate. Instead, he stopped and kicked me hard in the stomach. As I writhed on the ground, trying to catch my breath, he kicked again. This time, he only got me in the ribs. He made an attempt to stamp on one of my hands. Luckily, he missed that and Foot's bracelet. But there was another burst of fire close by. He pushed himself back against the wall of the house, and sidled off within the comparative safety of the dark shadows that lay all about the house. Someone else bounded over me and headed left for the parked cars. I don't know if he made it, but there was now a loud and pretty close battle taking place. I sat up and groaned. I felt queasy from the kicking. I knew I'd have some nasty bruises if I lived long enough for them to come out. My bottom was still on fire from Pakeshi's operation.

"Jesus!" I groaned. I put a hand up to my head. Pakeshi's operation! He'd been cutting that wireless thing out of me no more than twelve—perhaps fourteen—hours ago. It might have been days. And, at the lunch that followed, I'd been reflecting on the odd passing of time in the few days before. Now, it was even worse. I scratched my head and looked across the drive. There were three of Foot's men, laughing and singing Party ballads as they loaded shells about the size and shape of food tins into a piece of moveable artillery. Every few seconds, there would be a loud pop and the men would jump back. There was no point listening for any of the explosions. The night was suddenly alive with the bangs and crackles of a battle joined on both sides. Other of Foot's men took shelter behind the high brick pillars on each side of the gates. They bobbed in and out from the shelter, firing little machine guns into the darkness beyond.

There was a bang far overhead, and the sky became almost unbearably bright as another flare exploded. I heard a scream of pain and fear from one of the men at the gate. He'd fallen back and was twitching on the gravel. Sitting here, looking about as if I were a football match extra, was lunacy. Much longer in the rear of this battle, and I'd be joining Foot's man. I staggered up and got myself back in the house. Here, with a mixture of wails and sobbing, Macmillan's guests and his servants took what shelter they could. There was a smell of alcoholic vomit. Someone in a dinner suit was urinating against the post table. Incredibly, Kenneth Tynan had stripped off his trousers, and was abusing himself in front of Macmillan's cook.

"Have you come to take us to safety?" a minor BBC official pleaded. "Oh, please tell us what to do!" Someone else got hold of my arm and began tugging me towards the staircase. I shook myself free and tried to think. After all I'd been pouring down my throat that evening, it was a small miracle I could even stand up. But there was no doubt I could feel a delay between everything I saw and heard and its registering in my mind. And there was no doubt I'd have been generally sharper, given better foresight than I'd been exercising.

Michael Foot—yes, Foot! I shook someone else off who was under the impression I was there to save him. Foot had confirmed there was a bomb in the house. He'd be priming it, or whatever, before he got into his helicopter and set off for his meeting. Yes—I squeezed my eyes shut and tried to think straight—yes, he had his helicopter full of atom bomb stuff. Did Stanhope or anyone else know about this? Would they still be looking out for helicopters to follow once this house went up? I looked at my watch. Foot had mentioned a Russian submarine off Selsey at 1am. I tried to think harder. Birch Grove to Selsey, and perhaps five miles beyond that out to sea—How far? How long by helicopter? You might as well have asked me for street directions in Tokyo. But I looked at my watch. It was ten to midnight. About half an hour sounded reasonable, I told myself with an assurance that, if based on no evidence at all, quickly felt unshakable. That meant Foot should still be in the house. If he got his bomb going and blew us all up, it would be awful. If he got away to Russia with all that he said he'd gathered....

I stood up and swallowed. Stony sober, and I'd have laughed at myself. But I was at least three quarters cut. Between Michael Foot and the greatest world crisis since 1914 stood one timid little half-*babu*, eaten up with shame about his ancestry and self-loathing on account of the affections Nature had planted in his heart. "How would *you* respond if called on to serve?" Stanhope had asked me a hundred years and four days before in Westbourne Grove. It wasn't a question I thought I'd ever have the chance to answer without a big, heavy stick waved over my head. What would I really do for England? I thought. I stopped myself. If called on to serve, *what wouldn't I do for MY England*? I, at least, knew which side I was on.

"Has anyone seen Michael Foot?" I said in a firm voice that silenced everyone else in the hall. "Did anyone see where he went after we all left the dining room?" One of the servants suggested he was outside amid all the shooting. That didn't sound like the man I'd come to know. I willed the clouds to thin out and roll further back to the outer edges of my mind.

I might know where Foot had gone. Even though drunk, I broke wind at the thought of where he might be. It really was a matter of courage and shuffling the cards.

CHAPTER THIRTY FOUR

"Ah, Dr Markham!" Foot cried as I showed myself at the top of the stairs that led down to the deepest cellar in Birch Grove. "I can't say I've been waiting for you. But it's certainly in your interest to have found me."

I looked down the dozen or so wooden steps. Bathed in the brightness of a chemical lamp, Foot was pottering about in what had become his acid room. There was a forty gallon container in the middle of the room, and another one, still sealed, over by the wall. This was a huge container, its contents indicated by a red skull and crossbones painted on it. But Foot wasn't interested in acid for the moment. He'd just done with fussing over the box I'd noticed when he disposed of Krellburger.

"Is that your bomb?" I asked. "Do you suppose that little thing can blow this house up?" Foot grinned back at me as I went down the steps towards him. He'd picked up a canvas bag and was preparing to leave. Now, he put it down and gestured me towards him.

"The military arts really have moved on since Winston was hoping to direct them," he said with one of his giggles. "Don't tell me you thought bombs were still five times the size of oxygen cylinders—let alone black balls with sparklers set in them! Come and look at this." He waved me closer, and stepped back to show his bomb. He'd slid off a cover from the top that revealed a panel of buttons and an electronic number display. The panel was now lit up a sort of green, and flashing. "*20:17*," it said. "*20:16*, *20:15*, *20:14*," going down by one digit every second.

"In just over twenty minutes," Foot explained, "this will blow, and it will take most of the house with it. There might be a ball of fire and a shockwave. Or an observer outside might simply feel the ground shake and watch the dark shape of this house disintegrate. I rather fancy the ball of fire—so much more dramatic, not to mention so much more likely to divert attention from the helicopter that will have taken off a minute before. But we shall have to see." He laughed and walked again towards the steps. He paused and looked down at his bag.

"If you're still interested in my Boswellising offer," he said, "the least you can do is carry my bag. I'm not displeased by your smashing up of Harold's stupid plans. Short of what will happen in twenty minutes, it was the dramatic high point of the evening. It showed, nevertheless, an independence of spirit that you will need to curb if you wish to last long in Moscow.

"Oh—and you can bring the lamp as well. I don't fancy tripping over bodies or disordered rugs on my way to the roof."

It's one thing to stiffen your upper lip and say you'll do what England expects. It's something else to stand unarmed beside a raving lunatic who has a gun in his pocket. I looked about for a weapon. There was nothing of any use against a gun. I could go for him once we were in the main house. Perhaps I could brain him from behind with a handy vase or bust. Perhaps I might even raise the less useless of Macmillan's guests against him. I had to stop him from getting away. The question was how?

"Can this thing be turned off, Michael?" I asked, still looking at his bomb. There were dozens of buttons, and that counter was going down with surprising speed.

"The short answer is no," he said without looking back. "Once the six digit code is keyed in, the countdown can only be stopped by unscrewing the main panel—which, in any event, is booby trapped. These things are not made with safety in mind once they activated. But why would you wish to stop the countdown?"

"Just wondering," I said. I moved quietly round so that the bomb and the bench on which it sat covered about three quarter of my body. I looked harder at the panel, and tried to understand the Russian words and letters that seemed to explain the use of each button. There were dozens of them. Except for those that were numbered, each might have meant anything or nothing. I gritted my teeth and pushed a button at random. If it was supposed to do anything, it didn't show on the display. I pressed another with an arrow on it that pointed upward. Now, the time on the display dropped a whole minute. I pressed it again and again. The time dropped by two minutes.

Foot must have heard the gentle accompanying beeps. Already on the lower steps up to the main cellars, he now froze. He turned back to face me. He pointed his revolver at my head.

"Get away from that panel," he said sharply. He drew back the hammer and squinted as he took aim. "I may have left my killing box upstairs. But, if you press one more of those buttons, I'll shoot you on the spot." I squatted down behind the bench. My head was now covered by the bomb. I couldn't see the buttons on its panel. But I knew well enough where they were. I pressed the relevant button again. We must now have been down to sixteen minutes.

"Put the gun down, Michael, and stand over against that wall," I said. I pressed the button again. We hadn't more than fifteen minutes now—perhaps less. "If I take this down another ten minutes, you might as well sit where you are, and put your head between your legs, and kiss your arse goodbye." I let the fingers of my right hand wave provocatively just above the panel. I was sure he could see them. I heard shoe leather scrape on the floor of the cellar.

"If you move another inch, Michael," I shouted, "I'll keep that button pressed until it's gone all the way down. Do you suppose it will go down to zero? Or will it give you a minute's grace, so you can die above stairs amid Harold's pictures and the potted plants? Throw the gun over here, and come with me. We'll get everyone out into the drive, and you can call the surrender."

"Look, Anthony," Foot began. He cleared his throat and started again in a most reasonable tone. "Look, we'll never get everyone out of this house in time. And it's bloody murder outside. You really shouldn't imagine that anyone, on either side, will pay attention to me this far into the battle.

"Anthony, I've a better idea. I'll take out all my bullets and put the gun down. We'll then walk out of here together. We still have time to get upstairs. Or do you want to be the man who killed yourself and me, and everyone else in this house?"

"I want your gun, Michael," I repeated with serene conviction. "Whatever the risk, we'll do it my way. If you come any closer, or try running upstairs, I'll blow us all up. I'd rather not—but sooner that than let you make that submarine meeting. We're wasting time as it is. Would you like me to take us down another minute?" I poked my right hand an inch above the cover of the bomb and let my fingers wave about.

"You're a bloody fool, Markham," Foot shouted. I heard the snap of his revolver as he pulled the cylinder out. I heard the sound above my head of bullets thrown against the wall. "You can put your head out now," he called. I looked. He was standing about a dozen feet away. He held the unloaded gun in his right hand. As I poked my head higher beyond the cover of the bomb, he laughed bitterly and tossed the gun out of reach.

"Come on, then Markham," he jeered, taking up a fighting pose. "Let's do it fair and square, like in those shite novels that form the ballast of your mind. It's you against me. If you win, you and everyone else gets a chance out in the drive, and you can hand me over to Powell when he comes through the gates in his armoured car. If I win—well, you can at least tell yourself you tried."

I broke wind again. Whatever I'd been thinking upstairs, I hadn't supposed this would come to personal combat. I looked at Foot. He was pushing forty six, and—even forgetting his lungs—didn't look in very good shape. On the other hand, there was something confident about that fighting pose. He'd squealed for mercy the night before to Pakeshi. But Pakeshi had been armed and in total control. Now, Foot looked as relaxed and confident as any man can be who knows he has only limited time for crushing his opponent.

I took a deep breath and ran out from behind the bench. I took another breath and let out what I hoped was a fearsome cry. I launched myself at Foot. He stepped aside as I reached him, and let me crash into some broken cane furniture that was stacked in a corner. I heard him laugh as I pulled myself upright and wheeled round to face him. He was over by the bomb and was pressing buttons. A relieved smile on his face, he turned back to face me.

"You can't stop the countdown, Anthony," he cried triumphantly.

"But you can reset the manual override. I still don't have forever to dispose of you—but we are back where we should have been if you hadn't made your brave but ultimately futile gesture." He took off his spectacles and placed them on the bench. Without them, he looked younger and far less human. Though he blinked as he stepped forward, there was something low and predatory about him. I tried to stop shaking and stood up. I clenched my fists and tried to remember what I could of my last attempt at boxing. That had been in 1946, when I thought Briggs Minor had broken my nose. The oceans of drink I'd soaked up suddenly ebbed away, and exhaustion mingled with total clarity of mind. I could imagine how stupid I looked, as I bounced up and down and threw short punches at the air. In other circumstances, I might have joined in Foot's mocking laughter.

But now he fell silent. He held up both hands to his chest and stretched their fingers wide and straight. He looked at his hands and rubbed them together. He put them close together as if he had them about a throat. Keeping hands held in this position, he stretched his arms in my direction. He put back his head and howled. It was like a wolf in the zoo—no, it was like the monster in the most horrid German horror film. He howled again and rushed at me, hands still held out as if they already had my throat cupped in them. Oh, forget German horror films—forget the worst childhood nightmares from which you wake up screaming uncontrollably. This was indescribably worse. I saw the mad eyes, the mouth pulled open tight, the outstretched hands. Across the fifteen feet or so that had separated us, he raced straight towards me. From the corner of one eye, I saw the shadow he cast from the cold brightness of the chemical lamp.

As he came close, I bounced aside. Still bouncing up and down, I lashed out with a parody of a right hook. I got him on the nose. Hardly thinking what I'd done, I got him a left on the upper jaw that spun him about. Uncomprehending, I saw him lurch back and overbalance onto the floor. Now squealing as he had with Pakeshi, he had both hands cupped over his nose. As he straightened himself and sat up, he took his hands away and looked at them. They were covered with blood from the vessel I'd managed to burst in his nose. He whimpered and scrabbled his shoes on the brick floor as he pushed himself back against the wall and looked again at his bloody hands. For one lunatic moment, I did think of walking over to him and telling him to get up and fight like a man. But, as said, the alcoholic tide had fully ebbed. I looked across the room. I was now on the far side from the steps. I had a thought—if I could get past Foot and up the steps, I could lock him into this cellar. Now he'd cancelled my own interventions, we must still have at least eighteen minutes till the bomb went off. In that time, I could arrange something with those scared, sobbing creatures up in the hall. I could try to make sure Foot had no more victims that night.

"Not so fast, Markham," I heard Foot croak. I stared back from the lowest step. Still on the floor, he'd got hold of his revolver. I don't know how he'd found a bullet so fast—perhaps he'd had some in his pocket. But he rammed the cylinder back into place and aimed at me. I looked at the bloodied, hate-twisted face. I stopped and put my hands up. Foot giggled and pulled the trigger. There was a click and nothing. He swore viciously and fumbled with the cylinder. With a few deliberate clicks, he twisted it into place and aimed once more. I tried again for the steps. As the shot rang out and ricocheted from somewhere above me, I tripped and sprawled forward on the steps. I forced myself to my feet. So far as I could tell, I was unhurt. Like an idiot, I looked back. I looked straight over at Foot. Still sat against the wall, he was using both hands to steady the gun as he took careful aim.

A strange ringing—it was as if someone was rubbing on the rim of a wet glass—made me look away. I found myself now looking at the sealed vat of acid. The ricochet had gone into the artificial ceramic. It had made a little hole exactly where the mouth should have been on the skull and crossbones. Through this, the dark liquid was running as if from a drinking fountain. Even as I looked, I could see a pattern of cracks forming all over the wall of the vat. They radiated out from the single bullet hole, They extended and joined up and branched out in new directions. And, all the time, the artificial ceramic sang at me in the loud, clear voice of its own dissolution.

I stared again at Foot. Oblivious to the noise that seemed to fill the whole room, his lips were parted in an anticipatory snarl as he took a now unwavering aim and pulled back the hammer. He might have had the trigger pulled half back when the wall of the vat suddenly burst, and, with a loud and mighty flood, perhaps a hundred gallons of sulphuric acid poured out into the room.

Did I hear Foot's terrified shrieks above the corrosive hiss and slurp of the dark flood? I really can't say. The spell was broken, and I had the presence of mind to stagger, tripping and blubbering, to the top of those steps, and get myself out of the cellar before those clouds of hideous vapour could reach me.

My candle was where I'd left it, perhaps seven minutes before, in the big wine cellar. I stopped myself from rushing forward in blind panic. I wiped sweaty, trembling hands on my trouser legs, and reached for the holder. There was another cellar beyond this one, and then more stairs before we were back to ground level. It probably was madness to suppose I could get everyone out into the drive without being cut down in the crossfire of what must be a battle at or near its height. But that was the plan. And it was the only plan I had.

As I took another step forward, the door in front of me opened, and I looked into the intense glare of another chemical lamp.

"Oh, it's you!" Macmillan said impatiently. "I did hear that Edward had kicked you to death out in the drive. Now, I suppose I'll have to do the job myself."

CHAPTER THIRTY FIVE

"So Michael's bomb is down there, is it?" Macmillan grunted. Keeping the gun in his left hand, he passed me the chemical lamp and looked at his pocket watch. "If what you say is right, there's plenty of time to get up to the helicopter."

"I suppose it will have to be the hero's welcome for you in Moscow," I said bitterly. Now I was out of the deepest cellar in the house, I could hear the rattle of the guns again outside, and the regular thump of the artillery.

"In God's name, dear boy, not Moscow!" Macmillan cried with mock horror. "The problem with you historian chappies is that you spend so much time fussing about with the past that never understand what's going on around you." He laughed easily. He must have caught the look on my face, because he stopped his gradual progress towards the door and leaned against a wine rack.

"Oh, Anthony, Anthony," he sighed. "It's rather late for telling you anything at all. But a statesman's plain duty is to inform those he would lead—even if the leading isn't to be for very much longer. Listen, boy, did it never strike you as a little odd that I should be pressing on in a plot that had long since been about as confidential as the tips in *The Racing Post*? For months now, we've had Powell sniffing about, not to mention those silly Americans. Yet there I was, still plotting away and hurrying things forward.

"Well, on the one hand, there always *was* the chance that I could outrun everyone else. Halifax is still out of England. I still have all the authority of a Foreign Secretary. On the other—and I did hear Michael telling you in the billiard room about Plan A—I have always had a Plan B. In a few minutes, I will get into my helicopter and have myself put down just outside what I judge to be the maximum blast area from Michael's bomb. I shall have a pile of recovered nuclear secrets, and be the only survivor of a most dastardly plot that only I was able to foil." He stared again into my face and laughed so that his moustache quivered.

"Halifax had my full explanation weeks ago—not that he bothered reading it—and there is a full, if slightly biased, account on my desk in London of all my doings on behalf of Queen and Country. It may not be something that can be written up in my own lifetime. For all that, those in the know will be aware how an elderly Cabinet Minister, single-handedly and with reckless courage, pulled his country back from the edge of catastrophe."

"And you really think they'll believe that?" I sneered. I moved the lamp forward slightly, so my face couldn't be seen, and looked about for a weapon. Perhaps I could throw a wine bottle at his head….

"Do pull that light back a little," he said quietly. "I know what you're thinking. Whatever trick you pulled on Michael downstairs, you'll not be repeating with me." As he spoke, I heard a faint shuffling and grating behind me. I looked round. We were alone in the wine cellar. I thought at first it might be rats or mice. But the sound was becoming more distinct. It was coming from behind the door that I'd just closed. I swallowed nervously and let my mouth fall open.

"Help me!" came a ghastly croak from just the other side of the door. "Help me!" Because it had no latch, I'd only pushed the door to. Now, pushed from within, it swung open. I stepped further back to avoid the clouds of sulphur gas that were illuminated a dirty brown by the lamp still burning below. From those dense clouds emerged a tiny figure that crawled and dragged its way slowly across the floor.

"Help me!" it croaked again, moving with slow but desperate concentration away from the place of its utter shipwreck. I tried to look away from the blackened, hairless scalp and the claws, almost devoid of flesh, that served in place of hands.

"Oh, my poor, dear Michael," Macmillan crooned. "You do look a mess." He stepped past me and looked down at what had, just minutes before, been a cackling, triumphant Michael Foot. "You know, I can't help but suspect that you'd been planning to shit all over me. Nevertheless, I forgive you." He bent forward and pushed the barrel of his gun into the exposed neck. He pulled the trigger and the body jerked once. It was over.

"The punishment was just," he said to me. "And it was a mark of my forgiveness. Michael was, after all, a most distinguished President of the Oxford Union. Such a loss when he fell in with those ghastly Moscow people." He kicked the body and flipped it over. I tried to look away from the burned away face and the almost eyeless sockets. It was like beholding the face of an unwrapped mummy. But Macmillan pushed me with his weak right hand and pointed at the far door. "Come on, Anthony," he said. "Time and tide wait for no man—not to mention Russian bombs.

"And—ah—I'm putting my gun away. But I must warn you that, if you speak one word beyond this door, I will blow off both your kneecaps. I can tell you, from my experience in the trenches, that it is a most exquisitely painful injury."

Macmillan's butler had taken charge in the outermost of the cellars. He'd got servants and guests sat on the floor as if they'd been schoolchildren. The impression was heightened by the faint moan from about half of them of *O God, Our Help in Ages Past.*

"Excellent, Bellamy," Macmillan said with a return of his Edwardian manner. "You're a good man. Keep them together. Keep telling them that this is the best place for everyone to be when the bomb goes off."

Despite the threat, I wanted to shout a warning. But Macmillan already had me across the room and on the steps that led up to the main house. The door firmly shut, the hall was now empty. Still, however, the flares shone through the fanlights, casting a lurid glow over the paintings and the polished wood.

Macmillan stopped just before the main staircase and looked mournfully about.

"This was a beautiful house," he said—"yes, truly beautiful. My father would have been proud of the improvements I made to what was already one of the best houses in Sussex. Still, I can take if off the insurance."

"You're a bloody murderer," I cried, finding my voice again. I pointed back towards the cellars. "You'll kill them all."

"Oh, the staff, the staff!" he replied with a groan. "The house can be rebuilt. But how will I replace the staff? Oh, the sacrifices one must make." He righted a hat stand that had been knocked over and began a slow progress up the stairs.

"Come on, Anthony," he urged, pointing his gun at me again. "You aren't coming with me, of course. But I'd like you to see me off. After all the trouble you've caused me these past few days, it's the very least you can do."

"Harold!" a man cried from the first landing above us. "Harold! There's a helicopter on the roof. But the pilot won't take off without your instructions." It was the fat Welshman who'd been lecturing Foot on law reform. Macmillan paused and looked up.

"That is the case, Roy," he said. "Think of it as a lifeboat. But, you see, as with any lifeboat, it has limited room. And there is most decidedly no room in it for your bulk." Without seeming to aim, he raised his gun and fired off a shot. He got the Welshman in the stomach, who fell backwards and writhed screaming on the carpet. He hurried up the remaining stairs and silenced the screams with another bullet. He turned to me and smiled.

"I had promised young Jenkins that he'd be Home Secretary in my Ministry of All the Talents," he explained. "I don't suppose anyone else now will be so eager to abolish hanging." He looked at his watch. "But we must hurry," he sighed. Even on the most optimistic counting, we are fast running out of time." He looked once more at the solid elegance of polished wood about us, and stepped over the still body towards the next flight of stairs.

***

Up on the roof, the pilot already had the helicopter engine ticking over. Lit up from within, its glass and aluminium body gleamed from what was now a single, diminishing flare. Either sound didn't reach too well this high, or the battle was finally coming to an end. Had Stanhope's men given up? Or had they broken through? It was impossible to say.

"The battle looks to be over, dear boy," Macmillan said as if he were reading my thoughts. "Even now, in the relative dark, attackers will be creeping forward. It really takes me back to my young days in the trenches. Time, then, for such farewells as we can manage. I'd like to take you off with me. All else aside, you are a writer of most promising talent. The problem is that your account of what I've been up to would jar with my own." He moved towards the helicopter.

"You won't get away with this," I cried above the rising sound of the helicopter engine. "Stanhope at least will never believe your lies." Macmillan stopped and looked back.

"Anthony," he said, speaking loudly, "you must understand that the first thing anyone wants after a disaster like this is a narrative that makes sense of it. If my proposed narrative might seem bald and unconvincing to you, I am a politician. I will add to it a degree of artistic verisimilitude that will silence all doubts. When I am put down beyond that clump of birch trees in the distance, friendly hands will help me out, and uniformed men will salute me as I express my grief for all those I was unable to save." He put his good hand onto the frame of the helicopter and prepared to heave himself aboard.

"Oh," he shouted, turning back, "I'll make you one final promise. While you were alive, *The Times* was always too sniffy to carry anything by the likes of you. Once I have a spare moment, I'll see to a most glowing and regretful obituary. I may even write it myself." He laughed and made an ironic bow.

As he was about to turn again and climb aboard, another flare went up, and then another. Once more, we were bathed in their lurid glow. I thought at first Macmillan had been shocked by the sudden burst of light. Like one who's been turned to stone, he stood beside the helicopter, still looking in my direction.

I felt a hand strike me from behind and went sprawling onto the rain-soaked lead.

"Get down and stay down," I heard Pakeshi yell above the rising noise of the engine. He released the catch of his sub-machine gun and fired off a burst into the sky. He pointed it straight at Macmillan, who put up both hands.

"There's a bomb in the house," I shouted up at the dark-clad figure. "It will go off at any moment." I didn't think Pakeshi heard me, so shouted again. Now, he scooped me up with his free hand and hurried me towards Macmillan. Dropping me, he spun Macmillan about and frisked him. Out came the gun. It fell onto the roof. Pakeshi kicked it hard so that it flew out of sight.

"Get in," he shouted, pushing me at the helicopter. It was already swaying about a foot above the roof. There was no point asking what the bloody hell was going on. If we had a minute before Foot's bomb blew everything sky high, we were lucky. As I clambered in and tripped, I caught a glimpse at the pilot, who was pulling on levers and checking dials. I was about to sit up from where I'd fallen. But Macmillan was now roughly dumped on top of me. I heard Pakeshi shouting at the pilot to get us moving. Suddenly, the helicopter pitched and there was a bump that sent my face crashing against the metal floor of the helicopter. We were down again.

"It's the weight," the pilot cried. He pointed at the boxes that almost filled the back seats. "We're carrying too much weight." I thought of telling Pakeshi that fissile materials need lead sheathing. But he was already pulling vainly at one of the boxes with his free hand. It might have taken all four of us to get the thing shifted. For all he could move it, Pakeshi might have been trying to rip out the seats. The pilot fussed and struggled with his controls. But, even though the blades moved faster and fast overhead, the helicopter didn't manage more than a wobble.

"Get out!" Pakeshi screamed at Macmillan. He prodded him with the barrel of his gun. "Get out now!" There was a screamed reply, and pleading. But Pakeshi landed a kick in Macmillan's chest and sent him sprawling onto the roof. I pulled myself up into a seated position and looked out. In just a few seconds, we'd now managed to rise six feet or so above the roof. In the bright but inadequate light of the flares, I saw Macmillan scramble to his feet and raise his arms in a gesture of supplication.

We were rising higher. But there was a laboured sound of the engine, and the roof below seemed to be pitching like a turbulent sea. The pilot flicked a couple of switches and pulled frantically on a lever. I held on grimly to the tubular steel of one of the chair supports as we plunged again and twisted, Now, we were somehow ten and then twenty feet above the roof, and were moving across it. With more pulling of levers, the strangely arthritic helicopter swayed again, and I was looking down into blackness. I tried to pull myself properly up, but found that I had no control over any of my limbs. My hands were clamped immovably about the steel support. I looked up at Pakeshi. Holding on with one hand, he had his gun in the other, and was holding it as steadily as he could at something outside. I followed the direction of his arm. Back on the roof, I could see Macmillan. He'd got onto his knees. His hands were pressed against each side of his face, his mouth opened in a long, horrified scream that I couldn't hear.

There was a sudden crack, and the helicopter spun out of control.

"We've lost the tail rotor," the pilot screamed. He pulled again and again at his levers. It was to no effect. Every two seconds, I could look out at the roof. Now increasingly distant, Macmillan still knelt there, his hands raised again in despairing supplication. We were moving away. But we were spinning about and about as if on an out of control funfair ride. I remembered Foot's invisible light show. If the pilot hadn't been made aware of it, I was in no position to tell him. Would one of those beams shear us straight in two? I tried to shout a warning, but no words came out. Pakeshi wrestled again with one of the crates. Again, it wouldn't shift.

As we rose higher, I looked back for another two second inspection of the roof. It was now buckling and folding with a motion entirely of its own. On one spin, Macmillan was still there. On the next, he was gone. I couldn't see what happened next. Foot had been right to doubt if there would be a fireball. But I felt the shockwave. It hit us like a tennis racket strikes a ball. Still spinning round and round, we now turned over, and, with the sudden acceleration, I felt as if my innards were being forced into my chest. Suddenly, all our lights went out, and I had the sensation that we were falling.

I heard Pakeshi chanting something in a loud and oddly calm Hindi. The pilot was shouting encouragement at himself as he pulled and pushed on controls that might as well be attached to nothing at all. I felt the scraping of tree branches on the glass bubble that contained us. With a sickening lurch that tore me from my grip on the steel support and sent me into a somersault that ended with a smash into one of Foot's boxes, our descent stopped, and there was silence. Then, after a moment's apparent equilibrium, we turned on our side and fell again. It must have been no more than a second before we hit the ground. It seemed an age, nonetheless. Feeling like a bug that's been squashed underfoot, I was pressed harder and harder against a new place on the floor. The last I recall is a burst of incredible light inside my head.

***

"But he must be alive," I heard Vicky sobbing as if from a great distance. "He can't be dead. He really is the most beautiful writer Daddy ever contracted. His skin—his skin is *so wonderfully* smooth." I felt a hand thrust inside my shirt and take hold of my left nipple. It squeezed hard, and I felt long nails scratch against my chest.

"I do assure you, my dear, young woman," Pakeshi burbled happily—"I assure you on the authority of more certificates than the excellent Major Stanhope has had time to inspect, that my patient is very much alive. I shall, of course, feel happier once he is on a stretcher. But I do have the highest confidence in his capacity for survival."

I opened my eyes and tried to smile. Vicky fell back with a little scream. So far as I could tell, I was lying on damp earth. I could smell Pakeshi's foul, curry-laden breath somewhere close in the darkness. I blinked as a torch was shone into my face. Then the beam was turned away, and I could see Stanhope's grinning face above me. For the first time, I noticed how the grey hairs of his moustache began deep inside his nostrils.

"Is it over?" I asked weakly. The large face twisted into a broader smile.

"It is over, my lad," he boomed at me. "And, by God, you've done us all proud. You've done your duty to Queen and Country—and more than that besides."

CHAPTER THIRTY SIX

Big Ben was striking eleven as I presented my letter to the doorman at the Foreign Office. The uniformed man sat up and saluted me, He pressed a button on his telephone, and someone else came over to take my hat and coat. I ignored the offer of help and walked slowly towards the lift. I'd left my walking stick in Stanhope's club. It hadn't matched the blue of my suit, and I hadn't realised the effort involved in walking even a few hundred yards. But I got to the lift, and even managed a smile at the attendant as he pulled the doors shut.

Unpacked boxes of paper heaped on every available surface, Enoch Powell greeted me at the door of his office. We shook hands and made some desultory conversation about the state of my health. Then he guided me across to an armchair placed before his desk. I winced from the undrugged pain of all my bruises and cuts and settled into the soft upholstery. Powell stood over me with his desk lighter. I pursed still swollen lips as I sucked on the Capstan and waited for the faint wavering of shapes and colours about me to settle.

"Dr Markham," Powell said in his intense Midlands accent, "I am most grateful that you were able to leave your bed and attend on me with such promptness." I took out my cigarette and smiled carefully. It was Monday the 16th March, and the wireless in the carrying chair that had brought me here had been carrying reports from Berlin of the twentieth anniversary commemoration of Hitler's death. The flags in the Mall had been at half mast, and there was a small gathering of elderly national socialists shouting back at some half-hearted Communist Party protestors.

I looked at Powell. He seemed very pleased with himself. Well he might, I supposed. Halifax still wasn't back from Africa, but news of Powell's transfer from the India Office had been the lead story in the previous evening's news. If the official gazetting would have to wait another few days, Powell was to all intents and purposes already the new Foreign Secretary. He sat at what had been Macmillan's desk, a large portrait of Castlereagh behind him. It looked across at a portrait of Canning on the far wall. I twisted in the chair to find a point of least discomfort and tried for another smile.

"You will appreciate, Dr Markham," he continued, "that your services cannot be officially acknowledged. Even so, they have been considerable, and I am glad you are able to be here this morning to receive the private thanks of Her Majesty's Government." He paused and tried for a smile as his eyes looked straight through me.

"Since this meeting is covered by official secrecy," I said, "do you think you might be able to tell me something of what you were up to?" As if I'd accused him of dipping into the church collection, he raised his eyebrows. I took another suck on my Capstan and looked unwaveringly back. "Obviously, there was no Churchill Memorandum," I added. "At least, if the pages Macmillan had were genuine, what you got your agents to plant on me in America was a forgery. Can I suppose it follows that there were no Pressburg Accords—no shameful secrets about the destruction of America? Was all this just a game you were playing with Macmillan—a game you've now won."

Powell raised his eyebrows again. But there was now a knock on the door. As it opened, I heard the rattle of a refreshments trolley. I waited while a cup of what looked like brown, steaming treacle was place on a little table before me. I looked at it, and reached for a custard cream. Without turning, I heard the door close again. Powell was on his feet and walking over to perch by the window.

"It may be on account of their mixed parentage," he said, "that neither Mr Churchill nor Mr Macmillan was able to appreciate one simple fact." He held up a hand to silence what he thought would be a comment from me, and pressed on. "This, Dr Markham, is that there is room on this planet for only one English-speaking great power. All the talk one used to hear about the brotherly affection of the Anglo-Saxon powers was never more than an attempt to hide the jealous struggle of two close relatives for an estate that could never be divided.

"In 1917, in circumstances I do not have to describe, but that gave us no feasible alternative, we played the part of the apprentice in the old tale. We took out a book of spells and uttered the fateful words that called America to life within the greater world. During the next five years, we watched helpless as the Americans reduced that world to still greater chaos than it already knew. We could not stop them as they dictated a peace agreement that made a joke of the balance of power. We did stop them from building what they called 'a fleet second to none'—but only at the expense of nearly alienating of our Japanese allies in the East. Then, their own internal politics, and then the accident of their economic collapse, gave us a respite of fifteen years. It was never more than a respite. We could still watch the giant stretching its mighty limbs within its own confines—reaching out now with its cultural, now with its financial, arm into the world. We measured ourselves against that growing strength, and thanked Providence for the respite we had been given.

"Once we began rearming in 1937, however, it did seem as if our respite was at an end. As we strained every muscle for the coming renewal of struggle with Germany, we looked once more across the Atlantic for help, and watched again as our own money revived those torpid but vast industries. Had we gone to war in 1939 or 1940, there is no doubt that we should eventually have needed to repeat the spell we cast in 1917. And there is no doubt that the eventual defeat of Germany would have been as great in its own way a defeat for ourselves. Do you for a moment suppose that, folded in that gigantic embrace, we could have remained a great power? Do you suppose we might even have remained independent in any meaningful sense?

"Then, by one of those strokes of a Providence that, ever mysterious, have never been wanting in the history of our nation, the headlong rush into another Great War abruptly ceased. And what Providence supplied, the foresight of Mr Chamberlain and Lord Halifax secured.

"I am in no position to tell you what, if any, verbal undertakings were made in Pressburg. But such secret undertakings as may have been made did no more to the United States than the United States—in some other manner, perhaps—would have done to England and to Germany."

"And you think that the restored equilibrium that came out of

Pressburg can be continued forever?" I broke in. "Russia will get the Bomb within ten years—so, at least, Foot assured me. And Anslinger can't go on much longer. The Treaty of Pressburg, surely, was just another respite." Powell gave me one of his frigid smiles and walked over to stand beside the trolley. He poured himself a cup of tea and sipped with mild approval.

"Nothing, Dr Markham, is forever," he said. "The supreme function of statesmanship is to provide against preventable evils. By the nature of things, however, the artifices of one generation must be supplemented by those of the next. All we can do is try to ensure that our own prevention of evils does not raise up less surmountable problems for those who take our place.

"In a country like England, there is no shortage of wisdom and forethought. There is also no shortage of folly, and even of what may be regarded—if only in its effects—as treason. These qualities are not abstractions. They are manifest in the characters of men. If, from time to time, the Divine Providence gives chances, it is up to us to seize those chances. It is for us to ensure that men such as Harold Macmillan said he wished to raise to greatness shall remain in harmless obscurity."

Powell sat down again behind his desk. He looked past me at the portrait of Canning, and laughed without any sign of joy. I lit another cigarette and wondered when I could take myself aside for a shot of morphine that would get me through the rest of the day.

"Next year," he struck up again, "or the year after that, we shall stretch forth the hand of renewed friendship across the Atlantic. The Americans may sniff it with hostile suspicion. They may affect to detect a few spots on it of their own blood. They will ask by what tune of our own composition they are being called to the dance. But they will allow us to help them through their first and tottering steps. For the moment, things remain exactly as they have been for the past few decades." He looked at me and past me to the Canning portrait. "The balance of the old world is not yet in need of redress. Until such time as it is, the new world has no need to exist.

"If you have not yet seen them," he said with a change of tone, "this morning's newspapers carry more details of the unfortunate accident at Birch Grove. The loss adjusters have traced the explosion to the chaining in series of old and new home generators. There is, apparently, the slight chance of an explosion. When a house of that size is all lit up for a reception, the chance that the generators will all overheat and become unstable is unlikely but sufficiently possible for the insurers to justify asking no further questions."

"*No further questions*!" I sneered with a sudden loss of temper. "You make the country sound like a bloody police state!" I winced at the sudden expulsion of breath. But I was beginning to understand why Powell got on the nerves of everyone who had to work with him. There was another of his mirthless smiles. Then a light seemed to come on behind those hooded eyes.

"Come on, Dr Markham," he said with sudden humour. He reached out a hand to pull me from the chair. "Do please come over to this window." Wincing and choking back the pain as, supporting me, he squeezed hard on bruised ribs, I hobbled with Powell over to the window. It looked from a great height over Whitehall. Below us, hundreds and thousands of people went about their business. Men in their overcoats and hats, women in their elaborate clothing and high heels—they passed back and forth between Whitehall and a Parliament Square that, closed to traffic, was dominated by its toga-clad statue of Neville Chamberlain.

"Do you know, Dr Markham," Powell asked in a voice almost too soft for me to hear, "who those people are? Do you know what they are about—let alone what they are thinking? No? Well, we don't know either. We don't know because we make it our business not to know. In this country, we honour those who serve the nation, but think no ill of those who prefer to look purely to their own affairs. It is because of this that we do not need to boast—as the governments of other lands do—how we serve the public good, or how trusted we are by the people. It is something implicitly known in this country.

"And because we arc trusted, no one complains when we ask—or sometimes take—a favour. It requires a century of honest government to bring about an implicit trust of this sort. If Mr Macmillan's friends might have squandered it in at most a generation, this is a trust on which our whole way of life depends." He moved away from the window and let me follow him back to my chair. He smiled, now with a semblance of human feeling. "Of course the insurers will report as we have asked them. All else aside, your evidence and that of the one other survivor will be decisive."

"Another survivor?" I asked, nearly falling down in surprise. "Someone else got out of that horror alive?" I dropped back into the armchair and reached for my cup.

"Oh yes, Dr Markham," Powell said with the beginnings of real enjoyment. "You will be pleased to know that Mr Heath managed to hide himself in a cesspit. Its contents protected him from the worst of the explosion. Once he is out of hospital, he will confirm his resignation—the brush with death, he will say, has made him all the more determined to pass what time remains to him with the music that is the real pleasure of his life. Tomorrow morning, the Home Department will have a new Secretary of State. I spoke last night with Lord Halifax by telephone. He was pleased to accept my recommendation of Miss Margaret Roberts."

A woman as Home Secretary? I opened my mouth with surprise. But Powell paid me no attention.

"You may not know of Miss Roberts," he went on. "She only came into Parliament at the Grantham bye-election two years ago. She is, nevertheless, a young woman of great promise. Everyone who has met her is impressed by her grasp of important detail and her capacity for hard work. If this country is ever to have a woman Prime Minister, one could not hope for better than Margaret Hilda Roberts."

He paused again and got up. "But, Dr Markham, the morning will soon be over, and I am aware of the meeting that has been arranged with some lawyers. What the newspapers said about you was unpardonable. Some of it was no more than the coverage of a mistake by the authorities. But they do seem to have gone most scandalously beyond what was released to them. Major Stanhope tells me you have already been advised to settle matters out of court. I think I can predict, though, that the settlements to be proposed will be eminently to your satisfaction. I repeat that, if we do not often ask for them, the favours we do request are seldom refused."

He paused again and looked out of the window. Was there now a slight look of worry in the blank, fleshless face?

"One matter does remain outstanding," he said, sounding rather distant. "For all the newspapers will publish their retractions, I do accept that, for the moment, a certain damage has been done to your reputation. It is with this in mind that I have recommended you for a visiting professorship at the University of Dresden. Professor von Hayek is a personal friend as well as my opposite number in Berlin. For many years since his return to Germany, he has made a point of coming to England for a week in the spring, to spend time with me in the bookshops of York. There is a vacancy in the Department of History for an English professor, and, if I ask him, Hayek's recommendation will be taken by the authorities as law. I hope you will enjoy many evenings of debate with your new colleagues about the often troubled course of Anglo-German relations during the present century.

"Dresden is a most beautiful city. If you have any taste for the baroque, the view across the Augustus Bridge towards the Cathedral is, I am told, unforgettable."

I swallowed hard. This was the second time in a week I'd heard the praises of Dresden. But the meeting was over, and Powell was helping me to the door of his office.

CHAPTER THIRTY SEVEN

I stepped back into Whitehall at the stroke of twelve. The sun had come out, and people hurried about in still denser crowds to an early lunch. Pakeshi was waiting for me in a double carrying chair.

"To the Savoy, my good fellows," he cried brightly to the carriers. Even if I was rather slender, my own weight added to his made for a slow progress along Whitehall. "I did ask for a taxi," he said to me. "Sadly, even the most estimable and understanding Major Stanhope was unable to get a dispensation from the traffic rules." I sniffed and, despite the sun, was glad of the heating that was powered by the electricity radiated from overhead. We passed in silence through the happy crowds. I saw a class of schoolchildren looking solemn as their teacher stood beside the Cenotaph and lectured on its significance. I stared out at the new Home Office building. A combination of high renaissance and Greek revival, it gleamed white in the sun. Miss Roberts would be the first Home Secretary never to have governed from the old building.

"Did Mr Powell answer all your questions?" Pakeshi asked with a happy wave at some children who were looking at the curiosity of a brown face in Whitehall. I gave up on opening the small cardboard box he'd handed me. A properly weighted carrying chair gives the smoothest ride apart from a magnetised railway journey. Even so, this wasn't the place for digging a needle into your arm and hitting the right vein. I thought about my meeting with Powell.

"Most of them I didn't manage to ask," I said. "I'm not sure if he answered the ones I did ask." Or had he answered one? Talk about the Delphic Oracle! Pakeshi shrugged and dropped the subject. There were signs outside the Whitehall Theatre advertising a new play by Ayn Rand. Whatever her qualities as a dramatist, there was no doubt she had friends in the right places.

Trafalgar Square and all the streets that radiated from it were a solid jam of carrying chairs and rickshaws and pedestrians. The bronze mass of Leslie Barnes, the electrical genius, loomed from its plinth over the crowds of tourists who surrounded it. We made our way past the Dominion high commission buildings towards the shining new *façade* of Charing Cross Railway Station. Beyond that, the wheeled traffic began, and we had to wait for the correct lights before we could pass along the Mall.

"Isn't London beautiful?" I said, breaking the long silence. Pakeshi nodded, a look of solemn agreement on his face. Yes, London *was* beautiful. More than that—much, much more than that—it was all so very *normal.* Until the morphine had kicked in the night before, I'd been kept awake by recollections of all the nonsense spouted by Macmillan's Academy of Projectors. Thoughts of how they might have had their way with England, and thoughts that there were others, still alive, who might yet try the work of destruction, had chilled me. There might well be problems ahead. But London seemed, for the moment, unshakably normal. Everything was as it had to be. And everything would surely be as it had to be forever and ever. The Queen was on her throne. The pound was worth a pound. All was right with the world, under its English heaven. Yes, everything was as it had to be. And, if I'd nearly died to keep it that way, it was nice to think that I'd never be called on to do it again.

Oh, there's a definite pride in duty to Queen and Country—especially after it's been done.

Forty minutes and a 3s. fare later, I sat looking at the lunch menu inside the Savoy. Behind me, the salon orchestra played light selections from the later Schoenberg. I looked at Pakeshi, who was buried in the menu. Since I'd already thanked him for his surprise intervention at Birch Grove, there was no point alluding further to it. Since he'd politely evaded all questions of what arrangement he'd made with Stanhope, there was no point in raising that. Evidently, things had been settled with the Indian National Party. Not once had Pakeshi looked out of the rickshaw to see if there were any brown faces in the crowds we'd passed. He'd smiled happily enough at those children. But there was no trace of a hunted look in his eyes. I cleared my throat.

"I'll speak to Hattersley later on," I said. "But there's no hurry. I'll keep the flat going here in London. But it looks as if I'll be completing the Churchill biography out of England. I'll probably be away until Christmas." I looked harder at Pakeshi, who was still inspecting the menu. "I suppose you'll stay in Victory Mansions?" I hazarded. "If so, we must have lunch again when I come back for Christmas."

Pakeshi smiled and patted his bulging waistcoat. Suddenly, he looked at me. He laughed with good-natured humour and put the menu down.

"But did not Mr Powell tell you the full story?" he asked with suppressed mirth. "He was insistent that I should accompany you to Dresden as your personal physician. Though I have no German whatever, he tells me you are fluent.

"And there is, I am told, a most interesting factory outside the main city. The Germans say it is to manufacture synthetic penicillin. The ever-perceptive Major Stanhope assures Mr Powell that it may be to develop a new liquid fuel for rockets."

I'd scattered cigarettes all over the table before I could bring my hands back under control. Was that a smell of cannabis behind me? I suddenly noticed that the table was set for three….

Other Books by Sean Gabb

Cultural Revolution, Culture War: How Conservatives Lost England, and How to Get It Back, 2007, 105pp, ISBN: 0 9541032 2 X, £9.99/$20

Smoking, Class and the Legitimation of Power, 2005, 196pp, ISBN: 0 9541032 0 3, £18.99/$40

War and the National Interest: Arguments for a British Foreign Policy, 2005, 125pp, ISBN: 0 9541032 3 8, £18.99/$40

Dispatches from a Dying Country: Reflections on Modern England, Introduction by Chris R. Tame, 2001, 234pp, ISBN: 0 9541032 0 3, £20/$40

Books by Richard Blake (if you like one, you will like the other!)

Conspiracies of Rome, Hodder & Stoughton, London, 2009, 368pp, ISBN: 978-0340951132, £7.99

The Terror of Constantinople, Hodder & Stoughton, London, 2010, 420pp, ISBN: 978-0340951156, £7.99

Blood of Alexandria, Hodder & Stoughton, London, 2012, 502pp, ISBN: 978-0340951170, £6.99

Sword of Damascus, Hodder & Stoughton, London, 2012, ISBN: 978-1444709667, £19.99